MASSACRE!

The gunfire had died down and Billy saw what he feared most: the lodges were aflame. Not one or two lodges, but every single one in the camp was on fire. Five white men came into sight, and it so shocked Billy-Wolf that he reined up behind some willows to study the situation. It took a bit for the paralyzing truth to sink in.

Billy had never heard of whites attacking a village before. There must have been an awful mistake made. The Burning Hearts had never done anything to deserve being slaughtered.

As Billy watched the butchers shoot the wounded, a feeling new to him turned him bloodred. He felt pure, undiluted hatred for the first time in his young existence. The shooting went on forever, or seemed to. Each shot seared Billy-Wolf's heart like a red-hot poker.

Billy raised his bow, tempted to try a long shot.

He lowered it again. When the time came, he wanted to be absolutely certain he wouldn't miss.

MOUNTAIN MAJESTY

ASK YOUR BOOKSELLER
FOR THE BOOKS YOU HAVE MISSED

WILDERNESS RENDEZVOUS
PASSAGE WEST
THE FAR HORIZON
FIRE ON THE PRAIRIE

Mountain Majesty

BOOK SEVEN

FIRE ON THE PRAIRIE

JOHN KILLDEER

BANTAM BOOKS
NEW YORK • TORONTO • LONDON • SYDNEY • AUCKLAND

FIRE ON THE PRAIRIE

A Bantam Domain Book / April 1995

DOMAIN and the portrayal of a boxed "d" are trademarks of Bantam Books,
a division of Bantam Doubleday Dell Publishing Group, Inc.

The Mountain Majesty Series is the creation of Siegel & Siegel, Ltd.

ISBN 0-553-56460-9

Published simultaneously in the United States and Canada

Bantam Books are published by Bantam Books, a division of Bantam Doubleday
Dell Publishing Group, Inc. Its trademark, consisting of the words "Bantam Books"
and the portrayal of a rooster, is Registered in U.S. Patent and Trademark Office
and in other countries. Marca Registrada. Bantam Books, 1540 Broadway, New
York, New York 10036.

PRINTED IN THE UNITED STATES OF AMERICA

RAD   0   9   8   7   6   5   4   3   2   1

FIRE ON THE

PRAIRIE

Chapter

—1—

Second Son, warrior of the Burning Heart Band of the Tsistsistas, reined up and shifted to scan the wooded slopes behind her. For the better part of an hour she had felt that she and her mate were being followed, and now she was sure of it. "Someone is on our trail," she said in her quiet way.

Cleve Bennett, a powerful bear of a man whose golden mane starkly contrasted with his wife's long black hair, also drew rein. Hefting the heavy bow in his left hand, he looked in the direction she was gazing and spied a pair of squawking ravens that had just taken wing. "Here we go again, I reckon. They're as thick as fleas on an old coon dog."

His frustration was obvious, and Second Son could not blame him. Twice in the past week they had been forced to flee for their lives from hostile warriors.

"I won't be taken captive again," Cleve vowed bitterly. "I would rather go down fighting."

"Our hearts are one," Second Son said, for she, too, had keenly resented being held against her will throughout the long winter just past. Even though their captors had treated them decently, her spirit had craved freedom. She had almost forgotten what it was like to be able to do as she pleased, when she pleased. As so often happened, she'd had to learn one of life's many lessons the hard way: freedom should never be taken for granted.

"Let's see if we can shake them," Cleve proposed, and jabbed his heels into Socks. The sturdy horse broke into a trot.

Second Son did the same with Shadow, her mare. To their left flowed the mighty Columbia River, to their right reared sheer heights. They were following a well-defined trail that paralleled the river and she could hear gurgling and hissing from a long stretch of rapids.

Cleve looked over his broad shoulder but saw no sign of pursuit, as yet. He knew it was just a matter of time. Many coast tribes were hostile to whites. Others believed in the practice of slavery. He couldn't wait to get shy of this country, to set eyes again on the majestic Rockies and the vast prairie he loved so well.

Suddenly, a hundred yards to their rear, a sharp shout rang through the forest. An answering yell came from the right.

It was Second Son who first spotted the riders, a half dozen or so passing through a gap in the cliffs. A glance behind showed more warriors, some on the trail, some weaving through the thick pines. She realized with a start that the ones to the south were trying to cut Cleave and her off. "There!" she cried out, pointing.

Cleve took one look and goaded Socks to a gallop. He was beginning to think that joining the Beeville expedition to the Pacific had been the most harebrained notion he'd ever had. Between the hostiles and grizzlies and Spaniards, their life had become a series of deadly threats. He longed for the days when he could lounge around their lodge in the Tsistsista camp and not have to worry about whether he would be alive to greet the next dawn.

Second Son was trying to identify the warriors by their clothing and style of hair. In her own country, on the plains, it would be simple. The Arapaho liked to part their hair on each side and combed it straight up above their foreheads. Piegans loved to clip their bangs short and adorn themselves with colorful quills. The Absaroka were partial to two wide braids that hung in front of their shoulders, not behind.

But this was not the prairie, and Second Son knew little of the many tribes scattered between the ocean and the Rockies. She had heard stories, yes, of the Wenatchis, the Spokans, the Yakimas, and others, but she did not know any of them on sight.

A ridge appeared ahead. Cleve frowned on seeing the steep slope they must negotiate. It would slow them down, give their pursuers a chance to narrow the gap. He noticed his wife notching an arrow to her bowstring and did likewise, guiding his stallion by the pressure of his legs alone, a trick he had learned from his adopted people.

Cleve thought of their son, of young Billy-Wolf Bennett, and wondered for the umpteenth time whether they would ever see him again. By now the boy must think them dead. It bothered Cleve immensely. His sole consolation was that Billy-Wolf was safe and sound with the Tsistsistas. His wife's brother and nephew would take good care of the boy.

The crack of a rifle shattered Cleve's musing. One of the warriors had fired a fusil, an inferior trade gun no doubt received for prime plews. The man had wasted the lead. Hitting a target from the back of a racing horse was next to impossible.

Second Son was more concerned about a burly warrior who had pulled ahead of the others and stood a good chance of intercepting them before they reached the base of the ridge. This one carried a bow, an arrow already notched to the sinew string, and it was plain he was just waiting for a clear shot to loose the shaft.

The Tsistsistas knew how to use bows, too. Second Son held hers firmly in her left hand. She watched the burly man closely, and when he burst from the line of trees and whipped his bow up, she twisted and elevated hers.

The warrior saw and grinned, as if he found the

sight of a woman using a bow a source of amusement, even as he released his arrow.

A heartbeat later Second Son let her own fly. She had no time to see if it scored, for his streaked toward her almost too fast for the eye to track. He was a skilled archer. The shaft came so close that it clipped Shadow's tail. A few inches higher and it would have brought the mare down. The fact that the warrior had aimed at her horse and not at her told Second Son the war party intended to take them alive.

Her own shaft sped true. The warrior tried to veer to the side, but he was too slow by half. To his credit, he did not yelp in pain when the tip of the shaft sheared into his shoulder. The impact jerked him around and he went tumbling over his mount's rump.

Second Son had another arrow ready before the man hit the ground. She would protect Yellow Hair's back, even at the cost of her life, if need be. Several young warriors had been hard on the fallen man's heels and would shortly be in bow or rifle range.

Socks came to the slope and took it on the fly. Cleve checked to verify that his wife was right behind him, then lashed the reins to urge Socks steadily higher. If they could reach the top, he reasoned, they might be able to hold the warriors off.

Small clods of soft earth and bits of grass shot out from under Socks's pounding hooves, but Cleve paid little attention. Horses often sent dirt flying. In this instance, though, it would have paid Cleve to see where the clods were landing.

Second Son flinched when one struck her on the cheek. She went to rein to the left, but some dirt hit her squarely in the eyes. In pure reflex she blinked, and the harm was done. It felt as if someone had poured sand under her lids. Suddenly tears welled up and her vision blurred. She was unable to see more than a few feet in front of her. As a result, she did not see the log until it was too late.

The mare vaulted into the air to clear the obstacle. Going uphill, Shadow had to leap at an abrupt angle, so abrupt that Second Son, caught unprepared in the act of rubbing her eyes, had the misfortune of losing her balance and toppling backward.

So lightning quick was Second Son that the instant she felt herself starting to fall, she grabbed at the mare's mane to keep from being unhorsed. It was not enough to resist gravity. To her dismay, she plummeted, landing in high weeds that cushioned her fall. Unable to stop herself from rolling, she felt searing pain spear through her chest when her side smashed into a boulder.

Second Son still could not see. She could hear, though, and knew the foremost warriors were almost upon her. Rubbing furiously at her eyes, she rose to her knees. She had lost the bow, but she still had a knife, which she drew to defend herself.

As a warrior, Second Son was accustomed to fighting her own battles. Her pride was such that she could not bring herself to call out for help. Besides which, she would not let her mate suffer because of her mishap. Her features set in grim determination, she rose to confront her attackers.

Cleve Bennett was thirty feet above and climbing rapidly. He could never say what made him look back at that particular moment, but he did, and on seeing his wife about to be run down by a trio of painted enemies, he did what any man who loved his mate would do, even though he knew it might result in his capture, or worse. He turned Socks and charged down the hill.

The foremost warrior, a skinny man whose hair was adorned with two eagle feathers, held a war club. Snapping the weapon on high, he swooped down on the muscular woman before him. He saw her raise the knife to fend him off and and his eyes lit in appreciation of her courage.

To Second Son, the skinny warrior and his mount were no more than a vague blur. She was unsure where to strike, uncertain of which way she should dodge. The blur grew bigger and bigger. Second Son swiped at her eyes one last time. Abruptly, she could see well enough to note the club the warrior held. It was poised to strike. She tensed for the blow to come, a blow that never landed.

From above flashed a glittering shaft that pierced the skinny warrior through the heart. He died not knowing what had struck him, his lifeless form slumping to the side, the war club dropping from his limp fingers.

Second Son saw other warriors converging, some yipping like coyotes. She leaped at the dead man's mount, a sorrel, as it thundered on past, and succeeded in grabbing hold. As she swung up, a lance cleaved the space she had vacated. Another lance, poorly thrown, impaled the sorrel.

A squeal of anguish rent the air. Second Son tried

to throw herself out of harm's way, but the sorrel's front legs buckled and she was pitched hard onto her stomach. Dazed, she heaved to her hands and knees. The warrior who had thrown the second lance was mere yards away and bending to seize her.

Then Cleve was there. He held his bow as if it were a club and smashed the warrior across the face so hard the bow snapped. As the warrior sprawled to the ground Cleve wheeled Socks, leaned low, and bellowed, "Jump on!"

Second Son needed no prompting. She sprang, her sinewy arms locked with his, and the next moment he had swung her up behind him and they were speeding toward the top of the ridge. Only now the war party was much closer, and they were riding double.

The stallion did its best, but Socks was getting on in years. Cleve worked the reins frantically, to no avail. Halfway up the slope, they were overtaken by three warriors. Cleve would have given anything for a flintlock, but all he had was a knife. The way he saw it, they were as good as captured. He should have known better.

Not for nothing was Second Son one of the most widely respected Cheyenne warriors. Not for nothing had she honed her fighting skills on dozens of raids. Her prowess was regarded with deep pride by her people, particularly by many of her sisters, who secretly longed to do as she did but lacked her iron will.

Long ago Second Son had learned that the key to survival in close combat was to do the unexpected. A foe could not counter what he did not expect. So now, with a trio of bronzed forms closing in, she did the last thing any of them, including Cleve, would have anticipated.

The two nearest warriors were riding abreast. Their mounts were mere feet behind Socks when Second Son pushed off from the stallion, launching herself into the air. Catlike, she twisted in the middle of her leap so that she came down on top of the closest pursuer. She had hoped to reach the rider but fell short, ramming into the bay he rode instead. She caught hold of its neck, coiled, and kicked the startled rider in the stomach.

The bay reacted by angling to the right, plowing into the other horse, whose rider had to lift a leg to keep from having it pinned, or worse.

Second Son clung to the bay for dear life. If she slipped, she would fall under its thundering hooves. The warrior riding it had recovered and lashed at her with his quirt. The leather stung her cheek but did no real harm. She kicked him again, with all her might, driving both of her soles into his ribs, and lifted him clean off the bay. He squawked as he tumbled.

The spooked bay tossed its head, trying to dislodge Second Son. Over its shoulders she saw the other warrior trying to draw close enough to stop it. She managed to hook a leg onto its back to keep from losing her grip, then smacked the bay, hard, behind the ear. The anguished animal drew up short, directly in the path of the other warrior's mount.

It was as if the earth itself were in upheaval. There was a tremendous jolt, a splintering crack, and the bay went flying head over tail. Second Son was unable to hold on. Something thudded against her shoulders. She catapulted a score of feet and had the breath knocked out of her when she smacked into the slope.

Groggy from the shock, Second Son nonetheless rose. Her legs wobbled, and it was all she could do to stay upright. Somewhere a horse whinnied in pain, a warrior screeched in rage.

Hooves thudded beside her. A strong arm looped about her waist and she was hoisted onto a horse. Second Son blinked, thinking she had fallen into the clutches of the war party until she saw loving blue eyes fixed intently on her face. "I am all right," she said, to soothe Cleve's fear, and Socks surged to life under them.

Shadow had halted at the top of the ridge. Cleve drew rein next to the mare so Second Son could transfer, then they were off, heading down the far slope at breakneck speed.

A last glance showed Second Son horses and warriors strewn like broken dolls. Others were helping those who had fallen. One man, enraged, shook a fist at them but did not take up the chase.

Side by side, husband and wife, Second Son and Cleve, galloped for over a mile. They wanted to put as much distance as possible behind them. If not for their exhausted mounts, they would have gone even farther before stopping.

In a glade bordering the Columbia, Cleve sat and scoured their back trail. Only after several minutes had gone by and there was no hint of movement did he accept the fact that they had escaped. He exhaled loudly and wiped a hand across his sweaty brow. "I hope to high heaven we never have another shave as close as that one."

"We were lucky, Yellow Hair," Second Son said.

"*You* were plumb loco, pulling the stunt you did," Cleve scolded. "My heart was in my throat. I figured you were a goner for sure."

"I did what I had to," Second Son said, and let the matter drop. Alighting, she led Shadow to the river. The shore was flat, covered with gravel. She let the mare dip its muzzle into the cool water and squatted to splash a handful on her neck and face.

From long experience Cleve knew not to carp. He was upset, but at the same time he had to concede that if not for Second Son's bold gambit, they would now be in the clutches of that band. Riding Socks to the water's edge, he dismounted and ruefully regarded the quiver on his back. "I'll need me a new bow," he commented.

"We both will," Second Son said.

Cleve stared eastward. "Sooner or later we should reach Chinook territory," he remarked, referring to a tribe reputed to be friendly to anyone and everyone. Which made sense since the Chinooks were traders. Delegations came from far and wide to conduct business at the main Chinook village, located at the Dalles. "I just wish we had something worthwhile to swap for a good rifle and enough supplies to see us to the Rockies."

"Wishes are like butterflies," Second Son said. "They flutter about inside our heads, doing us no real good."

"Turning into quite the cynic, aren't you?" Cleve said. Reaching out, he tenderly stroked her chin. During their long captivity he had been denied her nightly company, and it pleased him immensely to have her constantly at his side once again. "I love you anyway."

There was no denying her man's affection, which Second Son told herself she should be used to by this time. But public displays were not the Cheyenne way, and even when they were alone, she sometimes felt self-conscious about showing him how she felt. Still, she had dearly missed being locked in his arms under a buffalo robe, their bodies entwined. "It is good that you do," she said, "since no other woman would have you."

"Is that right?" Cleve roared in mock fury, and before she could guess his intent, he looped his brawny arms around her waist and swung her in the air as if to heave her in the river. Her smile was priceless, as was the impulsive way she responded to his kiss.

Just then Socks nickered.

Cleve set Second Son down and turned. The woodland lay quiet under the late-afternoon sun, but he knew all too well how deceiving appearances could be, especially in the wilderness. Enemies lurked everywhere, men and beasts alike. "Maybe those jaspers aren't done with us," he speculated.

Second Son pulled her reluctant mare from the water and swung up. She assumed the lead this time. And while she knew that she should not let her thoughts stray, they did.

Once again, as she had so frequently over the past few moons, Second Son pictured their son in her mind's eye, pictured his grinning, vital features and recalled his carefree laughter. She longed to be with him, to see how much he had grown, how much he had matured.

How vividly Second Son recollected her last sight of him, standing proudly with her people and waving happily as Cleve and she rode off! It had never been her intention to be away for so very long.

At the time Second Son had believed Billy-Wolf needed time alone among the Tsistsistas, time to learn Cheyenne ways more fully, time to learn to stand on his own two feet. It had been obvious that while Billy-Wolf was as robust a boy as had ever lived, he was not as skilled in certain ways as other Cheyenne boys his age.

No one was to blame. Cleve had taught Billy-Wolf how to trap and shoot pistols and rifles and do all the things white trappers knew. Second Son had taught their son how to hunt and fight and the many practices of her tribe. And while Billy-Wolf was adept at those things they had taught him, he'd needed to polish those skills. He'd simply needed more experience to make him the equal of the other boys. Living with the Burning Heart Band should have put the finishing touches on his education into manhood.

Cleve, meanwhile, was keeping his eyes peeled for those warriors. He doubted the band would give up easily, not after several of their number had been wounded and one had been slain.

On the long trip west with Beeville, Cleve remembered being told that the tribes along the Pacific Coast were nowhere near as warlike as those found on the plains. Perhaps that was true in California, where the Spaniards, in the name of their church, had forced many Indians to convert to the white religion and treated the converts as little better than slaves.

But the same could not be said of the independent tribes living north of California and along the Columbia. They bowed to no man.

From a German named Wald, whom Cleve and Second Son had met before they were taken captive, they had learned of a trading vessel that had arrived at the mouth of the Columbia to do business with the Indians. The captain had made the mistake of daring to insult a visiting chief. The very next time the chief paid the captain a visit, the entire crew, with a single exception, had been wiped out, the ship plundered, and then set afire.

No sir, Cleve reflected. The tribes in that region were not to be taken lightly. Which was why he had about put a crick in his neck turning so many times to check behind them.

Eventually the blazing sun arced downward in the blue vault of sky and seemed to hover on the rim of the world, painting the horizon with brilliant streaks of red and orange and pink.

Cleve had noted the lengthening shadows with satisfaction. As a general rule, war parties did not attack at night. Second Son and he would have ten peaceful hours all to themselves. He could hardly wait.

On a low hill crowned by lodgepole pines they finally stopped for the day. While Cleve gathered deadwood and started a small fire, Second Son used her razor-edged knife to whittle a sharp point on a slender branch. He watched her glide off into the gathering darkness, his stomach growling as if it knew what was coming.

Within half an hour Second Son appeared as silently as she had left. Dangling from her left hand was a large rabbit. She had it skinned and butchered in no time.

Cleve made a makeshift spit and roasted the chunks of meat himself. The tangy aroma made his mouth water. He could tell by the way Second Son leaned forward on her haunches that she was equally famished. "Another day and we're still alive," he quipped to lighten her mood.

"And we will stay alive until we find our people," Second Son vowed. "I have been through too much to let anyone stand in our way." She glanced up at him. "How long, do you think, Yellow Hair?"

"White time, maybe six months. Five if we push real hard."

"Six moons," Second Son repeated, making it sound like forever, her face wearing a haunted expression.

"Don't fret," Cleve said. "I bet he's doing right fine. It wouldn't surprise me if he's one of the best warriors in the whole blamed tribe by now."

They locked eyes. Although neither spoke, they

shared the same thought and somehow knew that they had. It was a thought that summed up their innermost hopes and fears.

Yes, Billy-Wolf might be a fine warrior by now. Provided he was still alive.

Chapter
—2—

Billy-Wolf Bennett felt a tingle of excitement shoot down his spine. Rising as high as he could on the back of his stallion, Blaze, he raised a bronzed hand to shield his eyes from the bright morning sun and studied the two brown shapes on a distant knoll. "Do you really think so?" he asked.

"You have eyes," Rakes the Sky with Lightning replied in his laconic manner.

Billy-Wolf said nothing, but he doubted his sight would ever rival his cousin's. Strain as he might, all he could distinguish were stick figures. They might be horses or bears, for all he knew.

"They are buffalo," Lightning insisted, and nodded at the wide swath of prairie grass that had been flattened and churned by the tumultuous passage of thousands of hooves. "Stragglers from the big herd that went through here several sleeps ago."

"Why did they fall behind?" Billy wondered aloud. "They must know it is not safe being on their own, what with wolves and bears and whatnot."

"Perhaps they are old. Perhaps one is a cow heavy with calf and the other one will not leave her," Lightning said. "We will not know until we get closer."

Billy-Wolf glanced at his tall, strapping cousin, sitting there so calmly on a fine chestnut. They had grown very close since his folks left for California.

Truth to tell, to Billy's twelve-year-old way of thinking, Rakes the Sky with Lightning was the best warrior in the whole Burning Heart Band. Billy looked up to Lightning, hung on the young man's every word, tried to imitate him in everything. It had gotten to the point where some of the Tsistsistas liked to joke that Lightning was the only person in the village who could boast of having two shadows.

"We kill them by ourselves?" Billy asked, trying hard not to betray how nervous he felt at the prospect.

Lightning smiled down at the boy. "You have never killed a buffalo before, have you?"

"Not yet."

"Then it is time you did," Lightning declared, prodding his mount into a trot. He suppressed a smile at the look on his cousin's face. It seemed like only yesterday that he had gone on his own first buffalo hunt; his stomach had been tied into knots for days.

Clucking the paint into motion, Billy-Wolf caught up. He tried not to dwell on the many stories he had heard about various brave warriors who lost their lives to the great shaggy monsters that were the lifeblood of the band.

Next to grizzlies, buffalo were the most notoriously dangerous animals around. Bulls grew to be six feet high at the shoulder, weighed upward of two thousand pounds, and had a horn spread of three feet. Cows were not much smaller. Either could bowl over a horse or man with ease.

Billy-Wolf hefted the heavy lance in his right hand. He would much rather have his bow, since he would not have to get so close to the buffalo to bring one down. Unfortunately, it was back at the lodge. Lightning had brought him out to instruct him in hurling a lance from horseback, and it was just his luck that they had spotted the buffalo.

"If there is a cow with calf, we will not touch her," Lightning commented.

"She would be easier to catch," Billy said, although inwardly he cringed at the idea of killing any creature heavy with young.

"If we let her live, many winters from now her full-grown calf might feed a family in need," Lightning said.

"You think far ahead."

The warrior was somber. "A hunter must never waste game. If you kill for food, only kill as much as you can eat. If you kill for clothing, take only as many hides as are necessary." He paused and gazed westward. "Remember the Arapahos who visited us a short while ago? They claimed that the white trappers are well on the way to wiping out the mountain beaver. It is because the whites do not think ahead."

The statement jarred Billy's memory. Once, when he had been about seven years old, he had used a slingshot given to him by a trapper friend of his pa's to kill a pair of doves. He had not done it for the meat. Nor had he coveted their feathers. He had killed them for the sheer pleasure of killing them, and afterward felt so guilty he had been miserable. His pa had been upset but had not punished him, saying his misery was his just reward. Ever since, Billy never killed anything unless he had to.

A low whine drew Billy's attention to the two dogs loping along at his side. Snip and Jase had been with him ever since his family paid a visit to his pa's kin in the Little Sac country of Missouri. They had grown into fine specimens, as loyal to him as two dogs could be.

Billy grinned at Snip, the more protective of the pair. He would have to keep his eyes on them and make sure they were not harmed by the buffalo. To him, they were as much a part of his family as he was himself. He couldn't bear the thought of losing either one.

Lightning swung to the west rather than head directly toward the grazing buffalo. It would be prudent, he reasoned, to note the lay of the land before the chase began. Several summers ago a friend of his had made the mistake of blindly pursuing a small herd and been crushed when his horse had blundered into a steep gully and fallen on top of him. Lightning was not about to make the same mistake.

Minutes went by. They were fewer than a hundred yards off when the Kit Fox warrior confirmed that both animals were bulls. One raised its head and regarded them with interest but made no move to flee. Lightning decided his first guess had been the right one. They were old bulls no longer able to keep a harem. Left to themselves, they would eventually be brought down by wolf packs or other predators.

"I will take the bigger of the two," Lightning declared. He saw the boy nervously lick his lips. "If you do not want to do this, I will go on alone."

Billy-Wolf was stung by the mild rebuke. "I am the son of Second Son and Yellow Hair." He thought of how proud his parents would be when they got back and saw the robe he was fixing to have made from the critter's hide.

Lightning smiled, disguising the fact that deep down he was troubled. His aunt and Yellow Hair had been gone far too long, much longer than they had indicated. His uncle Singing Wolf, chief of the Burning Hearts, was of the opinion that Second Son and Cleve were still alive. It was a belief Lightning did not share, although he would dearly love it to be true.

Now both bulls were aware of the approaching riders and were standing with their legs splayed wide in an attitude of defiance. One snorted, then pawed at the ground.

"If they were any bigger they would be mountains!" Billy-Wolf breathed.

"You must aim for the lungs," Lightning said. "Their skulls are too thick for your lance to penetrate."

"What about their hearts?"

Lightning listened to a threatening bellow from the larger bull. "Hearts are much smaller than lungs. You must know exactly where to throw or the point will miss and the buffalo will run off with your lance sticking out of its side."

Billy-Wolf studied the animals closely. Both had hairy manes and beards, and long tails with tufts at the ends. Impossibly thick humps crowned their front shoulders. Past the humps, their backs tapered at a slant to slender rear hips. Their wicked horns were black. "So where do I throw to hit a lung? Into its side?"

"Aim right behind the foreshoulders," Lightning advised. "Then quickly get away."

"I understand," Billy-Wolf said. "The bull might try to gore Blaze or me."

"Or it might fall in front of your horse, which can be just as bad." The warrior slanted toward the knoll. "Stay close to me until I say to charge."

"Hold up," Billy-Wolf said. He slid down and stood in front of Jase and Snip. Gesturing, he snapped, "Sit! Sit!" until they did, at which point he commanded them to stay, then mounted. The dogs cocked their heads and watched him ride off, Snip whining, Jase fidgeting as if he were sitting on an anthill. "If they stay put, it will be a miracle," Billy muttered in English.

The bulls had moved closer together and glared at the two riders as if daring them to do something.

Rakes the Sky with Lightning was not fooled. Buffalo were belligerent, but they would rather flee than fight. He watched their backsides, and when the smaller bull's tail shot up, he took off at a gallop, trusting in the boy to stay close to him.

The sight of the enormous brutes wheeling and racing off set Billy-Wolf's blood to pumping wildly. Without being aware that he was doing so, he spurred Blaze after them. Buffalo were fast, but only over short stretches. He grinned as Blaze gained on them bit by bit.

The drumming sound of flying hooves filled Billy-Wolf's ears, beating in rhythm to the pounding in his temples. He noted the odd gait the bulls had and laughed aloud, half at them, half due to sheer exhilaration. Seldom had he been as excited as he was at that very moment.

Lightning heard the boy and smiled. It reminded him of his first buffalo hunt, and for a few seconds it was as if he were a boy again himself, racing through the high grass on his paint pony while whooping at the top of his lungs. Those had been grand times, learning to be a man. He envied his little cousin.

The bulls were going full-out, blowing noisily through their oversized nostrils, their heads bobbing as they ran. Muscles rippling, eyes wide, they ran as only creatures running for their very lives could run, exerting themselves to their limit, and beyond.

The larger bull was closer to Lightning. Ever so cautiously, never taking his eyes off the brute for an instant, he edged nearer, trying to draw within lance range. It bothered him that the smaller bull was on the far side, since it made Billy-Wolf's task that much harder. But they were committed. There was nothing he could do. If he were to swing wide and bring down the smaller bull himself, the boy might be offended.

For Billy-Wolf's part, all he had eyes for was his quarry. He was trailing Lightning by several yards when he started to guide Blaze to the left to go around both buffalo so he would have a clear throw. Then it occurred to him that maybe he should wait for his cousin to drop the other one before he moved in for the kill.

Lightning raised his lance on high. He was almost close enough. A few more yards would suffice. But as if the bull sensed its impending demise, it marshaled its strength and went even faster.

Slapping his legs against the chestnut's sweaty sides, Lightning again narrowed the distance. He thought he saw the bull glance back at him but couldn't be sure for the swirling high grass and the dust being raised. Patiently waiting for just the right moment, he rose, balanced for the throw.

Billy-Wolf saw, and marveled. He forgot all about the smaller bull. He wanted to witness his idol in action, to have a story he could share with his jealous friends for months and years to come. But even though he had his eyes glued to the tableau, he almost missed the throw.

It was a blur. One moment Rakes the Sky with Lightning had his arm cocked, the next, his arm was in front of him and the lance jutted from behind the foreshoulders of the large bull. That the throw had been accurate was attested to by what happened next.

The big bull crumpled, blood gushing from its nose. Its head drooped, its horns nearly scraping the ground. Uttering a last snort, the beast went into a forward roll that carried it over a dozen yards.

Billy-Wolf was forced to swing wide anyway. A glance revealed the bull lying still except for its twitching legs. Lightning had drawn a butcher knife and leaped down, ready to finish it off, but there was no need.

Now Billy had to do equally as well. The smaller bull had gained a good fifteen feet on him, so he knuckled down to make the distance up.

Blaze had never chased a buffalo before but took to the hunt like a duck to water. Long legs churning, the horse was capable of enduring a long pursuit.

Billy hoped that would not be the case. He kept expecting the bull to slow and held the lance ready to hurl. His arm grew tired, but he didn't care. His shoulder ached, but he ignored the discomfort. He had a chance to impress Lightning and he was not going to fail.

The bull ran on and on. How much time elapsed, Billy couldn't say, but when he risked a look back, he was upset to find that his cousin was no longer in sight. It was all on his shoulders; he couldn't rely on Lightning for help if something went wrong.

Presently Billy realized the bull had finally slowed. Not much, but enough to enable him to pull within ten feet. He was tempted to make the toss but knew his arm was too tired. He'd miss, and the bull would get away. In order to ensure success, he must cut the range by half.

Blaze heeded Billy's goading. He could see the bull's heaving flanks, see beads of sweat on its hindquarters. The hump, though, was still too far away.

The bull flagged even more. Billy-Wolf tensed. His gaze riveted to the spot behind the front shoulders where his cousin had struck, he hiked the lance as high as he could and steeled his sinews.

So intent was young Billy-Wolf on the proper spot to strike that he was slow to react to an abrupt change in the bull's movements. Too late, he realized the brute was whirling toward him. He tried to rein to the right and found himself looking down at the top of the bull's shaggy head. He saw the corded muscles, saw those awful horns. And, to his later keen regret, he screamed when the bull rammed into Blaze.

The stallion squealed as it went down. Billy was thrown clear of the saddle. The prairie and the sky switched places several times. And then he was lying on his back, his head spinning, his hands empty, while under him the ground rumbled.

Billy rolled without looking. The roll saved his life, for as he moved, the bull charged past. He leaped to his feet and cast about for the lance. All he saw was Blaze, still down, struggling to stand. He would have liked to see how badly his horse was hurt, but he had his own life to think of.

Spinning, Billy beheld the bull. It had stopped thirty feet away and was balefully regarding him. Perhaps if he stood stock-still it would wander off. He froze, the frantic beat of his heart so loud that he was certain the animal could hear it.

The bull shook its head a few times. It drove a hoof into the soil, tearing clumps of sod loose. Then, shoulders bunching, it dipped those deadly horns and attacked.

Young Billy-Wolf felt a few moments of raw terror. He was in the middle of the sprawling plain, with no cover in sight and without a weapon capable of slaying the beast. Other boys might have become too panic-stricken to move, and died right then and there. But in the short span of those terrible moments, in the midst of the most frightening experience of his young life, he reached deep within himself and proved that the blood of his warrior mother and courageous father pumped strong in his veins.

Billy whirled and ran. To a bystander it would have appeared as if he were fleeing in stark fear, but that was not the case. He had a plan, a desperate ploy that might work if he could survive one more charge.

The heavy thud of hooves grew louder and louder. He ran on, refusing to look, for fear it would drain his will to live. Only when he sensed the brute was almost upon him did he twist. The broad, hairy brow was six feet away. Those curved horns were ready to rip and rend.

Billy sprang to the side as far as he could leap. He was hit a glancing blow and something tugged at his buckskin shirt, tearing it. Landing on his side, he flipped onto his stomach and lay still.

Again the buffalo had flashed on by. Billy glimpsed its enormous bulk briefly. The grass closed around him and he made no attempt to stand. His idea was to lie there until the bull went away. After all, it wouldn't attack if it couldn't see him. Or so he hoped.

Silence descended. Billy thought he heard the buffalo stomping around. It brought to mind a tale about a warrior who once wounded a buffalo that vanished in some brush. The Cheyenne had been stranded afoot and had headed back for the village for another horse. That buffalo had come after him, seeking him out when he tried to hide. Had it not been for other warriors who wandered by, the man would have lost his life.

Would this bull do the same? Billy wondered. Off to the side the grass rustled and he spied the brown colossus weaving right and left as if searching for him. It was sniffing loudly, relying on its superb sense of smell to locate him. Billy hadn't though to test the wind and had no idea whether the breeze was carrying his scent to the creature or away from it.

The moments that followed were nerve-racking. Billy had never found anything so hard to do as lying there as still as the grass while the furious bull roved the area. Several times the animal came so close that it nearly found him. Once, the buffalo lumbered straight at him and was within several steps of stumbling over his body when it veered aside.

In due course the plain was quiet once more. Billy-Wolf still did not budge. He had learned from his pa and ma how to stay motionless for hours if he had to. It was a skill that came in handy when stalking an enemy or, as in this instance, hunting or being hunted by the more savage denizens of the wilderness.

The dull clomp of hooves warned Billy he was not as alone as he figured. A large form came straight toward him. Dreading that the bull had caught his scent, he was about to push up and run when he recognized Blaze.

Billy-Wolf rose and surveyed the prairie. The bull was hundreds of yards off, moving to the southeast at a leisurely pace.

A hasty examination of Blaze revealed no broken bones or wounds. He patted the stallion's neck, then climbed on and rode in ever-widening circles until he came on the lance. It had not been broken, either.

Billy-Wolf Bennett reined up. He had a decision to make. His cousin would understand if he were to explain what had happened and why the bull had gotten away. But could he go on living with himself, knowing he had turned tail?

The boy was torn. Then he thought of his parents, of his mother who was reputed to be the best warrior in the tribe, and of his father, who had once, armed with nothing more than an ax, tackled a bear.

"The Bennetts never run from trouble, son," Cleve once told him. "We don't go around stirring up grief like some folks do, but when someone wants to fetch us misery, they learn the hard way that getting us riled is the same as stirring up a nest of hornets."

"We never run," Billy-Wolf repeated aloud, and took off at a trot. Not north, back to his cousin. Not to the northwest, where the village lay. He rode after the bull to finish what he had started.

Blaze was not as eager this time around. The odor of the bull hung fresh in the air, and it made the stallion edgy. Billy had to keep poking his heels into its sides to prevent it from drawing up short.

The delay proved timely. Billy spied the bull rolling in a wallow. Dust sprayed in all directions as the animal wriggled on its back, its legs pumping the air.

The brute had already forgotten about him. Opting to take advantage of the situation, Billy bent low over Blaze and circled to approach the wallow from the south. Whenever the bull stopped rolling and sat up, he reined up.

The buffalo had not stopped cavorting when Billy completed his circuit. During the earlier clash he had let his excitement get the better of him, a mistake he was not going to make twice. He inhaled deeply, calming himself.

To the east rose a series of low hills. Billy happened to glance at them and spotted a gleaming pinpoint, as of sunlight reflecting off of metal. The light blinked out and he waited to see if it would reappear.

Since the village was only a few miles off, Billy guessed that it must be a Cheyenne hunter returning from a foray after antelope. Or it might be Singing Wolf, his uncle, coming back from the elk hunt, which many of the seasoned warriors had gone on.

On second thought, Billy realized it couldn't be the chief. Singing Wolf had left three days ago. Another week and a half to two weeks would go by before he saw his uncle again.

The reflection sparkled clearly on the crown of the second hill. Billy worried that it might be an enemy war party, or even a bunch of whites on their way to the high country to trap. After the light vanished once more, he promised himself that he would check later.

For now, Billy had the bull to deal with. He faced front and felt the short hairs at the nape of his neck prickle. The buffalo was upright and about to charge. But he wasn't the object of its wrath.

Snip and Jase, his cherished companions, had appeared on the scene. Their tails were erect, their hackles raised. Incredibly, they appeared to be about to tangle with the buffalo.

A second later the bull charged.

Billy-Wolf Bennett raised his lance and galloped to their rescue.

Chapter

— 3 —

Second Son was first to spot the fishermen and point them out to Cleve.

A dozen or so lithe, dark-haired men were in shallow water below some rapids. A few were naked, the rest wore leggings. Spears and clubs were about evenly divided among them. Spread out in a line, they were spearing and clubbing large fish with a skill that was uncanny.

Cleve had done his share of fishing. He knew how hard it was to hit one with a spear or an arrow, how the water itself added to the difficulty by making it appear a fish was in one spot when actually it was in another. These men were taking their quarry with such ease, they made the task look simple.

"What do you think, Yellow Hair?" Second Son asked. Her warrior instincts warned her to be careful, never to trust strangers until they proved worthy of trust.

"I'm mighty tired of being on the run," Cleve said. "It would be nice to sleep in a lodge for just one night. Maybe they're friendly. Maybe they'll invite us to their village."

"Or maybe they will try to lift our hair," Second Son said. She, too, was weary of always being on the go, but she was leery of offering the hand of friendship to those who might chop it off. The lure of a few creature comforts was not worth the loss of their lives.

"There's only one way to find out," Cleve said. "Besides, the trail goes right by them. Either we lay low until they're gone or else we detour to the south." He clucked at Socks. "Me, I'm partial to the direct approach."

Second Son moved alongside him. Even if he was making a mistake, she would face the consequences at his side. She loosened her knife in its sheath and held the crude lance she had fashioned the night before close to her right leg.

A boy on the bank spotted the riders and called out. All the men stopped what they were doing and turned. The tallest, a naked man whose frame was packed with muscle, glanced at his fellows, then stepped to the rocky shore. Once on land, he set the haft of his spear on the ground and waited for the newcomers.

To Second Son's seasoned eye, it was apparent by the tall one's bearing that he was a leader of men. He had a certain air about him, as if he had been born to greatness. She admired his lack of fear and the absence of suspicion. In a way, he reminded her of Singing Wolf, her brother, chief of the Burning Hearts.

As the warrior woman would soon learn, her guess was accurate. The tall man was indeed a chief. Chillarlawil was his name, and while he did not let on, he was quite amazed by the pair who halted before him. Never in his life had he seen a white man with hair the color of the sun. And the other, who had the watchful aspect of a battle-hardened warrior but in reality turned out to be a woman, was a wonder.

"Greetings, friends," Chillarlawil said in the tongue of his people. "On behalf of the Chinooks I welcome the two of you to our land."

Cleve glanced at Second Son. "I don't savvy this chatter one bit. Do you?"

Shaking her head, Second Son placed the lance across her legs to free her hands to make sign. Holding her right hand level with her shoulder, the fingers and thumb extended, she twisted her wrist several times. "Question." Her hands flowed smoothly. "You know sign language?"

Chillarlawil smiled, pleased they could communicate. "Learn many winters past," he answered. "We Chinooks. These"—he indicated the fishermen and the boys—"my people. We greet you, our arms open wide."

Cleve did not need Second Son to translate. After all the time he had spent among the Cheyennes, he knew sign as well as they did. "Cleve Bennett," he said aloud in English while tapping his chest, and then added in sign language, "This my husband, Second Son. We happy meet you."

Chillarlawil looked from one to the other. Had his eyes deceived him? The woman was the man's *husband*? Surely the man must not know hand talk very well.

Second Son noted the chief's confusion and allowed her mouth to curl upward. "Yes. Yellow Hair my wife. We on trail many sleeps. Make us happy meet friendly people."

Hearty laughter burst from the chief of the Chinooks. Chillarlawil found himself warming to this strange, mismatched pair. "Question. Your tribe confused about how marry?" he asked Second Son. "Question. May-be-so, your men like women, your women like men?"

Cleve joined in the mirth. For the first time in days the tension drained from him like water from a sieve. He felt that at long last they were among potential friends. "We happy explain after we rest."

Only then did Chillarlawil discern that the pair were in poor shape. They were both too thin, and in their eyes, when they stopped laughing, he detected a haunted aspect. "Come with me. I show where you stay." He swiftly donned his shirt and leggings, gave his spear to one of the boys, and walked eastward along the river.

Second Son saw the fishermen go on about their

business. Their utter lack of hostility reassured her that the strangers were in truth friendly. As she and Cleve were led over a rise, she gazed at the high walls of the gorge through which the rapids passed. Then a sound she had not heard in ages, the gaiety of playing children, rose to greet her, and she looked down on a tranquil scene.

A large village occupied a broad shelf bordered to the south by high bluffs. The lodges were of two types. Nearer the river were small dwellings made by placing bulrush mats over a cottonwood frame. One was currently being constructed by several women.

Nearer the bluffs were more permanent structures. These were plank affairs, some long, some short, and all with entrances that seemed to lead partially underground.

Canoes lined the shore. Huge racks had been erected behind them on which to dry fish. Many of the racks were completely covered.

People were everywhere; the village bustled with activity. Men were busy sharpening spears or mending nets. Others worked at carving canoes from yellow pine. Women were making clothes from sea-otter pelts and other hides. Several sat in front of lodges whittling the horns of bighorn sheep into various objects. Second Son passed one young woman who had nearly finished a large bowl. The craftsmanship was exquisite.

Cleve noticed that the Chinooks were not the only ones at the Dalles. Differently dressed Indians moved among them in perfect peace. None of them he recognized, which served to remind him of how very far away lay the land of the Cheyennes.

Chillarlawil was an observant man. He pointed to where several visitors in beaded buckskins bartered for candlefish oil and said, "Klikitats," Then, signing, he elaborated. "All tribes welcome here. Chinooks trade with everyone. No shedding blood allowed, ever. While you in village, no harm come you."

Neutral territory, Cleve mused. He'd heard this was the case, but until he saw it with his own eyes, he'd been skeptical. "Question. Many tribes Chinooks trade with?" he asked.

"Okanagons, Kalispels, Wenatchis, Wishrams, Sanpoils, Tillamooks, Nez Percé, Snakes," Chillarlawil signed, and stopped. "Many more."

The latter two tribes Cleve had heard of. "I surprised Snakes, Nez Percé, travel many, many sleeps. Their country far east this country."

"Chinooks have trade goods Nez Percé, Snakes no, find other places," Chillarlawil signed. "Shells, otter fur, slaves, other things."

Second Son was quick to pick up on the one sign word that reminded her of their awful winter ordeal. "Question. Chinooks keep slaves?" she signed.

"We no keep," Chillarlawil answered. "Other tribes bring slaves trade Snakes and Nez Percé for horses." He could not help but read the unrest her eyes betrayed. The only reason he could think of for her to be upset was that she and her "wife" had been slaves themselves. He sincerely hoped that wasn't the case and resolved not to pry. No one could blame him for doing nothing so long as he remained ignorant of the facts.

"We see band, warriors with horses, west of Chinook village," Cleve signed.

"That Broken Paw, Nez Percé. See them six sleeps past." The news disturbed Cleve since it meant the band would be coming through the village again sooner or later on their way eastward. He wanted to be long gone by then.

Chillarlawil halted at a small bulrush lodge that overlooked the raging waters. "Question? You like this?" he politely inquired.

"We thank you," Second Son signed.

"You rest now. Sleep may-be-so you like. Evening you honor me, come join my family for meal. Wife good cook." Chillarlawil indicated the largest plank lodge in the village. "Come when the sun rests on the horizon."

Second Son watched the chief walk off, then dismounted. Her initial elation had evaporated. There had been something strange about the way Chillarlawil reacted when she quizzed him on the slaves. Her warrior upbringing, which had taught her to regard anyone not of her own people or their few allies as likely enemies, reasserted itself. "I am uneasy, Yellow Hair," she said.

"Land sakes, why?" Cleve responded, genuinely puzzled. In his opinion, the chief had been as friendly as could be, and he looked forward with relish to partaking of Chinook hospitality, at least until dawn.

"I cannot say, but we must be careful," Second Son said.

Cleve scanned the encampment. Strangers being so common a sight, few of the Chinooks were paying any attention to them. None had shown the least little ill will. Were it not for the implicit faith he had in Second Son's intuition he would have shrugged off her suspicion as unwarranted. "All right. Careful it is. But for now, I could use a wash and a nap to tide me over."

"First the horses," Second Son reminded him. It was yet another example of her early training that she put the welfare of their mounts before their own. Without Socks and Shadow they would be stranded afoot, countless leagues from Burning Heart territory. Their horses were as essential to their journey as breath itself.

Together they took the animals to a secluded spot along the edge of the gurgling Columbia. While the horses drank and Cleve stood watch, Second Son stripped off her clothes and slipped into an oval pool screened from the lodges by a ring of trees. The water was cool and refreshing. She held her breath and dunked her head all the way under.

To Cleve, the sight of her glistening figure filled him with a familiar hunger. Because of the strain of their many narrow escapes and the feeling of always being in danger, they had not made love in more days than he cared to recollect. He longed to do so that very night, but knew Second Son would not let him touch her while they were in the village. Only when she was sure that they were completely safe would she let down her guard.

Second Son stood and wiped water from her shoulders and breasts. Totally unconscious of the beauty she radiated, she hastily donned her clothes and sat on a flat rock to wring out her lustrous raven hair while

Cleve took his turn. She marveled when he stripped bare, stood on a log, and dived cleanly into the pool. In many respects he was like an otter in the water, a skill her people had never developed.

Swimming always reminded Cleve of his childhood in Missouri. Many a summer day had been spent with his brothers at their favorite swimming hole, where they had rigged a rope from a high branch so they could swing out over the river and drop into its crystal depths. Those had been the days, he reflected. How innocent everything had been!

Cleve wanted to dawdle but washed and emerged to let the air dry him before he put on his worn buckskins. "We could do with a new set of clothes," he mentioned while inspecting a tattered sleeve.

"In time," Second Son said. "I would rather have a new bow and good arrows."

Cleve thought of the rifle he had lost. Obtaining another was going to be hard since they had nothing of value to trade except their horses, which they were not about to part with under any circumstances. Stealing one was also out of the question. So long as the Chinooks were being so sociable, he felt obliged to be the same.

Suddenly, from lower down the river, shouts and screams broke out. Alarmed, Cleve started toward the sounds without bothering to dress. He leaped onto a high rock that commanded a view of the village and the Columbia.

Second Son was only a step behind him. She saw a commotion at the water's edge, close to the fish racks. Men, women, and children were rushing from every direction. Many had ventured into the river, and some were gesturing at the other side. She did not understand why at first.

"Look!" Cleve bellowed, extending an arm. "That youngun is about to be swept away."

It was a boy no older than Billy-Wolf. Either he had been fishing or swimming and strayed too far from the placid water near the south shore, out past a towering island of solid stone in the middle of the river. Beyond the island, the channel narrowed, and rapids foamed over upthrust rocks. The boy was pinned against the island, his arms outspread for better purchase, trying to hold on as the current tugged at his legs and threatened to sweep him down the rapids.

"If he's swept away, he won't stand a prayer," Cleve mentioned.

Already five or six canoes had been launched, but the Chinooks were unable to paddle close enough to rescue the boy without imperiling their craft. A few braved the water on foot, edging slowly forward. The foremost man let out a squawk and would have been hurtled off his feet if not for the fast thinking of companions who pulled him back.

"Don't they know how to swim?" Cleve asked, and moved nearer the brink.

"They should throw a rope to him," Second Son said. Just then the boy wailed in despair and she saw him whisked to the very end of the island, where he managed to cling to a finger of rock. He gritted his teeth and held on, but it was only a matter of time before he weakened and the river won.

"Damn," Cleve said. He couldn't stand by idly

while the youngster perished. Bending at the knees, he executed a flawless dive. Second Son called his name, but he was already committed. The water closed around him and he arched his back and kicked to bring himself back to the surface. Stroking cleanly, powerfully, he swam toward the island.

Second Son almost dived in behind him. She stepped to the edge but hesitated, torn between her devotion and her knowledge of her limitations. She knew she was no match for Cleve in the water and might well find herself caught in the rapids. As much as it tore at her to hold back, she had to for both their sakes.

Among those who had gathered on the run was Chillarlawil. He had heard the shouts and knew that a boy was too far out. But he didn't realize it was his youngest son who had blundered until he stood at the canoes.

"Yelleppit!" Chillarlawil cried, entering the river. Of his six sons, the youngest was his wife's pride and joy. She doted on him, pampering him, and as a result the boy got into more trouble than all his other sons combined. It was strictly forbidden for any of the village children to wade out past a certain point in the river. Everyone knew that. Only Yelleppit would have been brash enough not to listen.

Chillarlawil was not much of a swimmer, but he was about to throw himself in and leave his fate in the hands of the Great Mystery, when women to his right started pointing up the river and jabbering excitedly. He looked, and spotted a pale log sweeping toward the island. Then he saw arms dipping in measured strokes and recognized the mop of yellow hair atop the swimmer's head. His knees went weak. The newcomer was trying to save his son!

Cleve swam strongly, confidently. So long as he stayed in the still water he was fine, but as he drew nearer to the island he felt the current increase. He resisted the tug, which grew stronger. By the time he was close to the east end of the rock slab, it took all his strength to fight shy of the rapids. Small wonder the boy had been sucked out.

"Hang on!" Cleve sputtered. "I'm coming!"

Yelleppit heard the shout and looked up. The words were foreign to him, and he figured they had been distorted by the roar of the rapids. Then he saw a golden-haired giant knifing toward him and was so overcome with amazement that he nearly lost his grip.

The boy had not been among the lodges when his father escorted Cleve and Second Son into the village. He had been playing near the canoes with friends, one of whom had dared him to go out beyond the point permitted.

Yelleppit had never refused a dare. He prided himself on being the bravest of his father's sons and had proved it time and time again. Usually, no harm was done. But the treacherous water had swept him off his feet before he could blink, and now he was about to be swept away again. His arms hurt terribly. It seemed as if they would be torn from their sockets at any moment.

Cleve was close enough to see the rising panic in the youngster's face, which is why he had yelled. He slanted to the left to skirt the bubbling tip of a submerged rock. Without warning, the current seized him in its irresistible grasp. He tried to reverse direction, but the river pushed him along as if he were no more than a bobbing piece of cork.

Since Cleve couldn't hope to resist the inexorable pull, he used it in his favor. Stroking with renewed vigor, he swam toward the end of the island. In his ears roared the hissing rapids. The projecting finger loomed before him and he thrust out both arms. By the merest hair his fingers caught hold.

Yelleppit gawked at the apparition next to him. He had met white men on occasion, but did not quite know if this was a white man or some new manner of creature. Then he heard the apparition curse lustily in the white tongue. The words were just as alien as before, but he knew the tone from trappers and traders he had overheard.

Cleve was in dire straits. He could not let go of the rock to grab the boy or the current would cast him down the river as if he had been shot from a cannon. Yet if he didn't grab the youngster and attempt to reach shore, he would grow tired and be swept away anyway. He was damned if he did, damned if he didn't.

"We'll make it!" Cleve fibbed to bolster the boy's spirit. The Chinooks were still trying to help, but none could get within twenty feet. He spied the chief moving to the forefront of the rescuers and prayed Chillarlawil would come up with a brainstorm to save them.

Someone did, but not any of the Chinooks.

Her face set grimly, Second Son rode Shadow at a

gallop into the Columbia. The water made the horse skittish and she had to prod it constantly to keep it going. Shadow plowed among surprised Chinooks, who parted to let the horse by.

Cleve's salvation was coiled in Second Son's hand. Over at the fish rack she had found a large coil of rope made from deer hide. Whether it would be long enough was debatable. She saw her man glance at her and held the rope high for him to see.

Chillarlawil also saw and divined her intent. He knew she would need something to weight the end of the rope and immediately stripped off his half-soaked shirt. After bundling it tight by tying the sleeves together, he intercepted her.

Second Son was perplexed for a few seconds when the chief shoved the bundle under her nose. He was so agitated that he forgot himself and tried to explain in his own tongue. She was on the verge of riding past him when, in a flash of inspiration, she realized how the bundle would come in handy.

Taking the bundle, Second Son quickly tied the end of the rope around the shirt. Hurrying on, she passed the last of the Chinooks. Shadow balked, afraid of the swift current, compelling Second Son to lash her with the reins. They were fifteen feet from Cleve and the boy when the mare stumbled and nearly went under.

Second Son hauled on the reins while leaning back as far as she could. Trying not to think of the swirling water, which rose as high as her knees, she backed up a short space and stopped.

Cleve wanted to whoop for joy. He looked at the boy, who had his eyes closed and was gritting his teeth against the strain. "Hold on!" Cleve encouraged him. "It won't be much longer."

Second Son let out enough rope for her to swing it in an ever-faster vertical circle. Thanks to the added weight of the bundle, she soon had the rope spinning like a whirlwind. At the apex of a swing, she released it. The bundle sailed toward the island, bobbed a few times, and was carried past the finger of rock before Cleve could grab it.

Willing herself not to be flustered, Second Son rapidly reeled in the wet rope and prepared to try again. She was concerned for the boy, whose face was scarlet. He could not maintain his hold much longer.

Once more Second Son whirled the safety line. She had to compensate for the angle and the current. When she was sure, she let the bundle fly. It hit the water about ten feet upriver from her mate and shot straight at him. All he had to do was reach and grab it.

Then the boy lost his grip.

Chapter

—4—

Snip and Jase could be as fierce as ravening wolves when the need arose. They'd had to be tough in order to survive. At an early age they had proven themselves to be the dominant dogs in the village, and Jase had acquired a nasty scar on his right cheek that resembled a miniature lightning bolt.

Later the pair had taken to driving off coyotes that prowled too close to camp. They had tackled a black bear once, and Snip had suffered a torn left shoulder. On another occasion, when they had been off hunting with their master, a roving grizzly had tried to run Billy-Wolf down. The dogs had distracted the huge carnivore while Billy made good his escape.

But never in their active lives had the pair of husky dogs gone up against a creature as huge as the bull buffalo that now charged toward them with its horns held ready to hook into their bodies.

They reacted automatically, Snip dashing to the right, Jase to the left. Snip, the light-colored of the pair and the heavier by fifteen pounds, snarled at the bull, which explained why the buffalo veered after him instead of Jase.

At first glance, it appeared as if the dog could easily evade its larger adversary. Snip flowed over the ground like tan quicksilver. But the bull, for all its bulk, was remarkably light and quick on its feet.

Billy-Wolf Bennett saw the buffalo swiftly close on his dog and hollered Snip's name in dismay. He raised the lance even though he was still too far off to make the throw.

Snip crouched, growling savagely, as the bull bore down on him. He barked a feral challenge a few times. Then, as the bull whipped its thick neck upward, Snip leaped, vaulting high, clear over the sweep of the buffalo's spearing horns. The bull's broad shoulder hit the dog a glancing blow, though, and it was enough to send Snip sailing. The dog landed on its side, stunned, trying weakly to scramble erect.

The bull slid to a stop. Spinning on the head of a coin, it glared and snorted.

Jase flew in from the left, barking frantically to draw

the buffalo's attention. The bull ignored the darker dog, dug in its hooves, and charged helpless Snip.

By then Billy-Wolf was close enough. He imitated his cousin's toss exactly, putting all the power of his developing sinews into the throw. That, combined with the speed of his horse and the momentum of the bull, was enough to drive the lance halfway into the bull's back.

Billy had not known if he was strong enough to embed the lance clear in the bull's lungs, as his cousin had advised. He'd hoped, at the very last least, to make the buffalo mad enough to forget about Snip and come after him. In this, he succeeded far better than he might have liked.

Driven mad by the pain, the buffalo uttered a bawling, rumbling cry and sped toward Blaze. Billy-Wolf wheeled and fled, flicking the reins for all he was worth, never taking his eyes off the onrushing beast. The bull drew closer and closer and he could see its dark eyes fixed on him, malignant pools of primal hate, the result of the torment he had inflicted.

Blaze raced like a chinook, mane and tail flaying. The buffalo's horns were mere inches from the end of the horse's tail when the enormous brute snorted a final time and fell. Its front legs buckled and the heavy body thudded onto the ground, then slid a good thirty feet. When it came to rest, the bull lifted its head high into the air, its tongue jutting from its mouth. The head waved in a circle once, slowly sank to the flattened grass, and was still.

It took a few seconds for the reality to hit home. Billy-Wolf hauled on the reins and sat staring in disbelief at the miracle he had wrought. He'd slain his first buffalo! Every boy in the tribe longed for such a day. His only regret was that his parents had not been there to witness his triumph.

Someone else was there, however, someone on one of the hills to the east. He was a large, lanky man whose hair had been slicked back with bear grease, whose buckskins were smeared with grime, and whose mouth contained several black teeth that were exposed when he grinned.

"Well, I'll be damned!" this apparition declared. "The sprout did it! I never would have believed it if I hadn't of seen it with my own peepers."

Chuckling, Rafe Hancock lowered his spyglass and slid back down the far side of the hill a few yards before rising. He considered himself lucky to have spotted the boy and the warrior who was galloping from the north before either of them caught wind of him. Their presence meant a village was nearby. And it wouldn't do for Rafe to stumble on an Indian camp.

Rafe was under orders to make his way in secret to a certain point along the North Platte River. The man who ran the whole shebang had made that point as clear as could be, and he wasn't the kind of man Rafe cared to rile.

After folding the spyglass in on itself and sliding it into his possibles bag, Rafe stepped into the stirrups of his gelding and resumed his interrupted trek to the northwest. He pulled a piece of jerked deer meat from the same bag and munched contentedly.

Things were looking up for Rafe Hancock. After two dismal years of trying his hand as a trapper, he had been about ready to call the frontier quits and head back to the States when he'd met the man he now called his boss. Who would have thought, Rafe mused, that the runt of a coon was as canny as a cornered painter? Who would have thought that thanks to him, Rafe had enjoyed acquiring more money each year than most trappers earned in a dozen of sweaty toil?

Yes, sir, Rafe reflected. Hooking up with that Mexican spitfire had been the smartest thing he'd ever done. The sole drawback was that working for the vilest polecat on the face of the planet had soured his reputation. None of the mountain men he had once called pards wanted anything to do with him. He was shunned, an outcast. And he would be a *dead* outcast if the trapping fraternity could prove how he had filled that beaded poke of his.

Once past the last of the hills, Rafe struck off on a direct course for the river. He knew it was not far off, knew that the Indian village might even be located somewhere along it, so he stayed on the lookout for more savages.

Although Rafe would never confess as much, he had a deep fear of the red devils, as he liked to call them, which stemmed in part from the fact he had nearly lost his hair to roving bands of Blackfeet and Piegans during his trapping days. It was his conviction that the only good Injun was a cold corpse. Every last one should be exterminated.

"Lousy Injuns," Rafe muttered. Just thinking about the red blight put him in a foul temper. He had half a mind to go on back and pick off the two bucks with his trusty flintlock. But he was already a day late reaching the North Platte, and his boss was not the most patient of men.

Three hours later a line of cottonwoods blossomed on the horizon. Rafe smiled. Where there were trees, there was water, and from the look of things, he'd found the river. He scanned the horizon, seeking a small bluff, a landmark visible from miles off. Since it was nowhere in sight, he bore to the west.

The bluff appeared about the same time as Rafe reached the serpentine belt of foliage. He became more alert, his thumb on the hammer of his rifle. Presently he smelled wood smoke. Reining up, he cupped a hand to his mouth and mimicked the call of a sparrow hawk.

From near the bluff came an answering *killy-killy-killy*. Licking his thin lips, Rafe rode on. He counted fifteen figures in the clearing yonder. A bear of a man with a red beard hanging down to a belly the size of a cooking pot came to greet him.

"As I live and breathe! Give this coon your paw. You're the last of the bunch, Hancock. We'd about given you up for dead."

"It'll be a cold day in hell before the lousy Injuns make wolf meat of me," Rafe bragged. It disturbed him to learn that everyone else had already arrived. He knew his boss's temperament all too well.

Other men greeted Rafe as he advanced to the string of tethered stock and dismounted. His moccasins had hardly touched earth when a firm hand clapped him soundly on the back and he turned to look down into the dark, cold eyes of the one man he feared more than Indians. More than anything. "Sorry I'm late," he blurted before he could help himself. "I was delayed leavin' St. Louis. Had to have my horse shod and the blacksmith was so busy I had to wait a few days before he could get to it."

It was a lame excuse, as Rafe knew. He thought that he would be cussed out, or worse. To his relief, the leader of their band beamed and clapped his shoulder.

"Those things happen, eh, amigo?" the short, wiry man responded. His swarthy, sinister features crinkled with sly mirth. "At least you made it, and in one piece. Tomorrow we can start for the mountains."

Rafe let himself be escorted to the fire and hid his astonishment when his boss handed him a cup of coffee. He'd never seen the man in such grand spirits and it threw him a little. "You're sure in fine fettle," he remarked.

"And why shouldn't I be, *compañero?*" responded the leader. "My time in New Orleans was *extravagante!* I bedded a different *puta* every night, drank myself under the table every other night, and gambled away my money in glorious style!" He inhaled and smacked his chest. "It was glorious!"

Red had walked over to the fire. "And now where to, boss? Up into the high country to waylay more stupid trappers?"

The other men assembled to hear the answer since they all had a stake in the decision. They had learned to trust their leader's judgment, but they all knew that their pickings the year before had been slimmer than ever and taken much more effort to acquire. Previous years had ended with each man being allotted two or three pokes as his share of the spoils. Last year each had received only one.

"I have been doing much thinking," the sinister man declared. "Stealing plews from the trappers is no longer as rewarding as it once was. Part of the problem is that the beaver become scarce. Part of the problem is that the trappers are much too careful." He grinned. "And part of the problem is that the stealing has become too much like work. Sí?"

"We agree, *mon ami*," a renegade named Landis spoke up. "But what else can we do? Fleecing sheep is all we are good at."

The leader poured himself a cup of black coffee and held the warm tin cup in his hands. "What would a shepherd do if his flock no longer produced wool? I'll tell you. He would get a new flock."

"What are you saying? That we head east and prey on those who travel back and forth between the settlements?" Rafe asked. It was one thing to waylay trappers in the remote Rockies, where there was no law other than survival of the strongest, quite another to contemplate rubbing out farmers and store clerks. One mistake, and they would be hauled before a judge or a vigilance committee.

"Do I look that dumb to you?" the boss snapped.

"No. Of course not," Rafe said quickly. If there was one thing their leader would not abide, it was an insult. Even an implied insult could prove fatal.

"Smart answer." The man leaned back and regarded them smugly. "No, I was thinking of the wagons which have been heading west to the Oregon country. I hear that each year more and more make the trip." Avarice animated his face. "Think of it, amigos. Those pilgrams, they take all they own of value with them. Money. Gold. Jewelry. Whatever."

"Damn!" exclaimed a stocky man named Avery, boggled by the prospect. "We'd be in bootle up to our armpits."

"That's right!" chimed in Webber, a man whose right eye had long ago been lost to a Sioux arrow. "Why, we'd be rich in no time!"

The leader chortled. "*Es verdad.* I thought you would see my point." Quaffing his cup in a few thirsty gulps, he smacked his lips and rose. "I say we head over South Pass. In the country beyond we will lay wait for the *estúpidos* who dream of a new life at the end of the rainbow."

"That's awful close to Confederacy country," Red mentioned, referring to the dreaded Blackfoot Confederacy, a loose-knit federation of the Blackfeet, the Bloods, and the Piegans. The three tribes shared a mutual hatred of all white men and made it a point to kill every one they came across in the most horrible manner possible.

"Sometimes one does not obtain great reward without great risk," the leader said. "But I would not be concerned. We have enough guns to hold off a large force."

"We'd better," Rafe commented, and took a sip.

The leader's eyes narrowed. "What does that mean, amigo?"

"Only that we might be close to a village," Rafe disclosed casually. "I spied on a couple of bucks out hunting buffalo early this afternoon." He saw the apprehension that crept over the gang. "Not to worry. They never caught a glimpse of me. I was too far off."

"Two Injuns," Red said. "That don't hardly mean a village is anywhere near."

"They had dogs, too," Rafe mentioned. "Or as least the sprout did. And you know as well as I do that Injun mongrels never stray far from a village. Injuns don't allow them to. It surprised the dickens out of me, seeing this pair."

Their leader had been about to pour himself another cup. He stopped, his voice oddly tight when he asked, "The one who owned the dogs was a boy?"

"Sure was," Rafe said. "With more grit than most men I've known. Hell, you should have seen him. A bull about sent him into the heareafter, and he mounted up and went after it a second time. I thought for sure he'd be gored, but he put a lance into the critter as slick as you please." He mentally reviewed the incident. "Now that I think of it, he must have been a breed. His hair was sort of sandylike, much too light to be a full-blooded Injun."

No one there was more shocked than Rafe when their leader lunged and grabbed him by the front of the shirt. "Describe this brat to me."

"I didn't get a good look at his face," Rafe said. He tried to pry the other's fingers loose, but it was like prying at the gripping talons of a hawk. "The only thing that caught my eye was his straw hair. Why? What difference does it make? Who cares about a stinking brat breed, anyway?"

Their boss seemed to regain control of himself and

let go. "This next is *importante*. Did the man with him have hair the color of corn?"

"Yellow? No." Rafe shook his head. He could tell the rest were as mystified as he was, but no one dared to probe deeper. "The other one had black hair, just like every other Cheyenne buck I've ever laid eyes on."

The blood drained from the leader's face. "Cheyenne?" he repeated softly, and then seized Rafe again. "Did you say Cheyenne?" Without waiting for an answer, he pushed Rafe aside and smirked wickedly, saying half to himself, "Can it be? After all this time has my wish come true? Old Cartland did tell me they have two dogs now."

Red cleared his throat. "What the hell is this all about? Do you know the breed?"

"I might know his parents," their leader rasped. "And if I'm right, it means we put off plundering pilgrims while I settle a personal score." He gestured toward their horses. "Mount up. We are going to go find the Cheyenne camp."

No one liked the idea much. Rafe made bold to comment, "What for? Ain't we asking for trouble? It's not like we can take on an entire village."

"Why can't we?" the leader retorted. "If I say we will, we will." Clenching his fist, he shook it at them, and there wasn't a renegade present who had the gumption to argue. "I swear to you, here and now. If these Cheyennes are the ones I think they are, then I won't rest until every last one is food for the maggots." Blood lust made his voice rise an octave. "Mark my words, hombres. A while back, a Cheyenne bitch and her bastard of a white husband made a fool of me. I vowed vengeance, no matter how long it took. And this is one vow that Julio Cardenas Morales intends to keep!"

A rosy crown was all that remained of the setting sun when Twisted Leg and her tired sisters hauled the heavy travois laden with buffalo meat and the hide into the Burning Heart village.

Billy-Wolfe Bennett rode in front of the travois beside his cousin. Their coming had been cried throughout the camp and many were on hand.

Billy's happiness was tempered by the absence of his ma and pa, and his uncle. It was a custom among the Cheyenne that when a boy his age did a remarkable deed, an adult family member would give a present to anyone in need, in honor of the event. But no one was on hand to honor him. Or so he mistakenly thought.

Rakes the Sky with Lightning reined up in front of his lodge and studied those assembled. "This day Wolf Sings on the Mountain has proven his medicine is powerful. It is fitting that I give the sorrel behind my lodge to Ghost Heart, who kindly cried the camp at my request."

The venerable warrior was elated. Age and disease had weakened him to the point where he could no longer get around without the aid of a cane. He had lost the last of his horses many moons ago and was too poor to trade for another. Holding his head high, Ghost Heart hurried off to collect his gift.

Billy-Wolf climbed down and trailed his cousin around the lodge. They were in time to see Ghost

Heart hug the sorrel, tears streaming down the old man's eyes. So overcome was the warrior that he departed with his head bowed low. "You did a good thing, Lightning," Billy said.

"I had a wise teacher," Lightning said. "One day I want to be a chief, like your uncle Singing Wolf. He has taught me that a true leader always puts the interests of his people before his own. One way is to make a habit of giving to those in the most need without stripping away their pride."

"Ghost Heart will be a happy man this night," Billy remarked.

"As you should be. Your parents will be very proud when they return."

The reminder brought a frown. Billy wondered how long it would be, if ever, before they showed up. When they had left for California, he'd brimmed with confidence that one day they would ride back into camp and the family would be whole again. As more and more time went by, though, and they failed to appear, his confidence waned. Of late, he had begun to doubt he would see them again and felt guilty for doubting it. He was their son. He was supposed to have faith in them.

After tending to their horses, Lightning and Billy Wolf walked around front. As they were about to enter the lodge a lean figure hastened toward them.

Eagle Stays in Air was the most influential man in the band, next to Singing Wolf. A noted chief in his own right, his acts of valor had been matched only by his boundless generosity. Now he halted and idly brushed at his gray hair. "I saw my old friend Ghost

Heart. His heart is full to bursting, and so is mine. Many times I tried to give him a horse, but he always refused."

The chief placed a hand on Billy's shoulder. "Perhaps, if you continue to do well, you will be asked to go on our next raid against the Pawnees and hold the horses for the warriors."

Billy-Wolf could scarcely believe his ears. Going on a raid was every boy's supreme dream come true, for by doing so he might earn the coup that would elevate his standing in the tribe. "Thank you," he said excitedly.

Eagle Stays in Air fixed a grave stare on Lightning. "Did you happen to see any sign of white men while you were out today?"

Immediately Lightning sobered. While the Burning Hearts had not had any dealings with the whites—except for their one white captive, whom they had later adopted and was now the wife of Second Son—they had heard many disquieting tales from other Cheyenne bands and friendly tribes like the Arapahos and Dakotas.

It was rumored that the whites were not to be trusted, that most spoke with two tongues. When offering the hand of friendship, they held a knife in the other. Some whites had boasted that one day they would own all the land between the great river and the mountains, and drive off any tribes who resisted.

Lightning had dismissed their prattle as vain raving until Yellow Hair had confirmed the fact that there were plans afoot in the village of the Great White Father to encroach on the land his people had roamed for more winters than any could remember. It would be a slow process, Yellow Hair had claimed. First a few would come, and then more and ever more, until there were as many as the grass itself.

"I saw no such sign," Lightning said. "Why?"

"Bear Shedding, on his way back from hunting antelope, came across the tracks of a horse with iron hooves near the hills to the southeast. The horse was heading north."

The mention of the hills jarred Billy-Wolf's memory. "I almost forgot. Today I saw something up there. It could have been a rider."

Rakes the Sky with Lightning glanced at the vanishing sun. "It is too late to check now. Tomorrow I will go find these tracks and follow them. If there are whites near our village, it is best if we can find them before they find us."

Chapter
—5—

Surviving in the wild was a tricky proposition. There were times when a mountain man had to use his brain in order to go on breathing. If, for instance, a free trapper knew that he was being stalked by a war party, he employed his wits to elude them.

There were other instances when taking the time to think a problem through often proved deadly, times when a man had to act on pure instinct, when his reflexes alone either proved equal to the occasion or he forfeited his life and possibly the lives of those who depended on him.

Years of frontier living had honed Cleve Bennett's reflexes to a razor edge. When he saw a need to act, he invariably did, and mulled over the consequences later.

So when the Chinook boy was torn from the finger of rock by the surging current, Cleve reacted automatically. He let go, too, pushing off and throwing himself to the left to snatch hold of the boy's wrist. The instant he did, he turned to the right, spied the bobbing bundle at the end of the rope, and girding every muscle in his body, launched himself at the rope. He had to fight the push of the current and the drag of the boy's weight combined. For a harrowing few moments it seemed that he would miss.

Then Cleve's clutching fingers closed on the line and the rope stretched taut. The water smashed at him, but he held on. He saw Second Son backing Shadow toward the shore and grinned as the mare slowly pulled them toward safety. In another thirty seconds they would be free of the current.

Then the rope gave a crisp jerk and Cleve nearly lost his grip. Raising his head, he saw Second Son staring at a point midway between them. He gazed at the same spot, and goose bumps broke out all over him. Whoever made the rope had not intended for it to bear much weight. It was beginning to split.

Cleve let himself go as limp as he could to ease the strain. Water got into his nose, his mouth. Sputtering, he tilted his head back and sucked in air.

Second Son had momentarily drawn rein. She

feared the rope would break if she kept on going. The chief, clearly mystified, was watching her closely. She bobbed her chin at the rope several times.

Chillarlawil took one look and understood. He knew they would lose his son and the white man if they did not do something swiftly. In desperation he glanced around, and hit on an idea. Barking instructions to those nearest him, he hastily stripped off his leggings. As others removed their clothes and passed the garments to him, he tied the sleeves and legs together. In short order he had a waterlogged buckskin chain twenty feet long.

Cleve saw the tall chief edge forward. He kept one eye on the rope, which had frayed another fraction, in part due to the boy, who was having difficulty keeping his head up out of the water and kept tugging on Cleve's arm. "Try not to move!" Cleve bellowed to be heard above the rapids, aware he was wasting his time since the boy did not speak English.

Yelleppit was terrified. He knew the white man had grabbed the rope and could not understand why the man's woman did not continue to pull them out and why the man himself was making no attempt to haul them to safety. He had kicked and pulled in an effort to goad the man into action.

But when the white man shouted at him, Yelleppit held himself still out of fear that the other might let go. He wondered if perhaps the man had been overcome by panic and was too paralyzed to move.

Chillarlawil had drawn within fifteen feet of the pair. The river tugged at his legs, nearly sweeping him off his feet several times. At last he could go no farther. He lifted one end of the makeshift line and heaved.

It splashed down a yard from Cleve, too far away for him to do anything. He had to go on clinging to the rope and hope against hope that the next cast came in time. He saw Second Son moving slowly back out toward them, reeling the rope in as she did so. Why she was doing this, he had no idea.

Second Son simply wanted to be closer in case the rope parted. She would not let her man be killed, even if it meant throwing herself into the rapids after him.

The chief had the end of the garment line in his hands again. Tentatively sliding his right foot farther, he concentrated, whipped back his arm, and threw.

This time the shirt at the end of the line hit the surface within half a foot of Cleve. Simultaneously, he felt the rope give and sensed it was about to break clean through. Could he grab the shirt before that happened? Taking a deep breath, he hurled himself at it. Once more the water buffeted him and nearly threw him backward.

Cleve's grasping hand found the bulky line and held fast. He would have been all right if the shirt had not been so slick. To his consternation, he slipped, losing a few inches of precious purchase.

Seeing his plight, Second Son chucked the severed rope and kneed Shadow forward. The mare balked, but she persisted. When she was abreast of Chillarlawil, she put her hands flat on Shadow's back and pushed into a crouch. Everyone there gaped, unable to guess her intent, which was made apparent when she leaped high into the air.

Cleve was filled with terror. Should she miss, she would be swept down the Columbia, and there was nothing he could do to help her while he still held the boy.

Second Son, however, had timed her spring just right. She landed close to the line of clothes and grabbed hold with one hand while extending her other toward Cleve. His hand had slipped again and he was about to be swept off. She caught him around the wrist, coiled her shoulders, and pulled. The strain was almost more than she could bear, but inch by agonizing inch she drew him near enough to get another, firmer, hold.

Now it was up to Chillarlawil and the Chinooks. A dozen men closed on the line, and at a word from their chief, drew it in. The current resisted but not for long. Chillarlawil uttered a happy whoop when the three were at long last out of its clutches and standing on their own two feet, a whoop echoed by the majority of his tribesmen. General rejoicing broke out.

Cleve, panting, hauled the boy around in front of him. Yelleppit was so exhausted he could barely stand. Chillarlawil took the boy and hugged him, his eyes reflecting the depth of his gratitude. Other Chinooks clapped Cleve and Second Son on the back. "I reckon we're heroes," he joked.

"What you did was foolhardy," Second Son scolded, then grinned. "My brother, Singing Wolf, is right. I know how to pick a fine wife."

"You might need to pick another if you ever do something like that again," Cleve responded. "You about gave me a conniption."

They were escorted to the bank by beaming Chinooks. Cleve was somewhat embarrassed by the fuss the Indians were making, doubly so when Chillarlawil saw fit to offer a short speech. There Cleve was, buck naked, with scores of strangers staring at him. Casually holding his hands over his manhood, he impatiently waited for the chief to get done.

Second Son knew her mate well and was amused by his discomfort. While nudity was frowned on among the Burning Hearts, the Cheyennes were not as fanatical about it as the whites. According to Cleve, many of his kind believed that the Great Mystery—or Great Spirit, as some trappers preferred—punished those caught naked in public by causing them to burn forever in a place called hell.

At least that was Second Son's understanding, but she had to admit that white beliefs in regard to the spirit world were hard to make sense of.

After all, everyone came into the world naked. And if, as the whites asserted, the Great Spirit created everyone, it must mean that nakedness was the natural order of things and not a sin, as Cleve called it.

Presently the crowd dispersed. Chillarlawil went with his guests. He would never be able to repay them for what they had done, but he could and did use sign to thank them for saving his son, adding after Cleve had dressed, "I tell my people act kind our new friends, act same Chinook act Chinook. I tell them Yellow Hair brother, Second Son sister. I tell them your hearts pure. Chinook village yours while you here."

"Our hearts sing thanks," Cleve signed.

"Question. We help Yellow Hair, Second Son?"

Chillarlawil suggested. "You speak, Chinooks do. Any want, sign words. I do for you as do for family."

The offer was tempting, although Cleve disliked imposing. They needed supplies, needed new clothes, needed a rifle or pistol or both. "Later we talk," he signed.

"I not let Yellow Hair forget," the chief said. "Expect me when sun low in sky."

On the floor of the bulrush lodge had been spread four or five soft otter hides. Cleve sank down with a sigh and folded the top one to make a pillow. Sinking onto his back, he propped a hand under his damp hair and permitted himself to relax fully for the first time in many months.

Second Son eased onto her side next to him and rested her head on his shoulder. She doubted that the Chinooks would do them harm, but she positioned herself so she could see the flap covering the entrance and curled a hand around the hilt of her knife.

Soon the regular rise and fall of Cleve's chest told her he was asleep. Half of her wanted to do the same and the other half wanted to stay alert, just in case. Fatigue won. She drifted into a fitful slumber broken once by the yip of a dog.

Suddenly Second Son came wide-awake. The interior of the lodge was much darker, and through a crack she noticed the sun about to vacate the sky. She also noticed the shadow of a man who stood just outside. Second Son began to draw her knife.

There was a rap on the side and the chief said something in his own tongue. The flap was thrown aside as Cleve snorted and sat up.

Chillarlawil smiled. "I trust both rest well. Time eat," he signed. "Chinooks hold great feast honor our new friends. All top men come, see, talk."

The long plank lodge was filled to overflowing. In addition to forty men, an equal number of women and half again as many children had been invited. It so happened that everyone wanted to see the courageous couple up close and talk to them.

Seated in the position of honor to the left of the high chief, Cleve and Second Son were treated to a meal the likes of which neither had ever partaken before.

Served first was a wild onion soup, garnished with herbs, so tangy Cleve guzzled his straight from the wooden bowl. Meat dishes were passed around; fish of several kinds, bighorn meat, deer meat, squirrel, and even a bark plate of roast grouse. Bitter cakes were plentiful, as was coffee received in trade with the British at Fort Vancouver. A boiled flour pudding laced with dried fruit was the last item. It had been so long since Cleve had sweets, he downed two huge helpings.

Second Son ate hearty but did not cram herself full as did her mate. She was keenly aware of the questioning gazes of their hosts. As the chief was to explain, a warrior woman was a novelty in their experience and they did not quite know what to make of her.

A pipe made the rounds. Cleve, as was his habit when in a sociable frame of mind, did most of the talking, or signing, for the two of them. When a Chinook wanted to know how it was that they found themselves in that region, Cleve told about their long trek from the prairie east of the Rocky Mountains to California.

The Chinooks were a curious people and asked many questions, mostly about the Diggers, the Indians at the missions, and other tribes. Cleve answered them all. He was quite pleased with how delightful the evening had been. As he accepted his sixth cup of coffee one of the men held up his hands.

"Question. White man come down river meet Chinooks?"

"No. We know Chinooks make home along great river," Cleve signed. "Not know spot. Find village accident." He paused. "We glad Chinooks kind. We no like be captives second time. One time plenty enough."

An invisible ripple went through those assembled. Cleve saw it, saw features cloud and smiles disappear and Chinooks whisper to one another, but he had no idea what had sparked the drastic change.

Nor did Second Son. Her intuition warned that the general mood toward them had taken an abrupt turn for the worse and she lowered a hand to her hip, within easy reach of her blade.

Chillarlawil knew the reason. He had been about to puff on the pipe but froze, hoping no one would see fit to elicit more information. He should have known better. Delashelwilt, who had long wanted to be leader and never lost a chance to make life hard for Chillarlawil, joined the conversation.

"Question. You slaves many sleeps ago?"

Cleve figured that he had made a mistake mentioning their captivity, but he did not see how he could avoid answering the question without offending those present. "Two moons past," he signed.

"Question. Name of the tribe?"

"They call themselves the People," Cleve hedged, since it was common knowledge that quite a few tribes called themselves by the equivalent of that name.

"Question. They let you go?"

Chillarlawil had to do something. He owed the yellow-haired white and the warrior woman for his son's life. Hiking his arms, he signed, "Enough. Chinooks no polite when pester guests many questions. New friends need long sleep. I say we let them go their lodge. May-be-so, Delashelwilt ask his questions when sun new in sky."

Delashelwilt was not to be so easily denied. Sweeping those around him with a sharp look, he signed, "I no mean insult new friends. One more question, I stop ask." He faced Cleve. "Question, Yellow Hair. Tribe take you captive let you go? Or you escape?"

Cleve hesitated. He did not like the nosy man's manner, and felt a lot depended on the answer. His natural inclination was to confess the truth, but when he glanced at the chief, something in Chillarlawil's eyes changed his mind. As much as he disliked lying, he signed, in effect, "We work hard, please our captors, they take pity on us. Decide we slaves long enough. Let us go our own country."

Chillarlawil jumped to his feet. "No more questions. They go now," he signed for the benefit of the couple. He motioned for them to follow and ushered them out into the cool night air.

"Question. Why escape important?" Cleve wanted to know.

The chief looked around to ensure that no one else was nearby. Leaning close so only they could see his hands, he explained, "I tell you time-past. Sometimes Chinooks trade slaves, not for Chinook use, for tribes on coast." He looked around again. "May-be-so, slaves escape. Tribe who find them have duty. Give slaves back tribe owns them."

Second Son heard voices raised in argument in the lodge. She did not need to know the Chinook tongue to deduce the fact that the Chinooks were squabbling over what to do about them.

"After brave deed you do, save my son, I not hand you back any tribe. Our hearts are one, all time," the chief went on to say.

"Question. We safe?," Cleve asked.

"May-be-so my decision, yes," Chillarlawil signed. "Other Chinooks may-be-so not think same, want hold you, find tribe you escape from." Sadly touching both of them, he went in.

"We must leave," Second Son wasted no time in saying.

"As soon as the village quiets down," Cleve agreed.

Shoulder to shoulder they crossed to their own little lodge. Where earlier they had been at ease, now both were tensed to lash out at any and every threat to their freedom. Cleve bent to lift the flap.

"Wait," Second Son said. "Where are our horses?"

Socks and Shadow were gone. They scanned the village without result. Second Son made a circuit of the immediate vicinity, trying to tell from the sign in which direction the animals had gone, but it was much too dark to read prints, even for a tracker with her skill.

"The varmints must have taken our animals so we can't ride off in the middle of the night," Cleve speculated.

"They must be nearby. I will go look for them," Second Son declared.

"Not alone," Cleve said. "We don't dare lose sight of one another until we're shy of this place."

Together they glided stealthily along the river to the fish racks. No one saw them since few Chinooks were abroad. Cleve was about to move into the open when Second Son grabbed his elbow and pointed.

A canoe was arriving from down the Columbia. In the poor light, few details could be made out. Three men occupied the canoe, two were wielding paddles. They did not appear to be Chinooks. Apparently they had visited the village previously, because after hauling their craft from the water, they made a beeline for the chief's lodge.

"I have a bad feeling about this," Cleve whispered.

Like twin ghosts, they wound among more bulrush lodges. From most, issued low voices, sometimes laughter. As Second Son, in the lead, rounded one of the structures, a large dog stepped from the shadows and growled, its lips curled to reveal its formidable teeth. She was all set to slit its throat when Cleve stepped past her and tossed something at the dog's feet. It lowered its head, sniffed a few times, gulped the offering, and walked off, pacified.

Cleve bent his mouth to her ear. "I stuffed some of that venison under my shirt to munch on later."

Southwest of the village a wide basin rich with grass afforded ample grazing for the few horses the villagers owned. Second Son and Cleve were almost there when they spied a small figure leading two horses to the east. Distinct white patches on the bottom of the lead animal's legs stood out clearly.

"Socks," Cleve whispered.

The figure leading them might as well have been deaf and dumb. He had no inkling anyone was within fifty yards until Second Son tapped his shoulder.

Yelleppit yelped and nearly tripped over his own feet. When he saw who it was, he smiled and offered the reins. "My father tell me feed horses new freinds while new friends eat big feast," he signed. "I sorry. I late bring horses back your lodge."

"We thank you," Second Son signed.

"No. I thank both new friends. You save my life," the boy responded. "I never see death close before. I have much think about. Plenty much." He looked from one to the other. "My heart glad may-be-so I help new friends someway. Please. Any way."

"I need rifle," Cleve signed, not meaning to be taken seriously. Few of the Chinooks owned guns, which were of little practical value to a people at peace with everyone and who mainly fished to fill their bellies.

Yelleppit pondered a moment. "Come with me," he signed.

Cleve was inclined to refuse. Every second they delayed increased the odds of their being discovered by

Chinooks bent on holding them until they were turned over to the tribe they had fled. Then, in the forest to the west, brush crackled and a horse nickered. Riders were approaching.

"Lead us," Cleve signed.

The noise filled Second Son with foreboding. It could be anyone, but ordinary travelers were rarely abroad in the deep woods after the sun set. Trying to follow a narrow trail through heavy timber in the middle of the night was inviting trouble. She made it a point to scrutinize the tree line as they crossed to the long plank lodge, but did not catch sight of the horsemen.

Both of them were surprised when Yelleppit guided them behind the building. He put a finger to his lips, then dashed inside through a narrow door. Inside, heated debate was still under way.

"What do you suppose the boy is about?" Cleve asked softly. "I doubt he owns a gun."

Dogs barked to the northwest, heralding the arrival of the riders. Shouts rang out and were answered. Second Son stepped to the corner to peek out. Many figures were gathering around a knot of horses almost at the limits of her vision. She could not identify the late travelers.

Over by the door, Cleve tapped his foot, anxious to be off. Minutes went by. He was listening to the babble of voices within when they abruptly fell silent. One man spoke, and there was the sound of feet moving toward the front of the lodge.

"We're not waiting any longer," Cleve whispered. He was in the act of turning to climb on Socks when

Yelleppit materialized, a rifle in his hands, an ammo pouch and powder horn hanging from his shoulder.

The boy held the gifts out to Cleve. When his hands were empty, he signed, "My father receive these many moons time-past from white man. He give them new friends. Show his heart good."

To say Cleve was overjoyed would be an understatement. He slung the pouch and horn across his chest, then caressed the rifle as he might caress Second Son.

"My father say he wish more ways he help," Yelleppit signed. "He tells you leave, quickly." The boy bent his head to hear the commotion to the northwest. "Question. You know who come village?"

"Question. Who?" Cleve asked.

"Broken Paw, the Nez Percé. Few his warriors hurt. One bad. They blame Yellow Hair, Second Son." Yelleppit paused. "Someone tell them you here. Broken Paw eager slit throats."

Chapter
— 6 —

Rakes the Sky with Lightning did not sleep well. He tossed and turned all night long, waking repeatedly. Half of those times he would lie on his back and stare up through the ventilation flap at the sparkling stars. The other half he would turn onto his side and stare with abiding affection at the lovely woman slumbering peacefully next to him.

Twisted Leg had been Lightning's wife for going on ten moons. Her name derived from a childhood mishap that resulted in her left leg being permanently bent. She limped when she walked, but otherwise the infirmity had not hindered her development into a full-bodied woman with a tender heart and pure spirit.

Many of the young men had shunned her because of her leg. They thought she would make a poor mate, unable to properly do the many tasks required of Tsistsista wives. Most had regarded her as a cripple.

But not Lightning. He had adored her from afar, seldom giving her leg a second thought. True beauty always came from within, and in his eyes she had more than any woman in the Burning Heart Band.

After a proper period of courtship, they had formally joined. Lightning would have liked for his aunt and Yellow Hair to have been on hand, but they had still not returned and he had not wanted to postpone the cherished event any longer.

Now, lying there in the dark, her warm breath fluttering on his cheek, Lightning gently placed a hand on Twisted Leg's swollen belly. It warmed his heart to think of the new life forming inside her, to dream of the son or daughter they would soon have.

At the same time Lightning was troubled and had been for some time. All due to the many stories he had heard about the whites, which in turn possibly explained a profoundly disturbing dream he had recently had. Lightning felt that he had seen a vision of the ominous future awaiting the Tsistsistas.

In the dream, Lightning had been out riding on the sun-drenched prairie with his wife. Suddenly an insect had smacked against his body. Then another, and another. Glancing down, he had seen what he mistook for a grasshopper and flicked it off his shirt.

More and more grasshoppers had flown into Lightning and his wife, and into their horses as well, making their mounts skittish. Gazing eastward, Lightning had been appalled to spy a huge, dark cloud of flying bugs sweeping toward them. In his dream, he had realized that these were not ordinary grasshoppers; they were locusts, the scourge of the plains, voracious insects that devoured everything in their path.

Then another one alighted on Lightning's chest and he reached up to swat it off. To his horror, he saw that it had the body, wings, and corked rear legs of a locust, but its tiny head was that of a bearded white man with teeth like tiny knives. Lightning swung at it, but the thing bit into his hand and clung fast, its teeth sawing into his flesh.

The roiling swarm swooped down upon them. Lightning heard his wife scream and tried to go to her aid, but he couldn't find her in the blinding cloud. The tiny terrors closed on him, encasing him from head to toe. He had felt them gnawing into limbs and torso, boring through his skin in a hundred places at once, felt them tear deep into his body and rip him apart from the inside out.

Lightning had snapped awake and sat bolt upright. Sweat had caked him, and his heart had hammered madly. He was not one prone to nightmares, which made the vision even more alarming.

That had been several moons ago, yet Lightning could not shake the deep unease that came over him whenever he thought about the encroaching whites. Knowing there might be some close to the village alarmed him. He wanted to find out who they were and what business they had in Tsistsista country.

Approaching dawn had painted the eastern sky with bands of striking pink when Lightning roused himself. Moving quietly so as not to awaken Twisted Leg, he dressed, took his bow and quiver, and slipped from the lodge.

Few Cheyennes were abroad. Lightning saw an old woman making for the river with a water skin. An old man stood in front of a lodge bearing a painted white buffalo on its side, arms outstretched to formally greet the new day.

Lightning had noticed that the elderly were always the first up in the morning, the last to retire at night. It was as if they were milking life for all it had to offer before they were called to the Great Beyond. Older people did not squander their time as the young were prone to do.

Going around behind the lodge, Lightning sought the swiftest of his six horses and mounted. He had told Twisted Leg his plan before they fell asleep so she would not be concerned when she woke and found him gone.

Turning the sorrel, Lightning was surprised to see her with a robe around her shoulders, her expression most odd. He kneed the horse over and leaned down. "I did not mean to disturb your sleep. You should go back in and get more rest."

"I will," Twisted Leg promised. Her warm palm caressed his face and neck. "Please be careful today. My heart is troubled and I do not know why."

Lightning smiled to reassure her. "I am always care-,ful," he said. "If there are a lot of whites, I will only spy on them, then come back to consult Eagle Stays in Air."

"Good." Twisted Leg lowered her arm. "Perhaps, though, you should take someone with you. Wolf Sings on the Mountain would be glad to go."

"My cousin is too young yet," Lightning said. "And I can travel faster alone." He rested a hand on her head. "Keep the fire kindled. I expect to be back before the sun is straight overhead."

"I will look forward to when my eyes drink in the sight of you again."

Those loving words lingered in his mind as Rakes the Sky with Lightning applied his heels and trotted eastward toward the distant green hills. He looked back once and his wife waved.

Twisted Leg was not the only one who watched him depart. Billy-Wolf had been staying with his cousin for several moons. He had heard the warrior leave, then seen Twisted Leg go out. Slipping from between Snip and Jase, he padded to the flap and peered out in time to see Lightning swallowed by the high grass. He knew where his cousin was going and would have liked to shadow him, but until he earned the status of a warrior, he knew that he must not overstep himself.

Billy scooted back to his blankets and crawled under them before Twisted Leg came back in. He thought it best not to let her know he had overheard their conversation. Closing his eyes, he feigned sleep.

"Are you hungry, Wolf Sings on the Mountain? Would you like your breakfast now or later?"

Flabbergasted, Billy didn't respond. He could not for the life of him figure out how she knew he wasn't asleep.

"There is plenty of pemmican," Twisted Leg said.

Realizing he was being silly, Billy faced her. "How did you guess?"

A sly grin creased her otherwise melancholy features. "Your breathing gave you away. That, and the moving flap." Twisted Leg glanced at it and gnawed lightly on her lower lip.

"Is anything wrong?" Billy inquired.

"No," Twisted Leg replied. It was only one small word, but the way she said it, the way she looked when she said it, gave Billy-Wolf the impression she wanted to bolt off across the prairie and bring her husband back no matter how hard he protested.

"He will be all right," Billy tried to soothe her. "Next to my mother, he is the best warrior in the band. My father has said so many times."

Bullets and arrows cannot tell good warriors from bad warriors."

Billy-Wolf wondered what she meant but decided not to ask. It might upset her more. Rising, he donned his britches and let the dogs out to do their business.

While Twisted Leg puttered around, downcast, Billy downed some pemmican. It upset him to see her so disturbed. She was one of the kindest people he had ever known. His mother once told him it had something to do with her leg, but his mother had not elaborated.

"I will be gone most of the morning," Billy-Wolf announced.

Twisted Leg studied him. "I trust you will not try to follow my husband."

"I would not think of it," Billy said, suspecting that she was fully aware that he *had* thought of it. Women had an uncanny knack for seeing through a man. Or so his pa liked to say.

Billy did not want to tell her that he had a surprise in store for her and Lightning. Several days ago he had been off exploring along the river and stumbled on a pair of ducks. They had taken frantic wing, the male raising a ruckus. Both had circled several times before flying off. On his way back to the village he had seen them returning to the same vicinity.

It convinced Billy that they were partial to that stretch of the river. They could even be nesting there. Since duck meat was a prized rarity among the Tsistsistas, and duck eggs even more so, he figured to repay the generosity of his cousin and Twisted Leg by fetching them an unexpected surprise.

The sun sat perched on the skyline when Billy-Wolf swung onto Blaze and headed westward. Snip and Jase dutifully tagged along, frolicking like playful pups. They had gone several hundred feet when Snip abruptly halted, raised his muzzle into the air, and sniffed loudly while walking in a small circle.

Billy slowed to scour the trees and prairie. Of the

two dogs, Snip had the keener nose. Often Snip had sniffed out game Billy would not otherwise have found. But this time he saw nothing to justify the dog's actions. Nor did Jase seem the least bit excited.

"It must be an old scent, fella," Billy-Wolf said. "Come on. I don't aim to take the whole day."

The dogs fell in behind Blaze. As the animals and their devoted master wound off through the strip of woodland flanking the river, none noticed the parting of tall weeds or the relieved face that stared after them.

"That was too damned close for comfort," Rafe Hancock declared. "If that brat had yelled, half the village would be here before we could blink."

"I ain't afeared of no mangy redskins," Red said, slowly standing. "Let them come."

It was well-known among Morales's band that Red Fletcher had a temperament to match the color of his hair and was too reckless at times for his own good, so Rafe didn't argue. He crept to the edge of the prairie, then into the high grass, until he came to a cluster of their companions, all squatting low so as to be invisible to prying eyes.

"Any sign of the boss yet?" Red asked.

"Non, mon ami," Landis said. A former *coureur de bois* from Canada, he spoke French more fluently than English and affected a blue cap tilted on his head at a rakish angle.

"What the hell could be keepin' that greaser?" Webber interjected.

Rafe couldn't believe his ears. Slapping the older man on the arm, he said, "What's gotten into you, old hoss? Are you looking to give up the ghost? 'Cause that's what will happen to you if Morales ever hears you using that word. You know he can't stand it."

"Look, Hancock," Webber said while scratching his grizzled chin, "I ain't about to kiss his ass. Sure, I'll call him sir and bend over backward to suit him when he's around, but when he's not here, I'll be damned if I'll tread softly. The man is a thievin', back-shootin', lyin', skulkin' son of a bitch. He ain't God."

From the grass to their left a flat voice chilled the blood in their veins. "How thoughtful of you to bring the difference to our attention, señor."

Julio Cardenas Morales snaked out of the growth and crouched in front of them. His flat eyes resembled those of a rattler's about to strike. None of them wanted to be in One-Eye Webber's moccasins.

The old man mustered a wan grin. "Hell, Julio, I didn't mean nothin' by that crack. I've ridden with you since the day Yoder was kilt. If I didn't think you were a savvy leader, I wouldn't be here. You know that you can count on me."

"How glad I am to hear that," Morales said suavely in his clipped accent, masking his inner fury for the time being. He did not think it wise to provoke ill will when they were about to engage in a perilous undertaking.

Rafe thought it best to change the subject. "So what's it going to be? Do you still think this might be the right band?"

"Yes," Morales said, "even though I saw no sign of

that bitch, Second Son, or that meddler, Bennett. I did see a boy ride off who might have been their son. Too bad I wasn't closer to him."

Rafe and Red glanced at one another. Only then did Rafe realize it must have been the same brat he'd spied on from the hills, but he was not about to own up to the fact.

"I have been counting," Morales said. "There are only twenty-eight lodges, so the red vermin do not outnumber us all that much." His brow knit. "In fact, now that I think of it, most of the males I saw were either very old or very young. I think many of the warriors must be off on a raid."

"But what if you're wrong?" another man asked. "I don't mind admitting that some of us don't much like the notion of going up against a whole village."

"Who else thinks that way?" Morales asked, and was secretly amused when no one had the courage to confess. He knew they feared him, and indeed he fanned their fear since it was his sole means of keeping the motley, murderous crew in line.

The previous leader, Yoder, had relied on brute strength. The leader before Yodder, Jules Terrebonne, had resorted to animal cunning to maintain his rule. But Morales used fear as his tool for molding their actions to the pattern of his thoughts. He reveled in his power over them; he gloried in leading cutthroats who acknowledged no other authority.

Julio Morales had never aspired to be anything other than what he was. He liked to steal, he liked to kill. So it was perfectly fitting for him to devote his wily energies to doing those things he loved best of all.

Only twice throughout his long and checkered career had anyone gotten the better of Morales. Once, Cleve Bennett had spoiled an ambush that would have netted Julio thousands of dollars in plews. Another time, Second Son had shamed him. Those two defeats had festered within him like an incurable sore. Thinking about them rankled him so badly that he wanted to lash out and slay everything in sight.

"No one speaks, eh?" Morales said. "It is just as well. We have work to do." He gestured eastward. "I sent five men on around the village. In half an hour they will fire the grass. That will be our signal to hold up our end."

"Maybe we should wait," Rafe proposed, not because he wanted to, but because he was afraid of the consequences. "You want to get your hands on that boy, don't you? Let's spread out and snare him when he comes back."

"How thoughtful you are, amigo," Morales said sarcastically. "But the longer we wait, the greater the chance of being discovered. No, we will attack when I say to attack. So all of you see to your rifles and pistols. It would not do for any of you to have a gun misfire when a savage is about to cave in your skull with a war club or tomahawk."

Rafe Hancock twisted and gazed wistfully westward. He told himself that if he'd had any sense, he would have let that boy see him so the alarm would have been sounded and Morales would have been forced to call off the attack. But he had acted without thinking. There was no sign of the boy anywhere now. All Rafe could do was hope the kid would come back soon and spot them before they saw him.

Unfortunately for the renegade and the Tsistsistas, such was not to be. Over a mile off, young Billy-Wolf Bennett rode at a leisurely pace along the riverbank. He wanted to avoid spooking the ducks by coming on them too suddenly, as he had the last time.

The morning was made for hunting. Billy inhaled deeply the crisp, cool air and admired the clear vault of blue high overhead. Birds sang merrily in the trees, and across the river several deer were quenching their thirst. Moments like these were the ones Billy lived for.

Jase and Snip had gone off by themselves. Billy had not tried to call them back, since they would be likely to scare off the ducks long before he set eyes on his quarry. He came to the area where he had seen the pair, climbed down, and tied Blaze to a tree.

Like his cousin, Billy had seen fit to bring a bow this day. He notched a shaft on the string before advancing cautiously. Having never hunted ducks before, he had no knowledge of their habits and thus no idea of where to focus his search.

Did ducks stay on the water all the time except for the female when she was nesting? Did they like to spend time on shore, off and on throughout the day? What did they do at night? Were they always quick to take flight when they perceived a threat? How close could a warrior get to them? Which tactics were best?

These were the sort of questions Cleve had advised Billy to consider every time he went after game. "Know the habits of the animals you hunt and you're halfway to filling the supper pot," his pa had once said.

Billy had taken the words to heart. He'd spent many a day doing nothing more than observing wildlife, learning the ways of the many and varied creatures with which he shared the land. Buffalo, he knew as well as he knew himself. Deer, antelope, rabbits, squirrels, and many more, he had studied until there was nothing new left to learn about them.

Ducks were different. They did not come in great numbers to Cheyenne country except in the fall, and then mainly to the west.

Geese were also seldom seen, although Bear Shedding liked to tell how, many winters ago, when he was a boy, the Tsistsistas had been encamped far to the east and one morning emerged from their lodges to see the field of wild grain next to their village covered with geese. Everyone—warriors, women, and children—had grabbed whatever was handy and raced into the field to dispatch as many geese as they could before the flock took wing. "It was a marvelous slaughter," Bear Shedding liked to say. "For many sleeps my little stomach was full every night thanks to those geese."

Billy would have liked to see a field full of geese one

day. Then again, there were many sights Billy had grown fond of seeing. The visit to his pa's home a while back had fired his imagination with thoughts of new lands, new people. He would dearly love to visit California, as his folks had done.

Thinking of them saddened the boy. He tried hard not to let their prolonged absence affect him, but sometimes his guard slipped and he was ravaged by the hurt. His misery was compounded by the depth of his love for them. A few boys he knew were not overly fond of their parents, but not so Billy-Wolf. He adored them more than life itself.

Shaking his head to dispel his thoughts, Billy hiked westward. The water was so clear he could see the bottom, and he noted with interest the meandering of a number of fish, another type of game he had infrequently gone after, and then always in the company of his pa.

Time went by. Billy drew up, debating whether to go back for Blaze. He did not like to leave the horse unattended, easy pickings for rival tribes on a raid. About to turn, he heard a series of low quacks from somewhere up ahead.

Billy dropped into a crouch and investigated. Around a bend the river widened. Bathed in sunlight near the middle were the pair of ducks, swimming side by side. Billy raised the bow but didn't fire. He needed to reduce the range.

For a while Billy contented himself with watching to see if they would paddle closer to the bank. When it became obvious that they were content where they were, he sank flat and crept through the brush to a better vantage point. He had to hold the bow in front of him to avoid snaring it on the vegetation.

A log fifteen feet from the water offered Billy an ideal spot to wait for the right moment. He noted the rich green plumage of the male and wondered what kind of duck they were.

The female broke off and strayed in Billy's direction. His fingers tightened on the arrow, but he was premature. She swam in a tight loop and rejoined the male.

Patience was not Billy-Wolf's strong suit. His mother and father constantly pointed out that it was essential for anyone who aspired to be a competent warrior or hunter, but try as he might, Billy's impulsive nature often spoiled his attempts at self-control.

In this case, Billy grew tired of waiting. The ducks did not appear to be paying any attention to either shore, so he saw no harm in slowly rising to his knees so he could loose a shaft from concealment. He thought the log would hide him, thought the ducks would not fly off if he did not make any sudden moves.

How disappointing it was, then, when the very instant that Billy raised his head above the log, the pair flapped their wings and were airborne before he could snap the bow up. Annoyed at himself for spoiling everything, he leaped to his feet and angrily shook a fist at the fleeing waterfowl.

When they were specks in the sky, Billy-Wolf

turned to retrace his steps. Through a break in the trees he saw something that galvanized him into flight every bit as speedily as the ducks—a wide wall of smoke rising far to the east, right about where the village should be.

Chapter
— 7 —

"I don't get it," Cleve said while surveying their back trail for the umpteenth time since they had slipped from the Chinook village the night before. "There should have been some sign of them by now."

"We have worked hard to shake them," Second Son. "Be glad we succeeded."

"Have we?" Cleve questioned. As clever as they had been, he found it hard to accept that the Nez Percé war party had lost the sign. Yes, it was possible to wipe out hoofprints with grass and limbs, and to cover horse droppings with leaves and dirt, but any halfway competent tracker easily saw through such ruses.

Second Son did not see why her man was being so glum. She had perfected the art of disguising a trail to the point where a few could follow her if she did not wish them to. Yellow Hair should have more confidence in her ability.

They were no longer anywhere near the Columbia. Since too many Indians either traveled the waterway in canoes or paralleled its course on the shore, they had decided to swing to the south and bear due east later on. That way they could avoid being seen by parties who might inform Broken Paw.

Cleve was finding it difficult to stay as alert as he should. They had been on the go all night and half the morning, pausing briefly every so often to give their horses a breather. He would have liked to stop, find a comfortable spot, and curl into a ball, but they were better off pressing on until they knew beyond a shadow of a doubt that they had given the Nez Percé the slip.

Second Son saw him yawn and suppressed one of her own. She, too, was weary, but she shut the weariness from her mind, a trick she had learned during her early days as a warrior. By refusing to acknowledge her body's demands, she could push herself farther and faster than she would have dreamed she could. It was the secret of her superb endurance.

Even Second Son had limits, though, and she could feel the fatigue gnawing at the edges of her senses. By the end of the day she would have to rest or she would be worthless.

The terrain was much more rugged than either of them had anticipated. Steep mountains, deep gorges, and a network of ravines posed formidable barriers, which they negotiated with seasoned skill.

When a narrow stream appeared, Cleve made for a small pool and climbed stiffly down. "What say we let the horses drink their full? Half an hour shouldn't be too long."

A tiny voice in Second Son's head warned her to take only a few minutes and press on, but she overrode it with logic. Cleve was right. They and the horses needed a longer break. Slipping to the grass, she dropped the reins and stood back while Shadow dipped her nose into the sluggish water and gulped.

Cleve went straight to a pine, sat with his back propped against the trunk, and motioned for her to join him.

"One of us should keep watch," Second Son said. She did not know whether to be amused or annoyed by the fact that he was the one who insisted the Nez Percé must still be after them, yet he was all too willing to let down his guard simply because he was tired.

But that was ever the way with Cleve. Second Son found him a constant source of surprising contradictions. Sometimes he behaved just like a Tsistsista warrior would; at other times he acted contrary to all reason. Sometimes he was manly in the extreme; at other times he acted like a small boy. Perhaps that was the secret to understanding white men, she mused. They were all boys in men's clothing.

Second Son walked a few yards to the north and gave the ridge they had descended, and the forest beyond, a close scrutiny. For as far as she could see, the woodland lay undisturbed and tranquil, deceptively so since there were those out there who would slay her and her man without a second's hesitation.

That was ever the way in the wild. One moment a person might be riding along without a care in the world, and the next moment be locked in deadly combat with a savage beast or two-legged enemy.

Second Son had long ago accepted the uncertainties of life. Since they couldn't be avoided or shunned, since they were as inevitable as breathing and eating, she took each one as it came and made the best of whatever situation she became embroiled in. Adapting was the key. Either a person learned to adapt to life as life presented itself or life had a nasty habit of sweeping those unwilling to adapt off the face of the earth.

Second Son thought of Chillarlawil. It was most distressing that Broken Paw had come along when he did. The rifle had been a generous gift, but she was sure the kindly chief would have helped them even more than he had if the Nez Percé had not shown up.

Thinking of the rifle turned Second Son toward her mate. He was still awake, the rifle across his thighs. It was too bad she did not have a suitable weapon of her own.

Second Son was about to venture into the trees in

search of a limb to use as a temporary bow when she heard the faint clink of a hoof on stone. Whirling, she swept the ridge from top to bottom.

"Did I just hear what I think I heard?" Cleve asked at her elbow.

"You did."

"Damn. I was sort of hoping they wouldn't catch up before nightfall, so we'd get a decent night's sleep for once."

"Is that all you think of?" Second Son said testily, more upset at herself than at him. He had been right, after all. She had been too confident in her ability to disguise their trail, and in the wilderness, too much confidence could prove as fatal as too little.

Cleve glanced at her and noted the rare tension in her face. "Oh, I think of other things now and then," he quipped, and stroked her arm to accent his meaning.

That was another thing about Cleve that never failed to amaze Second Son. The man could never get enough of her. No matter where they were or what they might be doing, all she had to do was give him a certain look and he would be on her like a bear on honey. She suspected that he never really stopped thinking of it. Of course she was flattered, but it seemed to her that when they were fleeing for their lives through unknown country, the least he could do was keep his mind on the matter at hand.

"I was only joking," Cleve said.

To the northwest, an owl hooted. It was answered

by another to the northeast, and a third less than two hundred yards to the north.

"Not very bright, are they?" Cleve commented. "Owls never make a peep during the day."

"They have spread out," Second Son said. "They seek to ensnare us in this small valley."

"But they're not in front of us yet." Cleve dashed to the horses and brought both back. He had no objections to Second Son taking the lead since she could read the lay of any land much better than he. They forded the stream, crossed a grassy tract, and began climbing the next slope.

Cleve stayed on the lookout for the Nez Percé. He was itching to try the rifle. All he wanted was a clear shot, just one to let the warriors know they had better keep their distance or, better yet, call off the hunt while they still could.

It was doubtful they would. Cleve knew enough of Indian ways to realize the Nez Percé would not rest until they had redeemed themselves in their eyes and the eyes of their people.

Broken Paw, the band's leader, would be held to account for every life lost, for every man wounded. He had already been defeated once, at great cost. If he went back to his village now, his prowess as a leader would be diminished. His medicine, the people would say, was bad. To prove himself, to be able to hold his head high when he returned, Broken Paw must avenge the defeat.

Second Son reined up on a high bench and turned Shadow. The bird's-eye view enabled her to glimpse furtive riders moving toward the stream from three or four directions at once. Apparently the Nez Percé did not yet know that their prey had slipped the trap.

"I count eight," Cleve said.

"Nine," Second Son corrected him as the last of the painted warriors rode into the open near the spot where they had dismounted. "See that big one?" she said, pointing at a man who gestured angrily at the others.

"Broken Paw," Cleve concurred. "And from the look of things, he's none too happy."

They melted into the pines before they were spotted, Second Son in front as before. Shadow and Socks were tired but did not let them down. Until the middle of the afternoon they pushed on through magnificent country rife with game and amply watered. It surprised Cleve that they saw no sign of Indian habitation. It was peculiar, such prime land going to waste.

Then they came on another, much smaller stream, and as Second Son dismounted, an impression in the mud along the water's edge caught her eye. She squatted for a better look.

The track was a human footprint, but quite unusual for two reasons. First, the person had been barefoot. Second, the sole had been heavily callused, indicating the maker went barefoot all the time.

A shadow fell across her and Cleve whistled. "Look at the size of that coon. He must be as big as a redwood."

"He was here not long ago," Second Son deduced from the dampness of the mud flattened by the man's weight. She glanced up. "He might be watching us, Yellow Hair, as we speak."

Cleve hefted the flintlock and pivoted. The woods were quiet enough, but he swore he could feel baleful eyes fixed on them. It must be nerves, he told himself. "Let's light a shuck to the southeast. We'll stop for good about sunset."

Pushing on was a challenge. The timber grew thicker. There were deadfalls everywhere and dense briars to be skirted. They made slow headway, so slow Cleve chafed at the delay. His frayed nerves kept him imagining that someone was stealthily dogging their steps, yet whenever he checked, he saw no cause for alarm.

Shortly before they decided to stop, they entered the heaviest forest of all. Cleve noted the long shadows and remarked, "At least we gave Broken Paw the slip for a while."

"For a while," Second Son stressed. "But he is most persistent. The only way for us to stop him for good will be to kill him."

"Fine by me. I'm awful damned tired of running," Cleve groused. The game of cat and mouse they were playing with the Nez Percé war party was delaying their homecoming, keeping them from Billy-Wolf. It rankled him so, he wanted to throttle the one called Broken Paw with his bare hands.

Darkness overtook them when they were in dense timber. They made a cold camp in a clearing no bigger than their bulrush lodge at the Chinook village. Cleve set to work building a crude bed out of pine needles and brush, but Second Son stopped him.

"There is danger here, Yellow Hair. I feel it in my bones, as you like to say. We must be on our guard at all times."

Cleve listened to an idea she had and went along with it. Both of them sat in the middle of the clearing, backs to one another. Second Son looped Shadow's reins around her left wrist, and he did likewise with Socks's reins. That way no one would be able to steal their mounts. Better yet, no one could get at them without going past the horses, which were bound to act up if they caught a strange scent.

Cleve could feel the warmth of Second Son's body through his buckskin shirt. He leaned his head back until it rested against hers and sighed. "I'll never object to quiet, boring village life again. If there's one thing this trek has taught me, it's that the grass sure isn't greener on the other side."

"The other side of what?" Second Son inquired.

"The fence," Cleve clarified. He'd forgotten that while Second Son spoke English quite well, she still had problems with figures of speech.

"Which fence?"

Cleve sighed again. "Never mind."

Second Son didn't understand the allusion. She had seen a fence once, in Missouri when they visited his family, and as best she could recall, the grass had been the same shade of green on both sides. Perhaps, she reflected, it was another of those nonsensical white sayings she would never figure out if she lived to be a hundred.

Suddenly a familiar feeling came over Second Son, the feeling of being spied on. The nape of her neck prickled, her hands tingled. By this time the woods were so dark she couldn't see more than eight or nine feet with any clarity, so try as she might, she couldn't spot whoever lurked in the gloom. It might be one of the Nez Percé, she mused, sent on ahead. But somehow she doubted it. Her choice for most likely culprit was the owner of those huge, naked feet.

Cleve sensed a change in her posture and twisted his neck to see her profile. "Something wrong?" he asked softly.

"We are being watched," Second Son said while unwinding the reins from her arm. "I will go see who it is."

"Let me," Cleve said. "I have a rifle. All you have is a knife."

"It is all I need," Second Son reminded him. Among the Tsistsistas, her prowess as a knife fighter was second to none. Handing him the reins before he could protest, she slowly drew the blade and held it close to her leg so whoever was in the forest might not notice. "I will not be long."

"I'd rather—" Cleve began, but it was no use. She was gone in the blink of an eye, disappearing silently into the wall of vegetation without rustling a single leaf. He yearned to leap up and follow, only he knew she would be upset if he did. And he should know better than to worry. How many times had Second Son done the same thing, only to come back later with her knife dripping the lifeblood of an adversary?

Just inside the forest, Second Son crouched and paused to let her eyes adjust to the slightly dimmer conditions. There was no moon, only starlight to see by, which in the clearing had been ample, but here among the tightly packed pines and thickets it was as if all the stars had blinked out, leaving her in an inky soup. She must be careful not to move too fast, not to make any noise.

The silence was unnerving. No insects buzzed, no breeze stirred the trees. It gave her the false impression that she was all alone and at the same time made her feel vulnerable.

Second Son moved deeper into the growth, a single step at a time, stopping after each to look and listen. She had taken only four strides when off in the night something moved. She could not say what it was or exactly where, but the whisper of motion was unmistakable.

Moving behind a trunk, Second Son sought to determine if the lurker was coming toward her or moving away. She could not. The air hung as still as the mountain itself, affording no clues. If it was the barefoot man, he was either uncommonly clever or had the senses of a wild beast.

Just when Second Son was about to move on, another whisper reached her. Only it came from an entirely different direction than the last time. Either there were two people, or the first one had traveled some thirty feet without her being aware of it.

Second Son did not think there were two. And since she was more than a match for any one man, she elected to take him by surprise before he did the same to her.

Angling into the growth, her moccasins making virtually no sound on the thick carpet of spongy pine needles underfoot, Second Son cautiously wound through the minty pines until a blackberry thicket barred her path. There wasn't a person alive who could go through the center of a blackberry patch and not make noise, so she went around, bearing to the right.

The next instant Second Son halted, riveted by a strong sensation of someone or something close to her, so close she might reach out and touch whatever it might be. A scan of the trees did not reveal a thing. She went to move on, then thought to gaze into the murky depths of the blackberry bushes.

Second Son felt her skin crawl when she beheld a large, dim shape and discerned the dull gleam of large eyes fixed on her. She sank onto one knee so she would not be as plain a target, and the figure promptly sped off, moving so fast she couldn't keep track of where it went. Not once did she hear a twig snap or the scrape of a plant being pushed aside by the passage of the large form.

How was that possible? Second Son wanted to know. It was as if whoever she had seen had no substance to him, or else was able to move through the night more quietly than she ever could. The idea was disturbing.

So far the lurker had made no attempt to harm her. Second Son could return to Cleve and inform him that in her opinion the barefoot man did not pose a threat to them. Cleve would accept that because he trusted her with his life.

But Second Son wouldn't do it. Her opinion was

one thing, proof another. She reversed course and sped around the thicket on the left side. Although she moved as swiftly as a jackrabbit, the big man had vanished again.

This time, though, there was a clue to guide her. As Second Son stopped to check the thicket, a pungent odor assailed her nose, like the rank stench of a person who had not bathed since the day he was born, a foul reek akin to that of a wet bear or the hind end of a horse suffering digestive problems. It almost made her gag.

Second Son breathed shallowly and rotated on her heel, testing the air as she turned. The odor was stronger to the southwest, so she went to the southwest, advancing as warily as only a true warrior of the Tsistsistas could.

Presently it dawned on Second Son that she was much farther from the clearing and Cleve than she had originally intended to go. She was so far, that if she needed his help it was doubtful he would reach her in time. Which did not stop her from going on. She had fought her own battles long before Yellow Hair claimed her heart and soul, and marriage had not weakened her sinews or her will to apply them as necessary.

The timber began to thin out as Second Son climbed steadily higher. She came on more and more boulders and short open spaces where the grass grew sparse. After a while the wind could be heard howling over the summit, which loomed like a gigantic black wall that blotted out a portion of the night sky.

Second Son finally concluded that she had gone far enough. She had not heard or seen anything in quite a while. Whoever had been spying on them must have been scared off.

As the warrior turned, a twig snapped to the west. Second Son never hesitated. She sprinted toward the source, going from cover to cover, determined to catch the elusive ghost if for no other reason than to soothe her battered pride. Comanches, Blackfeet, Bloods, she had snuck up on them all at one time or another. Why, then, was she finding it so hard to catch a barefoot man as big as a grizzly who stank like a skunk? It was humiliating. Her brother would say she was losing her skill.

After covering twenty yards, Second Son halted. The wind whipped in stronger gusts, stirring her long hair despite its being braided, warrior fashion. To her right a cluster of vertical boulders stood like silent sentinels guarding the mountain. To her left, the slope inclined steeply to a barren shelf.

Second Son faced the boulders. If the man had not run off again, that was where he would be. She catfooted toward them, the knife level at her waist.

Had it not been for the rattle of loose pebbles rolling down the slope behind her, Second Son would have been taken completely by surprise. As it was, she barely whirled in time to defend herself against a hulking figure who hurtled toward her brandishing an upraised club. She ducked under a blow, then stabbed, but her thrust was neatly evaded.

The man skipped to the right, Second Son danced to the left. They circled, her attacker dwarfing her, making her wish she had gone back when she'd had the chance.

This close to the man, the awful stink was overpowering. Second Son held her breath, bunched her legs, and thrust at the giant's gut. He blocked it with his club, nearly knocking the knife from her hand. Second Son retreated to gain room to swing but was thwarted when she backed into a boulder.

The giant shot the club up, then down. Second Son dived to one side and heard a thump above her. She rolled when she hit. The club thudded into the ground, missing her by a fraction. Pushing to her feet, she barely avoided a third swing.

Suddenly Second Son had the opening she needed. The giant's side was fully exposed, his arm bent away from her. Taking a short step, she rammed the blade into his ribs. It should have stopped him in his tracks, or at the very least made him howl with pain and rage. Yet neither occurred. Instead, he dropped the club and was on her before she could draw the blade out, his massive arms encircling her waist and hoisting her into the air.

Second Son threw back her head and opened her mouth to voice a cry that would bring Cleve at a gallop, but the breath whooshed from her lungs instead of sound. She struggled fiercely, trying to yank her arms free. She kicked wildly. And she had no more effect on the giant than a mosquito would have on her.

A pale face filled the warrior's swimming vision. Agony lanced her chest. Her lungs were seared as if by fire. Second Son tried to butt the man in the nose but could not find the strength. She made a last, valiant attempt to turn the tide by kneeing him in the groin. Then the black of night engulfed her, and the last sensation she experienced was of something wet and sticky touching her forehead.

Chapter

— 8 —

Billy-Wolf Bennett's eyes were not the only ones to fill with fear on beholding the wall of smoke. Eagle Stays in Air had been rubbing down his favorite warhorse in front of his lodge when the animal jerked its head from his grasp and nickered. The horse had never misbehaved before, which was partly why Eagle relied on it more than any other horse he owned. He took a step back to regard it quizzically.

In doing so, Eagle glimpsed the prairie to the west of the village and felt a chill constriction in his chest.

A thick, wide wall of smoke ran from north to south for hundreds of yards, ran from practically the edge of the river to well past the southern end of the encampment. And thanks to the prevailing wind, which on nine days out of any given ten blew in from the northwest, the flames making the smoke were rushing toward the lodges.

Eagle was amazed that no one had noticed sooner, but then it was the quiet hour of the morning when most of the women were inside. And most of the men, he was acutely aware, were off on the great elk hunt with Singing Wolf.

"Fire!" Eagle yelled stridently. "Fire in the grass! Gather your little ones and whatever else you can carry and flee for your lives!"

In his excitement, Eagle Stays in Air did not question the cause of the blaze. All that mattered was the safety of his people, especially the women and children left in his care.

Eagle ran to the next lodge and threw the flap wide without bothering to announce himself. Inside, Wears Red, his niece, was sliding her infant into a cradle board. "Hurry!" Eagle coaxed. "Try to cross the river before the flames reach us."

Others had taken up the hue and cry, and worried Tsistsistas were scurrying every which way. Men were herding frightened horses, women herded anxious children. The village dogs were left to fend for themselves, their yips and barks adding to the uproar.

Eagle stood near the center of the village and jabbed a finger at the river. "Across the water!" he shouted. "It is our only hope!" He ran off to help where he could, while all around him utter bedlam engulfed the camp.

The din was so loud that it woke up Twisted Leg. In her condition she tired all too easily, and of late she had been taking several short naps throughout the day. She rose on her elbows, bewildered by the racket, and wondered if an enemy war party was to blame.

Twisted Leg heard the word *Fire,* and thought she understood: one of the lodges was ablaze. She had to roll onto her side and push with all her might to get to her feet. Holding a hand over her swollen belly, she hurried to the entrance and leaned down as far as she could to peek out.

Her lodge, like the others, opened to the east. Twisted Leg did not see a fire. She did spot Eagle Stays in Air. Many of her people were gathered around him and more came every moment. He was advising them to stay calm, saying he would lead them to safety across the river.

Twisted Leg thought she had better hurry. If the Tsistsistas were abandoning the village, she did not want to be left behind. Turning, she hastened toward a parfleche filled with pemmican and other food. It would not do for her to go without nourishment for very long; she had the baby to think of.

Suddenly Twisted Leg heard many loud popping sounds, attended by screams and screeches. She did not know what to make of it until she was bending to go through the opening. To her horror, Eagle Stays in Air and eight or nine others were lying in spreading pools of blood. More popping sounds rose above the din, sounds she realized must be rifle fire, and more Tsistsistas dropped, some dead when they hit the ground, others wounded, groaning and writhing in torment.

The village was under attack! Twisted Leg was so scared, she couldn't collect her wits. Should she hide in the lodge and hope the raiders overlooked her, or should she head for the river as Eagle Stays in Air had advised? She wished Lightning were there, for he would know what to do. He was always so calm in times of crisis.

Twisted Leg bit her lower lip, hard. She had to be the calm one now, because if she fell apart, the innocent child in her womb would pay the price.

Another step disclosed a fire raging to the west. A heavy shroud of smoke swirled ahead of the roaring blaze, pushed into the village by the wind. Twisted Leg's nostrils filled with the acrid odor. She beheld four lodges being rapidly consumed by crackling flames, witnessed some of those flames leap from a burning lodge to another, which until that moment had been untouched.

But the fire was not the worst of the nightmare. Advancing into the village in skirmish order, barely visible in the thick smoke, were white men, laughing fiends who shot down Tsistsistas in cold delight.

Twisted Leg saw a little girl, named Yellow Petal, rush screaming into the open. She never heard the particular rifle that fired, but she did see the little girl's brains explode out the front of her head.

Yellow Petal crashed down and slid a few feet in the dust.

The whites were exterminating the Tsistsistas! The numbing insight made Twisted Leg feel faint. She sagged against the lodge. Why would any whites do such a thing? her brain shrieked. Didn't they know that Yellow Hair, one of their own, lived with the Burning Heart Band, was, in fact, an adopted member of the tribe?

Twisted Leg saw an old warrior charging the whites. It was Bear Shedding, armed with a bow, his gnarled fingers hardly able to hold it. He spotted her and smiled encouragement.

This time Twisted Leg heard the twin gun blasts. They came from close behind her lodge. Bear Shedding was flung like a crumpled doll onto his back and made no attempt to rise. She would be next if she did not get out of there.

Once, six winters ago, long before Twisted Leg became Lightning's mate, she had nearly lost her life during a Pawnee raid. The raiders had been after horses, but when caught in the act, some had been cut off from their fellows and forced to flee through the heart of the village instead of out across the prairie as they would have preferred.

She had been in her father's lodge, sewing. On hearing war whoops and harsh cries, she had limped outside to see what was going on and nearly blundered right into a fleeing Pawnee. The young warrior had been as startled as she, and without thinking, he had elevated a war club to smash in her

head. For a few moments she had stared into the
grim face of death.

Then an arrow had pierced the Pawnee's chest.
Lightning appeared at her side, asking if she was well,
and when she blurted that she was fine, he pushed her
back inside and ran off to fight. It had been her earli-
est true inkling of his affection.

Twisted Leg had lived, but a day did not go by that
she did not recall that young Pawnee's face and the
fear that had welled up inside of her when he raised
that heavy club of his.

That fear was nothing compared with the fear
Twisted Leg now experienced. This was only the second time her life had ever been in danger, and she discovered that it made her knees like mush and her
stomach churn with butterflies.

Still, Twisted Leg would not let her fear get the best
of her. She had spent a lifetime conquering a cruel infirmity, building an ordinary, respectable life for herself
through the sheer force of her will. She had refused to
be branded a worthless cripple when in her heart and
soul she was as unfettered as the wind.

Now that iron will served Twisted Leg in good
stead. Girding herself, she shuffled eastward as rapidly
as she could. As always, the limp slowed her, but she
willed herself to ignore it and go faster. All around her
was chaos. Bodies littered the ground. Panicked
Tsistsistas, mostly women and children, ran every
which way. The men and older boys had rallied to resist the whites, but there were not enough of them and
few had bows. Tipis burned brightly, like oversized

candles. The smoke was so thick she could have cut it with a tomahawk.

Twisted Leg reached the next lodge and hurried around it to put it between her and the vicious white men. If she could put a few more behind her, she might be able to slip northward into the brush lining the river. From there she could easily cross to the far side.

In her haste, Twisted Leg nearly tripped over the bloody body of Wears Red. She was about to go around it when an infant wailed and the bundle in the cradle board moved. Quickly, Twisted Leg stooped. The baby was alive and unharmed. She stripped off the cradle board, her fingers flying. Tearing the last strap loose, she rose with the cradle board clutched protectively in front of her. The infant kept on bawling, too terrified to be soothed no matter how gently she talked or held it.

The delay had proven costly. A glance showed Twisted Leg several whites within a stone's throw of where she stood. She ran awkwardly on, hopping unevenly every other step, for it was impossible for her to run with a steady, smooth gait, and she was so heavy with child and doubly burdened by the cradle board that she could not hop well. She passed another lodge, made for a third.

Somewhere to Twisted Leg's rear, a white man yelled excitedly. A rifle boomed. Simultaneously, an invisible fist slammed into Twisted Leg's right shoulder. She was sent stumbling and fell to her knees, but somehow she managed to keep her hold on the cradle board so the baby wouldn't be hurt.

Stunned by the blow, Twisted Leg glanced down at herself and was horrified to see blood streaming from a hole in her beaded buckskin dress. It took a moment for the reality to sink in, and it was as if a bolt from the heavens had struck her. She had been shot!

Twisted Leg shifted. A white man thirty feet away was hastily ramming a lead ball down a rifle barrel. She resisted a wave of dizziness, pushed erect, and lumbered on by the next tipi. Acting on impulse, she turned to the side. The move saved her life. The rifle blasted again, but the ball ripped into the lodge instead of into her.

It would take the man a bit to reload, Twisted Leg knew. She hurried toward the river, plunging into a wispy smoke cloud rather than going around it. The terrified infant began to cry louder, its tiny arms and legs pumping in agitation. "Be still, little one," Twisted Leg whispered. "They will hear you and know where we are."

Weakness came over her, whether from the blood loss or the shock, Twisted Leg could not say. She willed her legs to keep moving, but her body slowed of its own accord. Frantic for the lives of Wears Red's baby and her own unborn child, and for her own life as well, she looked back to see if the white man was still after her.

No, he wasn't.

A different man was.

Twisted Leg went all numb inside. This new one wasn't white. He was smaller and darker and his face was a cruel mask lit by sinister glee. He had a rifle tucked to his shoulder, but he did not seem to be in any rush to shoot. No, he was playing with her, letting her fear mount in order to feed his sadistic pleasure.

Unexpectedly, the smoke thickened, burying Twisted Leg in its depths. She couldn't see the cruel man and he couldn't see her. Encouraged, she limped off. The river was not all that far away. She might escape yet.

Twisted Leg's left foot struck an exposed root. Pausing, she saw that she had reached the brush, and that the smoke was gradually dispersing. She hunched down as she hiked on, her bad leg lancing pain through her whole body but nowhere near as much as the shoulder wound. The front of her dress was now drenched.

A few more steps and Twisted Leg was in the clear. The river flowed in plain sight up ahead. Holding the cradle board closer, she hobbled toward her goal. She was the length of a lance from the water's edge when a mocking laugh made her breath catch in her throat.

Julio Cardenas Morales took precise aim. He was thinking of a saying the gringos had, something about killing two birds with one stone. Well, Morales was going to go them one better. He was going to shoot three with one lead ball.

That the pregnant woman was a cripple meant nothing to him. That she held an innocent infant meant even less. The idea of mercy was so foreign to his nature that he never entertained it. The concept of compassion was as alien to him as the concept of doing honest work for a living.

Morales saw the woman's pleading eyes, saw her start to mouth an appeal to be spared. Her stupidity was almost laughable. His finger curled around the trigger and the rifle thundered. The cradle board fell from her limp fingers and she landed heavily on her side. He thought she was dead, but when he advanced to make certain, she moved her head to look at him.

Those eyes of hers bothered Morales. There was something about them, an element that made him feel as if all the rottenness and vileness of existence festered within him. It was disturbing, this feeling. He had to stop her from staring. Setting down his rifle, he pulled both of his smoothbore pistols and stood over her.

"*Puta.* You get what you deserve, eh?"

The woman merely stared. Sadness etched her calm features, sadness and a tinge of regret.

Morales could not bear to have her look at him like that any longer. He extended the right pistol and shot her in the breast, then extended the left and shot her in the belly. He had half a mind to draw his butcher knife and slice open her stomach.

Someone began calling his name. Morales jammed the pistols under his belt, scooped up the rifle, and headed back, reloading while he walked. The firing had died down, except for an occasional shot. Flames crackled loudly; every lodge in the village was burning, just as Morales had intended.

The fire itself had leaped from dwelling to dwelling,

but the ground around the tipis was largely untouched, since most of the grass had long since been grazed off or worn down. To the south of the encampment, the burn was still in progress, flames sweeping in a broad line to the southeast.

No doubt the prairie fire would burn for days, reducing hundreds of thousands of acres to charred ruin. Many hundreds of animals would be slain, rabbits and prairie dogs and perhaps a few buffalo, burned to a crisp. The mental picture made Morales smile.

Rafe Hancock materialized out of the smoke, several other renegades trailing him. All were coated with soot and grinning like kids given the birthday present of their dreams. "I reckon we bagged most of them, Julio," he declared. "No sign of that boy, though. Or of Bennett and his squaw."

Morales listened to the loud wails of despair, the groaning and moaning of the wounded. "Amuse yourselves. Finish off those still alive. Check all the bodies—"

"Lookee there!" Red interrupted urgently, pointing. "One of the bucks is coming back!"

Over a quarter of a mile distant a lone Cheyenne warrior raced madly toward the devastated village. His quirt rained down on his mount without cease.

"Look at that jackass," Rafe said. "He's so worked up about the vermin he calls kin that he ain't watching out for his own self." He raised his rifle. "He'll be easy to pick off once he's a mite closer."

"Don't waste the lead," Morales said.

"How's that, boss?" Webber asked.

"Wait and see."

They complied, and relished every moment. They saw the fire line leap to the north, consuming the dry grass at an incredible rate. Within no time the blaze had spread out over a front hundreds of yards in length and kept on growing by scores of feet a second. At the same time the wind swept the line steadily eastward, toward the onrushing warrior.

"Don't that idiot see he's in for it?" Webber wondered. "Look at 'im. He's not slowing at all."

"Maybe he thinks he can jump the flames," Red said, and snickered.

"Or maybe he just don't give a damn," Rafe mentioned. He would never admit it to the others, but he sort of admired any man—even a stinking Injun—who would put the welfare of his own before all else.

Morales chuckled. "He'll never make it."

And the Mexican was right. The warrior galloped straight at the billowing line of flame and smoke. At the last possible moment he tried to sail his mount up and over. It was a brave effort, but the one thing horses feared more than anything else was fire and this horse proved no different. No matter how superbly trained it might be, the intense, searing heat and the blinding, stinging smoke make it balk at the worst of all times. It slid to a stop in the very middle of the flames, then reared.

"He's done for now," Red declared.

The animal's anguished whinny carried clear as a bell across the plain. They saw the warrior topple into the flames, try to rise, and be blanketed by smoke. The horse fled, much of its hide burned, its tail ablaze.

"Ain't that a hoot!" Webber laughed. "I bet a pack of lucky wolves will be tastin' fried horseflesh before the day is done."

Landis had joined them and witnessed the warrior's demise. *"Pardonnez-moi, mes amis,"* he piped up. "But if one Indian come back, maybe more be on their way, *non?* Maybe many more, I be thinking."

The thought jarred Rafe Hancock. "Frenchy has a point. We didn't see many bucks. A lot of sprouts and old farts, but hardly any warriors in their prime. They must be off on a raid somewhere, and we sure as hell don't want to be here when they show up."

Morales wasn't worried, but he could see his men were, and did not care to provoke a tug of wills by forcing them to stay any longer than they had to. "Post two men to keep watch. The rest of you, kill any Injuns still alive. We don't want to leave witnesses." He pulled a pistol to reload it. "Soon as we're done, we'll ride out. Now get to work, you lazy slugs."

The renegades enjoyed themselves immensely. Working in pairs, they went from body to body. Those Cheyennes not fortunate enough to have been slain outright were treated to a variety of mutilations. Some had their throats slit and bled to death. Others had their eyes or tongues gouged out and then were dispatched, or, if Webber found them, were stabbed so many times they looked more like sieves than corpses when he was done.

Webber made a game of it, trying to see how many

times he could stab each one without inflicting a fatal wound. An elderly woman surprised him the most. He had to stab her fifty-three times before she gave up the ghost.

Morales also went from corpse to corpse, but he was searching for Second Son and Cleve Bennett. It disappointed him beyond measure when he found neither. But it also gave him an idea, which he decided to share with his companions once they were all gathered together.

"Where to now, boss?" Red asked. "To South Pass, to find us some ripe pilgrims who need plucking?"

"In due time," Morales said. Given that his men would be as glad to go up against a war party as that warrior's horse had been to jump the flames, he knew he had to choose his next words most prudently. "First, I have a *favor* to ask of all of you."

Rafe was immediately suspicious. "*You* want to ask a favor of *us*? Since when? Usually you tell us what to do and expect us to do it or die."

"Which is as it should be," Morales said suavely. "But this time I need to ask because what I have in mind is most risky. You need only do it if you agree to help."

"Spell it out," Webber said.

Morales gazed at the smoldering ruin of the nearest lodge. A child had been trapped inside and its blackened limbs jutted into the air like the legs of an upside-down black spider. "I do not like to leave a job half-finished, and this one is not done. As Frenchy pointed out, the warriors have not been accounted for."

"So?" Red said.

"So it occurs to me, amigo, that maybe these warriors will come back, find their village gone, and vow to never rest until the guilty have paid." Morales bobbed his chin at the charred child. "Think a moment. Would you do any less if you were in their place?"

"Son of a bitch," a late arrival snapped. "I knew we shouldn't of done this! The bucks will spend the rest of their lives hunting us down. They'll dog us from one end of the country to another, if need be."

"*Sí,*" Morales said, "unless we end it, here."

"How?" another renegade demanded, and all of them leaned forward, hanging on the next words.

It was not easy for Morales to keep from smirking. How sweet leadership could be! He had them right where he wanted them, and now he tightened the noose. "How? I'll tell you." Morales paused to keep them on edge a few seconds longer. "We go up into the hills and make camp. We keep watch on the village through our spyglasses. And when the warriors return, we set up an ambush and finish it. Then we can go on about our business without having to look over our shoulders every minute of every day."

"You always were a cagey cuss. I like it, boss," Red said. "Count me in."

The others chimed in with similar sentiments. All except Rafe Hancock, who wisely kept his mouth shut. Rafe had a hunch there was more to the Mexican's plan than Morales let on. Such as their leader not giving a damn about the warriors. The real reason Morales wanted to hang around was to get his hands on the Bennetts. Which made Rafe think of the breed brat.

That kid would probably be the first to show.

Chapter

— 9 —

Cleve Bennett was beside himself with worry. All morning he had crisscrossed the vicinity of where he had last seen his cherished wife, to no avail. There was no trace of her. It was as if the earth had yawned wide and swallowed her whole.

Only Cleve knew better. Either she had been taken captive, or slain. He tried not to dwell on the latter. She had to be alive, he told himself over and over and over. He convinced himself that she was being held somewhere against her will, and that all he had to do was find the trail her captors had taken and they would soon be reunited.

There had to have been two or three involved, maybe more, Cleve reasoned, since Second Son was more than a match for any one man. Somehow they had jumped her and prevented her from crying out, which in itself was a remarkable feat. Very few possessed the skill needed to take her by surprise.

The sun was directly overhead when Cleve reined up and sat slumped in the saddle, dejected by his failure. He had tried his best and it had not been enough. But he wasn't willing to concede that she was lost to him forever. He would keep hunting for however long it took—days, weeks, months if need be. He would never rest until he held her in his arms once again.

Which was all well and good so long as Cleve discounted the wild card in the deck. He wiped a sleeve across his brow, then surveyed the countryside to the north. Sooner or later Broken Paw and the war party were going to show up, and then what would he do? He couldn't take on nine seasoned warriors all alone. Nor would he let them drive him off, not unless Second Son went with him.

So far, Cleve's luck had held. The Nez Percé had not appeared. It was too much to hope, he mused, that they had given up and headed back to the Columbia. More than likely, they had temporarily lost the trail but would pick it up again soon enough. Then the grease would really hit the fire.

Cleve put a hand behind his neck and rubbed sore muscles. As he tilted his head back he happened to see a golden eagle soaring high on the currents above the mountain. From that high up, the eagle had to be able to see for many miles.

The insight spurred Cleve to action. He goaded Socks up the slope, leading Shadow by her reins. The higher he went, the more he could see of the surrounding landscape. It was his hope that he'd spot a tendril of smoke or else Second Son and her captors.

Presently the timber thinned out, to be replaced by open patches dotted by boulders. He spied a convenient shelf about a hundred yards off and made for it. As he went around a boulder the glint of sunlight off of metal caught his eye. He drew rein and looked to the right. A gasp escaped his lips. In a twinkling he was off Socks and on one knee with Second Son's knife in his left hand.

Dry blood caked the last few inches of the blade. Cleve felt his own race through his veins. Dizziness nipped at him. He shook it off and slowly stood. There was no reason to panic yet, he assured himself. The blood might be hers, but it might also be someone else's.

The ground, though hard, bore evidence of a scuffle. In loose dirt next to a boulder Cleve found the clue that confirmed the identity of her attacker—the track of a large, naked foot. Either the same man had dogged them most of yesterday afternoon, or there was an entire tribe of big, barefoot men traipsing around the mountains in the central part of the Oregon country. He doubted very much that such was the case.

Where had they gone? was the crucial question Cleve needed to answer. He climbed on the stallion and rode to the shelf. The scenery below was magnificent, but its beauty was lost on him. His sole concern was his wife. Search as he might, he couldn't find her.

The position of the sun revealed that there were seven hours of daylight remaining. It seemed like a lot, but not when Cleve considered the vast scope of the wilderness he must search. Resigning himself to a long day on horseback, he rode along the shelf, bearing westward.

Farther along, part of a facing slope had buckled, leaving an incline composed of dirt mixed with earthen clods. It was ideal for preserving tracks, and Cleve discovered four of the naked variety. These were the clearest yet. He spent five minutes examining the break and came to a reluctant conclusion.

There had only been one man, probably an Indian, since never once in all his far-flung travels had he met a white man who liked to go barefoot all the time.

Indians, yes. There had been the Diggers west of the great Salt Lake, and some of the tribes along the California coast. It was rumored that several tribes living in the southwest desert country also routinely shunned footwear, but Cleve had not seen them with his own eyes, as yet, and could not say whether the claim was mere hearsay or fact.

Even so, the presence of a barefoot Indian meant a whole tribe must inhabit the region, a tribe of which Cleve had never heard and that might be as intent on exterminating whites as the notorious Blackfoot Confederacy.

As if having the Nez Percé to worry about wasn't enough, Cleve had to rescue his wife while keeping his eyes peeled for hostiles who had every advantage: they outnumbered him, knew the lay of the land far better than he did, and were able to hold their own against a skilled Tsistsista warrior like Second Son.

Mounting, Cleve commenced tracking. From the depth of the prints, which he had compared with his own, he guessed the man was burdened with extra weight, such as the body of an unconscious woman. He marveled at the length of the Indian's stride and how effortlessly the kidnapper surmounted obstacles that would have daunted him. At one spot, for example, the barefoot man had leaped over a log, hardly breaking stride, a feat requiring muscles of steel.

Cleve Bennett held his new rifle close to his waist and cursed the day he had agreed to accompany Beeville and Walters. If anything happened to Second Son, he would never forgive himself. His wanderlust was to blame, the same craving for new sights and new experiences that had taken him from Missouri to the untamed frontier, and from there deep into the uncharted Rockies.

There was no harm in a single man gallivanting all over Creation, Cleve mused. But once a man set down roots, once he took a wife and they reared a bunch of younguns, the man should have the common sense to stick close to wherever he and his wife called home, if only for the sake of their family.

Cleve knew Second Son would say he was being silly, blaming himself for something over which he had no control. But he couldn't help himself. He loved her more than life itself, and the prospect of losing her made his heart heavy with sorrow.

Gazing sadly at the crest of the mountain, Cleve

Bennett asked himself aloud, "Second Son, where the blazes are you?"

Unknown to Cleve, the warrior was wondering the same thing herself. She had revived a while ago in pitch-black darkness and learned her wrists and ankles were securely bound. Quite naturally she assumed it was still night, and that she was lying near where she had been attacked.

However, when Second Son rolled onto her back, she saw there were no stars. Nor was there any breeze. It was as if she had been thrown into a deep, inky pit.

The comparison was not that far from the truth.

When Second Son tucked her legs under her and rose onto her knees, her left shoulder brushed a hard object at waist height. When she wriggled closer, her probing fingers roved over a rock jutting from an earth wall. She inhaled deeply and realized the dank scent of dirt hung heavy in the air.

Was that the answer? Second Son pondered. Had the giant cast her into a hole in the ground and covered it to hide her from prying eyes? She rose as high as she could, but the top of her head still did not brush the ceiling of her prison.

Then Second Son heard a slithering noise, as of scales on a rough surface, and she entertained the disturbing idea that there might be snakes or lizards in the pit with her. She remembered seeing a rattlesnake den once, where dozens upon dozens of snakes of all sizes writhed and hissed in a gigantic roiling mass. Watching them had made her skin crawl, and she had been glad to be on a ledge above the pit instead of down in it with them.

Second Son listened, but the noise wasn't repeated. She searched her prison carefully and thought she detected a thin gleam of light ten feet above her and to the right.

Muscles rippling, Second Son tried to free herself. The rope refused to budge. She ran her fingers over it and ascertained that it had been made from hard-twisted grass, not hide or cured leather. Remembering the rock that jutted from the wall, she positioned herself in front of it and began rubbing the rope against the dull edge. It would take a lot of time, but eventually she would sever the rope.

Hardly had Second Son started than there was a thud overhead, then a loud swish. She glanced up into sunshine so glaringly bright she had to squint to see, and even then the dazzling radiance eclipsed all else. It took a while for her eyes to adjust. When they did, she could hardly credit their testimony.

Above Second Son, holding a crude latticework cover made from entwined brush and limbs, towered an enormous hulk of a man, the giant with the naked feet. He studied her, his expression neither friendly nor hostile.

Second Son had expected him to be an Indian, and in her mind had pictured him wearing buckskins, as did the Tsistsistas, and armed as would be a member of her tribe, with a lance or a bow or a war club. She was wrong in every respect.

The man had the build of a bear. His shoulders were corded knots of muscle made all the more broad by a pronounced hump between his shoulder blades. In keeping with his bearish image, the hide of a grizzly covered his powerful torso. His brow was low and sloped like the shell of a turtle. His eyebrows were as thick as woolly caterpillars. Legs resembling tree trunks supported his great weight.

The strangest aspect of all had to be the man's eyes. They were mismatched, one dark brown, the other a pale gray, and the right was a full finger's width higher on his face than the left. Combined with the hump and fingernails that had been filed to a point, he looked more like some fierce otherwordly predator than a human being.

Second Son glanced at the spot where she had stabbed him. The bear hide was caked with dry blood, yet he did not appear to have been seriously hurt. "I am Second Son, of the Burning Heart Band," she said in her language. "I mean you no harm, big one. Why have you done this to me?"

The misshapen figure made no reply. He did set the cover to one side and crouched on the rim, his immense club balanced over his left shoulder.

"Can you speak?" Second Son reverted to English. "Which tongue do you use? Frenchay, maybe? I know a few words. *Je regrette.*"

Flat eyes regarded her dully. The giant parted his thick lips but didn't say anything. He did scratch under an arm and sniff his fingertips.

"Do you know sign?" Second Son inquired, mystified by his silence. "If so, untie my wrists so we can talk with our hands."

The man bent his head to stare at her face.

Straightening, he looked all around as if to assure himself that no one was spying on him, then started down the short incline toward her.

Thanks to the sunshine, Second Son could see that she was in a small cave. She tried to back away from her captor, but bound as she was, she couldn't move very well. He was on her before she went a foot, his bulk blotting out most of the light. A hand coated with calluses closed on her arm, pinning her in place. Up close, it was apparent that his nose had been broken once and not reset properly.

"I mean you no harm," Second Son stressed, doing her best to stay calm, not to let rampant fear claim her. She had to keep telling herself that she was a warrior, and that come what may, she must not shame herself in her own eyes. "Cut me loose and you will see for yourself."

The giant reached up and scratched his mane of unruly black hair. Grunting, he glanced to the left. Second Son did the same, thinking there must be something there worth her attention. It was a trick. The instant she turned, he pounced, his left hand closing in her own hair. She was yanked off her knees and dragged toward the opening.

"There is no need—" Second Son tried to say, but had to grit her teeth to resist waves of agony that rippled down from her scalp. She thought her hair would be ripped out by the roots before they emerged from the cave, but it stayed intact and she was unceremoniously heaved up and over the edge.

Second Son glimpsed a barren slope below, a cliff above. She tumbled, rolling down the slope, unable to stop herself even though she dug in her elbows and feet. A rock ripped open her cheek. Another gouged her neck. Battered and bruised, she ultimately slammed into a small boulder. Stunned, she struggled to sit up, but her body wouldn't respond to her commands.

The crunch of heavy feet on stones alerted Second Son to the giant's approach shortly before his iron fingers closed around her neck. She was snapped into a seated posture and propped against the boulder.

Displaying no ill will, the giant inspected her closely. He plucked at her clothes, pulled on her braids, sniffed at her neck. All the while he grunted. Then he squatted and simply stared.

"What do you want?" Second Son demanded. So far he hadn't laid a hand where no man other than Yellow Hair was allowed to touch her, but she had no idea how long his restraint would last. She had to persuade him to cut her loose. Shifting, she extended her arms and wagged her wrists. "Free me. I will not try to hurt you if you do not try to hurt me."

Yet another grunt was the giant's response. Extending a finger, he jabbed her in the chest. When she looked at him in blank confusion, he jabbed her again, harder.

"What do you want?" Second Son asked, at her wit's end. "Make it plain so I can understand."

The giant pursed his lips. He was motionless for a while, then a slow grin creased his craggy visage and he jabbed his own barrel chest. "Modoc," he said in a deep voice more like the rumble of a bear than a human tone.

The word meant nothing to Second Son, so she shook her head. It was gratifying to know he wasn't a mute because now she might be able to communicate.

"Modoc," the giant repeated, touching his chest once more. His brows arching, he touched her chest, too.

At last Second Son guessed his purpose. "Tsistsista," she said proudly, holding her head high. "I am Tsistsista."

"Tssss—" the giant attempted to form the word.

"Tsistsista," Second Son encouraged him. "I am Second Son, a warrior of the Burning Heart Band. I am willing to be your friend if you will release me."

He ignored her appeal and tried several times to say the name of her tribe. With each failure he grew increasingly upset, and after the fourth attempt he growled like an animal and smacked his fist on the ground.

"Why are you upset?" Second Son sought to soothe him. "Learning another's tongue takes time and patience. Do not be so hard on yourself."

She might as well have been talking to a tree. The giant pounded his fist a few more times, glared at her awhile, and seized her right ankle. Before she could guess what he was about, he stomped off down the slope, dragging her in his wake.

"Stop," Second Son protested. A rock poked into her back, low down, making her wince. "Let me walk." She tried to tear her leg loose, but his grip was unbreakable. Another rock tore into her, ripping her shirt and gashing her skin. A damp, sticky sensation spread slowly toward her hip. "Why won't you listen?"

The slope ended. Second Son felt grass under her and exhaled in short-lived relief. Trees closed around them. Brush tore at her, broken limbs snagged her clothes. In desperation she kicked his arm, but it was like kicking a log.

They had covered a considerable distance when suddenly the giant released her and halted. Second Son ached abominably. She tried to sit up and received an unexpected boost when her captor grabbed the front of her shirt and braced her against the rough trunk of a pine.

Second Son saw a small spring a few steps to the left. He had brought her there to drink, she figured, and watched him cup a huge hand to the water and slurp noisily. When he faced her, she thought he would force her to drink from his palm. To her surprise, he bent over her feet and began undoing the knots.

The giant was slow and clumsy. Often he stopped and peered at the knots as if trying to recall how he had made them in the first place.

Second Son sat perfectly still, not daring to disturb his concentration. This was her chance to escape and she wasn't going to spoil it. While he slowly loosened her ankles she quietly tried to loosen her wrists by rubbing them against the trunk and exerting all her strength against the rope. She managed to gain a little play in the coils, but not enough.

Presently the giant stopped and glanced up at her. "Modoc," he declared, tapping himself. "Modoc."

"A very stupid Modoc," Second Son corrected him while smiling sweetly. She had to make him believe that she was not about to offer any resistance, that she would do whatever he wanted.

"Modoc," he said.

"Modoc," Second Son repeated.

Pleased by her brilliance, the man renewed his assault on the knots. His grimy nails nipped and pried until he had the last one undone, and the rope slid off. Picking it up, he grinned, showing blackened teeth.

"Yes, you did well," Second Son said softly to keep him off his guard. "Now my wrists." She shifted and extended her arms so he would comprehend. He did, but he merely uttered one of his guttural grunts, then pointed at the spring.

"So that is how it will be," Second Son said, never losing her smile. Tucking her legs under her, she slowly stood. The circulation had been cut off for so long, she tingled from the knees down. Shuffling slowly, stalling to buy time to recover fully, she moved past the Modoc.

Second Son squatted rather than knelt. With her arms behind her, the only way she could drink was to bend her mouth to the water. She took several swallows, pausing between each one so she could furtively scan the woods on the other side of the spring. There was ample cover, if she could just reach it.

The giant snorted and gestured.

"Just one more sip," Second Son said, and dipped her lips to the cool liquid. She drank while fixing one eye on him. When he turned away to gaze back up the mountain, she exploded, vaulting over the spring and into the undergrowth. His sharp cry was seconds late. She looked back to see him wading through the spring, his club waving in frantic circles.

Once the vegetation hid her from his sight, Second Son sheared to the right and ducked behind a tree. No sooner had she crouched than he pounded on past on the original course she had taken. For one so large, he was fleet of foot. His wits were another matter.

Second Son did not move until he had disappeared. Standing, she returned to the spring, skirted it, and entered the forest twenty paces farther to the north. She heard her captor barging around like a man run amok, down the slope. He realized that she had eluded him and he was not taking it well.

Resorting to the stealth she had spent a lifetime acquiring, Second Son pushed on. After an interval, the crackle of brush to her rear died, as did the Modoc's gruff bellows. She had time to think about him, and she came to several conclusions.

It was Second Son's opinion that the giant must be an outcast. Perhaps due to his monstrous appearance or gargantuan size or both, he had been banished to the wild to live as best he could. Or else he had left his people on his own, maybe unwilling to tolerate their gawking stares or the mocking whispers behind his back.

Since the Modocs didn't live anywhere along the Columbia and no one in Walter's expedition had heard of them, Second Son pegged the tribe's location as somewhere in northern California, many sleeps to the south. She need not worry about encountering any more of them. Once she had escaped the giant, she would be safe.

Fresh in Second Son's memory was her clash the night before. All too vividly she recalled how silently the giant moved, how swiftly. She had been caught once; she would die before she let him get his hands on her a second time.

As much as Second Son would have liked to free her wrists, she pressed northward for the longest while. The sun soared to its zenith and arced westward. She had climbed to a ridge below a gap, which might be a pass to the far slope, when she stopped to rest briefly.

Second Son scoured the area and settled on a jagged rock as the means to rid herself of the rope. Wedging it between her feet, she pressed the grass fibers to the edge, then sawed back and forth. Strand by strand, the rope parted. It was hard work. Presently she paused to let the pain in her shoulders subside.

Where was Yellow Hair? Second Son wondered. He would not have stopped hunting for her, unless the Nez Percé had found him first. From the summit she might be able to spot him and attract his attention.

The clatter of pebbles below snapped Second Son's head up. Cleve would have to wait. For flying up the mountain toward her was the giant Modoc, and if looks could kill, she would be dead long before he reached her.

Chapter

— 10 —

Twelve-year old boys, by their very natures, are impetuous. They rashly rush into situations more mature heads wisely avoid.

Billy-Wolf Bennett was no exception. When he set eyes on the wall of smoke, cold fear clawed at his heart and sent him racing toward Blaze. His people needed him. He must reach them swiftly.

There were only two likely causes of the fire, that Billy could see. One of the Tsistsistas might have carelessly set the prairie alight, which was a slim likelihood since Cheyennes learned at an early age to treat fire with great respect and never, ever to start one where the flames might spread out of control.

That being the case, it was more probable that someone else had been responsible. Raiders, perhaps, one of the many hostile tribes eager to count coup on the Burning Hearts by whatever means necessary.

Billy-Wolf thought of Twisted Leg, all alone and so vulnerable in her condition, and his feet fairly flew. Jase and Snip materialized out of the woods. They seemed to sense his urgency and loped silently at his side, their tongues lolling.

Billy regretted having left Blaze so far away. The smoke had broadened and thickened by the time he reached the horse and vaulted onto its back. As Blaze broke into a gallop faint popping sounds heightened Billy's rising terror. Soon a chorus of distant screams carried across the high grass.

Raids were a regular occurrence. Twice, maybe three times a year, the Burning Hearts were forced to defend themselves from roving marauders. Sometimes the raiders were only interested in stealing horses and escaping unscathed. At other times, their enemies were intent on exterminating as many of the Tsistsistas as they could.

Billy was a veteran of a dozen or more attacks. Once he'd been taken captive by the Shinni, or Comanches as his pa liked to call them. If not for his folks and cousin, who tracked the Shinni down and rescued him, he would have been whisked far to the south and never seen any of his people again.

Perhaps, Billy-Wolf told himself, another small boy was at that very moment being thrown over the back of a raider's mount. Perhaps it was one of his friends. He listened for the war whoops of the defenders, for signs that the raiders were being stiffly opposed.

Then it hit him. Singing Wolf and most of the warriors were gone, off on a grand hunt. The few warriors left, even with the help of the old men and boys, would be no match for a large war party.

Billy-Wolf sped madly along the strip of woodland, taking reckless risks. He hurtled over logs best avoided, plowed through thickets best skirted, and passed under tree branches so low they tore at his hair and shirt. He didn't care. His personal safety mattered little when so many were in need.

The gunfire had about died down when Billy saw what he had been dreading: lodges were aflame. Not one or two lodges, either, but every single one in the camp was on fire. And scattered among them were the bodies of Burning Hearts, of men, women, and children. The sight so infuriated him that he nearly charged into the village without regard for the consequences.

Just then five white men came into sight, and it so shocked Billy-Wolf that he reined up behind some willows to study the situation. It took a bit for the paralyzing truth to sink in. The Tsistsistas had been attacked by a large band of . . . white men!

Billy had never heard of whites attacking a village before. The thought boggled his brain, muddled his thinking. There must have been an awful mistake made, he reasoned. The Burning Hearts had never done anything to deserve being slaughtered. He wished his pa had been there, because surely Cleve would have stopped the whites from committing the atrocity.

Then another man walked around a burning tipi, and Billy-Wolf gasped. He recognized the renegade Morales, whom his father had pointed out to him at a rendezvous years before as one of the vilest killers on the frontier.

"That polecat crossed me once, son," Cleve had said, "and I made the mistake of letting him live. It's a mistake I'll correct if he ever causes me grief again." His pa had frowned. "You're to stay shy of that man, no matter what. He hates your ma and me. If he could, he'd cause us no end of misery. We have to make sure he never gets the chance."

The words echoed in Billy-Wolf's head like peals of thunder. Was that why Morales and his band had struck the village? To kill his parents? Or did Morales know they were gone and had done it out of sheer spite? A man that vicious, his pa had once said, was "wicked to the bone."

Billy-Wolf saw more renegades spreading out through the encampment and changed his mind. Were he to go riding in there, he'd be throwing his life away. A volley would bring him down before he could unleash a single shaft.

As Billy watched the butchers shoot helpless, wounded Tsistsistas, a feeling new to him turned him bloodred, a feeling so raw, so strong, that he quivered with the intensity of it. He felt pure, undiluted hatred for the first time in his young existence, a hatred so overwhelming that a crimson haze settled before his eyes.

Morales had ambled nearer to the river. Billy raised his bow, tempted to try a long shot. He lowered it again because when the time came, he wanted to be absolutely certain he wouldn't miss.

The shooting went on forever, or seemed to. Each shot seared Billy-Wolf's heart like a red-hot poker. He couldn't stand to look after a while and turned toward the river, tears brimming in his eyes. The death rattle of a woman so affected him that he thought he would break down and sob. But he didn't. Crying was for children.

Some of the renegades had gathered a small herd of stolen horses. These were driven ahead of the band when Morales and company departed. Laughing and yipping like frolicsome wolves, the killers rode due north, toward the river and the willows fringing it.

Billy-Wolf was upset with himself for not guessing sooner. The prairie to the south and east still burned. To the west, the grass that had been lit to start the fire still smoldered. The butchers only had the one avenue to take.

There was no time to flee. Quickly sliding off Blaze, Billy gripped the animal's bridle and dropped onto his knees, pulling the horse's head down low to the grass. It was a trick he had practiced a few times but not mastered to his satisfaction. Blaze often balked and made a racket doing so. If that happened now, Billy knew the cutthroats would be on him before he could escape.

The stallion sank halfway to his knees, then bobbed its head, refusing to go any lower. It tried to stand. Billy had to hold on with all his might, using his weight for leverage. He threw an arm around its muzzle to keep it from nickering and giving him away.

Morales was almost to the trees. He was busy talking to a beefy man with a red beard, both gesturing happily at the ravaged lodges.

Billy-Wolf put his mouth to Blaze's ear. "Lie down, boy," he said softly. "Do it, or I'm liable to be maggot food before the day is done." He pulled harder and was rewarded by the horse lying flat on its side. Immediately Billy lay on top of it, a hand over its mouth.

A feral growl reminded Billy of his dogs. Snip and Jase were crouched in the grass beside the willow, tails twitching. "Shush!" Billy hissed. "Stay!"

Like Blaze, the dogs only listened when they felt like listening. Billy feared they would go after the renegades no matter what he said. Jase started to rise, and Billy snapped a finger to get the dog's attention, then smacked the grass. "No, darn you!" he growled. "We're dead if you don't behave!"

Discovery loomed anyway, since the stolen horses were trotting directly toward the spot. Spooking them to throw the renegades into confusion seemed Billy's best bet, and he prepared to rise up and screech at the top of his lungs.

The wind must have shifted, because the very next moment several of the foremost horses behaved as if they had caught the dogs' scent. They lifted their heads high, pricked their ears, and slanted to the right to swing wide of the thick willows. The killers herding them were caught by surprise. Shouting and whistling, the men tried to turn the animals back on track. But after all that had happened, the horses were not inclined to obey.

Billy smiled grimly. Thanks to his dogs, the butchers were too busy to so much as glance his way. Snip, he noticed, was coiling to spring, so he snaked over Blaze's neck and placed a restraining hand on the dog's shoulder.

Twisting, Billy counted the gang. There were sixteen, including Morales. They forded the river and turned to the east, one of their number twirling a fresh scalp on the end of a finger.

Billy-Wolf did not allow Blaze to rise until the killers were lost in their own cloud of dust. Tying the reins to the willow, he notched an arrow in case there were stragglers, and crept from hiding. The putrid stench of charred flesh was enough to bring bile to his mouth. He covered the lower half of his face with one hand and slowly advanced.

The carnage was worse than Billy had thought it would be. Seeing the corpses from a distance in no way prepared him for the stark horror of beholding, up close, the blasted, burned forms of people he had known and loved. He saw an old woman, Sparrow Tail, who had been shot twice, then bludgeoned until her head split like an overripe melon. He gazed on a little girl of four, Rainbow, whose intestines had been torn from her sliced stomach. His stomach wanted to heave, but he refused to be weak.

Closing his eyes, Billy calmed himself. He had witnessed death many times before, but never so many dead at once, all victims of a horrible slaughter. Or were they all dead? He knew that he must keep looking, on the off chance that one of the Tsistsistas was still alive.

Half an hour later Billy had been disabused of the notion. There were nineteen bodies, which in a quirky manner was encouraging since it meant that a number of Cheyennes were unaccounted for and might have escaped. They had the smoke to thank, for without it they would surely have died.

Billy went to where Lightning's lodge had stood. No one could have told a dwelling once occupied the spot if not for the smoldering poles and bits of blackened hide. He poked among the debris for sign of Twisted Leg but did not see her.

Jase and Snip were cowed by the gore and bloodshed. They slunk along with their tails between their legs, avoiding pools of blood, occasionally sniffing at bodies with their hackles raised.

Billy ignored them until they both growled at once. They were gazing out over the blackened plain to the east. He looked, filled with dread that the renegades had spotted him and were coming back. No riders were in evidence, and he was about to turn away when something moved, something at ground level, a figure every bit as black as the remnants of the grass itself.

The logical conclusion was that it must be an animal, and while Billy felt sorry for any beast caught in the inferno, more important matters claimed his interest. He was going to go in search of the Tsistsistas who had escaped, when the figure tried to stand on two legs and instead pitched onto its face.

It was a man! Billy realized. Jogging to Blaze, he climbed on and started off at a gallop but promptly slowed on seeing tiny fingers of flame scattered everywhere. The prairie was still on fire. Since he didn't want Blaze harmed, he gingerly picked a path toward the crawling figure.

Forty yards out, Billy-Wolf nearly rode over a pair of bodies, that of a woman and her daughter scorched beyond recognition. They had fled the village, only to be caught in the flames when the fire roared across the plain. Judging by their contorted features, their deaths had been excruciating.

Billy wondered if the rest of the missing Cheyennes had suffered a similar fate. It shocked him to realize that he might well be the sole unharmed survivor, that if he hadn't gone duck hunting, he might be lying there as well.

He didn't see how the man had survived. The smoke alone could have killed anyone; he recollected his pa once telling him that smoke was every bit as deadly as fire. And the flames had been so hot they had blistered the flesh of that poor mother and daughter.

Billy noticed that the warrior had stopped moving. He halted and went the last ten feet on foot. Tattered leggings were all that remained of the victim's clothes. His naked feet were coated with blisters, his back caked with soot and sores. The fire had burned his long hair clear down to his scalp. Kneeling, Billy gently rolled the man over and received yet another jolting shock.

It was Rakes the Sky with Lighting, or what was left of him.

His chest and neck had been badly burned. The skin had been seared from whole sections of both arms. His fingers were intact but he would not be using them to tie his moccasins for a long time. And while the right half of his face had not been touched, the left had been horribly burned.

"Oh, Lightning," Billy whispered, aghast. His cousin's chest did not appear to be moving and he tentatively reached out to touch it when the warrior groaned low and long.

"You're alive!" Billy exclaimed. Bringing Blaze over, he slung his bow and stood next to the prone form. Lightning was much heavier than the boy, and he didn't see how he could get his cousin in the saddle. But he had to try. Stooping, he slipped an arm under Lightning's shoulder and hoisted him up. The older man groaned again and his eyelids fluttered.

"Can you hear me?" Billy-Wolf asked. "I need your help. We have to get you on my horse, but I cannot do it by myself. I need your help."

Lightning gave no indication that he had heard.

"Please. You must lend a hand," Billy-Wolf pleaded. "The ones who did this to you might take it into their heads to return. We have to get out of here." He shook his cousin a few times. "Please."

The warrior's left eye was burned shut, but the right snapped open. Cracked, blistered lips parted, and what came out could only be described as the sum total of all the pain ever experienced by humankind. Lightning looked right and left, his cry choking off when he saw Billy. He tried to speak but could only croak.

"There is no need to talk," Billy-Wolf assured him. "Just try to stand. Can you do that for me?"

"Wolf Sings on the Mountain." The words were breathed, each syllable rasped as if it would be Lightning's last. He looked toward the village and said plaintively, "Twisted Leg?"

"I do not know," Billy said. "I searched, but she was nowhere to be found. Maybe she got away."

"Must . . . find . . ." Lightning said, and could not go on. He had known pain in his time but none to match the agony he was now enduring. Pain filled every fiber of his being. It made thinking hard, speech more so.

"Can you stand?" Billy-Wolf asked hopefully, afraid his cousin would pass out on him.

In answer, Lightning gritted his teeth and heaved upward. He thought he was ready for the anguish it would provoke, but he was deluding himself. The previous torment was as nothing compared with this. His vision spun, the world faded to gray. He took several halting steps, not knowing where he was going, and he was about to fall when his flailing hands came into contact with a sweaty hide.

"It is Blaze," Billy said, seeing his cousin's confusion. "Hold on to him and I will give you a boost." He placed an arm around Lightning's lower back and accidentally brushed his hand against a blister, which ripped open. "Sorry," Billy mumbled.

The warrior barely heard. His forehead rested on the horse and his eyes were closed. He attempted to call up the last ounce of his waning strength so he could mount as the boy wanted, but his limbs were so weak his legs threatened to buckle. "Must hurry," he urged. "I do not feel well."

Billy-Wolf bent and linked his hands. "Here. Put your foot in this."

All Lightning saw when he glanced down were blurred objects where his legs should be. "You must help me," he said, and grimaced when fingers closed on his singed ankle.

As if Billy did not have enough to worry about, Blaze picked that moment to shy, to start to walk off. Billy grabbed the reins in the nick of time or his cousin would have dropped like a rock. "Hold still," he chided the animal, and patted its neck. "This will be over with soon if you do not act up."

Lightning was having trouble hearing. "What was that?" he asked, uncertain if the boy had addressed him. "You want me up?" Even though he had a frail grip on the horse's mane, he clenched his fingers and pulled.

Billy wasn't ready. He felt his cousin slipping and clamped both arms around Lightning's lower legs. As the warrior sagged he thrust upward. "Grab on!" he cried.

Through a swirling haze, Lightning responded. He exerted himself to the limit, calling on every vestige of strength he had left, draining himself dry in the process but marshaling the energy to clamber up onto the stallion, where he collapsed on his belly. His senses swimming, he tried to sit up, but his body was too heavy.

"You did fine," Billy-Wolf said, and almost clapped his cousin on the back. Catching himself in time, he mounted behind Lightning and turned Blaze around.

Since Billy wanted to avoid jostling the warrior, he held the horse to a walk as he rode back toward the river. He entered the trees not far from the north edge of the village. As he picked a path with care he suddenly stumbled on two bodies, that of a woman and an infant.

Billy stared, and felt all sick inside. The tears gushed again, but he fought them off. He glanced at Lightning to verify that his cousin was unconscious. Swinging wide to the right, he went to a gravel bar.

The water was cool to the touch. Billy splashed some on his face and neck, then did the same to Lightning. He'd hoped it would bring the warrior around, but Lightning merely groaned and muttered a few unintelligible words.

"What do I do now?" Billy asked himself aloud. He knew that his cousin was in no shape to travel very far, that it would be best to find somewhere to hole up while Lightning mended, somewhere close to water, as the warrior would need a lot of it in the days ahead. He remembered a bank about half a mile away. The bottom had been eroded out many winters ago during a flood. When the river receded, it had left a sizable hole, which Billy had crawled into one day to see if any critters called it home. The empty hole had been spacious and dry.

"It'll do right fine," Billy said, simply to hear his own voice. The discovery of Twisted Leg had destroyed his last hopes that he would find some of the Tsistsistas alive and well. Sorrow tore at his soul and would have ripped it asunder if he had let it. But he had to hold himself together awhile longer, for his cousin's sake.

Billy remembered a trick his ma had taught him and rode into the middle of the river before turning westward. In an hour or so the current would wash all traces of the hoof marks away, ensuring no one could track them.

On closer examination, Billy-Wolf realized that Lightning hovered at the brink of death. Many of the burns were so severe they would have killed a lesser man. The left side of the warrior's face, even if he recovered, would never be the same.

"Why did this have to happen?" Billy asked the empty air. *"Why?"* He glanced at the puffy clouds drifting sluggishly on the air currents and recalled the day his pa had explained the white version of the Great Mystery. God, the whites called it, and claimed that this God looked down with love and compassion from a lofty lodge in the sky, known as heaven. Billy never had fully understood. But he did wonder.

He wondered again, now. How could a loving God allow innocent people to be massacred? Why would a compassionate being stand by and do nothing while women and children were brutally butchered? It seemed so wrong, people being made to suffer the way they did. What had Twisted Leg ever done to deserve her horrible fate? The answers were beyond him.

Billy-Wolf just knew that he must not let the events break him, that he must not give up. "The Bennetts have never been quitters, son," Cleve liked to say. "And I expect you to uphold the tradition."

"I'll try Pa," Billy said, wishing more than ever that his folks would at long last show up. The vicious raid had added to his anxiety by reinforcing his fear for their safety. If they were alive, he mused, they would have been there long ago. Their absence must mean that they had suffered a fate similar to the Burning Heart Band.

Billy-Wolf located the cavity. Dragging Lightning inside took twice as long as he thought it would. Once he had the warrior's head nestled on a makeshift pillow of bent grass, he brought water and trickled the liquid between Lightning's lips.

The whole time, Billy-Wolf kept resisting an impulse to cry as he had not cried since he was a baby. He had to be strong for both their sakes, and do what he could to nurse the warrior back to health. In the meantime he would keep his eyes skinned for other

Burning Hearts. Singing Wolf should return soon, and once the chief did, it would be safe to leave.

Billy intended to answer the prompting of his heart and do what he should have done long ago. He was going to find his parents, or die in the attempt.

Chapter
— 11 —

Second Son took one look and bent with renewed vigor to the task of sawing through the grass rope. The giant Modoc was taking prodigious strides, but he was slowed down by the steep slope and the treacherous footing. Loose stones and dirt spewed out from under his churning feet. Several times he slipped but managed to stay upright.

The warrior's arms seesawed back and forth, her sinews corded. She put her entire weight into the effort, pressing so hard on the jagged edge of the rock that she accidentally cut her left hand. Blood flowed, rendering the rope slippery. She wriggled her hands, trying to slide them loose of the loops, but the rope refused to give.

And meanwhile the Modoc had climbed to within twenty feet of where she crouched. His club was overhead as if he planned to smash her skull, but the look on his face was more one of hurt than fury. He took another bound, fell to one knee when the earth shifted under him, and snarled in frustration.

Second Son glanced over her shoulder and saw that she only had a few more tough strands to sever and she would shear the rope in half. Another time or two should suffice. She arched her back and rammed the rope against the sharp edge. It gave, not all the way but enough for her to tear her hands free, and as she did so an enormous shadow fell across her and she looked up into the sweaty features of her irate captor.

Not again, Second Son thought, and launched herself at him, low down, her arms catching him around the knees even as she threw her shoulders against his thighs. On flat ground he would have been able to keep his balance, but not on that slippery slope. Yelping, the Modoc tumbled.

Second Son let go and rolled to a stop. She shoved into a crouch and saw the giant doing the same. He swung the club halfheartedly, narrowly missing her head. Backpedaling up the grade, she kicked dirt and stones at him as he tried to seize her ankles.

It took a few moments for the new sound to register. With a start, Second Son realized a horse was bearing down on them from above, at a gallop. She twisted, and her heart soared to see Cleve rushing to her aid, his rifle pressed to his shoulder.

The Modoc also saw, and stopped in amazement. Straightening, he gawked dimly at Socks, the club falling to his side.

Cleve had been about to fire, but when he saw the giant lower the weapon instead of trying to use it, he hesitated and, in doing so, reaped calamity. He hauled on the reins to bring Socks to a halt. The dependable animal tried to obey, but its momentum was too great. Its hooves were unable to find purchase, and the next thing Cleve knew, Socks was hurtling down the slope out of control and all he could do was hold on for dear life.

"Yellow Hair!" Second Son shouted as he shot past her. She tried to grab his arm and pull him from the saddle, but it all happened too fast.

The Modoc's dull wits warned him too late that he should move his ponderous bulk out of the way. He threw up his hands as Socks slammed into him, and then all three of them were down, giant, horse, and mountain man, catapulted out of control by the collision.

Second Son ran after them, barely able to see more than a few feet due to the choking cloud of dust spewing into the air. She held her breath to spare her lungs and swatted at the cloud in a vain bid to see better. Then, abruptly, it cleared, and she saw the three forms below her.

The Modoc was hurt. He was on his side in front of

a boulder, a hand pressed to his ribs, wincing as he attempted to stand.

Socks was cut and bruised but otherwise appeared unhurt. The horse had risen halfway and was vigorously shaking dust from its coat.

Cleve, however, lay still, as if sleeping. His head rested next to a small boulder; his arms were outflung. The rifle had smashed into the boulder and lay a few feet away, the stock splintered.

Second Son gave no thought to the gun. All she had eyes for was her mate. Her breath caught in her throat as she slid to a halt next to him and saw a spreading puddle of blood under his head. "Yellow Hair?" She knelt and carefully turned him over. The blood drained from her face when she beheld the severe gash on his forehead and the damaged flesh around it.

Propping her man's head on her thighs, Second Son drew his knife and sliced off part of his sleeve. Cutting the buckskin into wide strips, she made a crude bandage and applied it to stanch the blood flow. Cleve made no sound. She tenderly touched his cheek, then gave his shoulder a few nudges to revive him. It did no good.

"Yellow Hair?" Second Son said again, softly. She had seen enough wounds to know he was in a bad way. Her probing fingers found no other wounds, which was small consolation.

Again a shadow fell across the warrior. In her worry over her mate, she had momentarily forgotten about the Modoc. She coiled, prepared to plunge the blade into his stomach. His expression, and the fact his hands were empty, stopped her.

The giant's brow was furrowed in confusion. He kept glancing from Cleve to Socks and back again. When the horse suddenly lurched erect, he recoiled a step and made as if to flee for his life.

It dawned on Second Son that the mighty Modoc was scared to death of horses. She was proven right when Socks walked toward them and the giant promptly retreated an equal distance, his hands extended as if to ward off an attack. Under different circumstances, his antics would have been comical.

Rating him no threat at the moment, the warrior bent to her man and tried once more to bring Yellow Hair around. Cleve showed no reaction. The bleeding had slowed but not yet stopped, his face felt warm to her touch.

Socks stood over them and dipped his muzzle to the blood. He sniffed a couple of times, then tossed his head and stepped back.

Second Son needed to get Cleve to water. She gently laid him flat and stood. Up near the pass stood Shadow, ground-hitched. The Modoc was thirty feet away, watching.

Slipping her arms under Cleve's, Second Son lifted him as high as she could. He was a big man, and heavy, much too heavy for her to hike him onto Socks. She tried twice and each time had to give up. Baffled, she gazed around for a means of propping him up so she could slide under him and boost him into the saddle, and saw the giant come toward her.

Second Son had not let go of the knife. She braced Cleve with her shoulder and raised it to slash.

The Modoc halted, staring at the blade. He gestured and spoke in his tongue, and when Second Son made no reply, he took another step, his frightened gaze on Socks. Acting as if he expected the horse to tear into him, he sidled closer to Cleve.

Unsure of the giant's intentions, Second Son held her ground. He poked a finger at Cleve, at his chest, and at Socks, and repeated the motion while inching nearer. She turned so the blade continued to point at his stomach. Her shoulder slipped, not much but enough that Cleve started to topple over, forcing her to make a snap decision since she couldn't catch him and keep the knife fixed on the giant. She went to prop her mate up.

The Modoc beat her to it. His enormous arm closed on Cleve's shoulders, his other hooked behind Cleve's knees, and with about the same ease as she would lift a feather, the giant swung Cleve onto Socks. The instant Cleve alighted, the Modoc sprang to one side, his body held as if to ward off an attack by the stallion.

Second Son leaped under Cleve and thrust her hands up to keep him from falling. She glared at the giant, who was so fascinated by Socks that he failed to notice. He behaved like someone who had never seen a horse before.

Was that the answer? Second Son reflected. A number of tribes in the interior, the Diggers among them, hardly ever saw horses and regarded the animals with a mixture of primitive fear and superstitious dread. A Digger would no more go near a horse than he would a coiled rattler. The Modocs, Second Son mused, must be the same.

The knowledge didn't solve the problem of what to do about the giant. Second Son was at a loss. After his brutal treatment of her, she would just as soon slit his throat as look at him. But there was something about him, a childlike quality that reminded her distinctly of young Billy-Wolf.

Second Son made up her mind when the Modoc picked up the shattered rifle. She coiled her legs, thinking he would use it as a club to brain her. Instead, he studied the broken weapon a moment, then, wearing a lopsided grin, he awkwardly held it out for her to take.

"Thank you," Second Son said.

The Modoc had already forgotten about her and was gaping in wide-eyed wonder at Socks. He about jumped out of his bear hide when Second Son bounded onto the animal's back and wheeled the horse to go up the mountain. She climbed with exquisite skill, avoiding stretches where Socks was bound to slip. On reaching Shadow, she simply bent and snatched the mare's reins. Then she headed for the pass.

Second Son was not surprised to see the Modoc follow at a distance.

Among the Chopunnish, or Nez Percé as most called them, the name of Broken Paw was well-known.

He had counted his first coup at the age of fourteen, taken the scalp of the Piegan who slew his uncle at fifteen, and proven himself a notable warrior by the time he turned twenty.

It was Broken Paw who led a successful raid deeper into the heart of Blackfoot country than any man had ever done before. Not only had he stolen dozens of horses, he had clashed with the feared Blackfoot warrior Brings Down the Sun and killed the man in personal combat witnessed by warriors on both sides.

That had been the greatest day of Broken Paw's life, in his opinion. He had returned to the village in triumph to show off the stolen stock and recount his exploits. The word spread quickly, and before long Broken Paw was looked on as a gifted and brave man who would one day assume the mantle of leadership.

Two winters had passed since that eventful day, and Broken Paw was looking to add to his fame. He went on raids every chance he could in the hope of doing more noteworthy deeds.

Once each year, though, Broken Paw took a break from his never-ending quest to exalt himself and journeyed to Chinook territory. Everyone believed that he went to trade, but the secret truth was that Broken Paw had a passion for the sea matched only by his passion for power.

The passion had been kindled on Broken Paw's first visit to the Great Water, when he had yet to see seven winters. His father had taken him on a whim, and thereby changed his life forever. The rolling waves, the pounding surf, the tangy salt air, they had gotten into Broken Paw's blood, as it were.

It filled Broken Paw with an intense inner peace to sit on a hot beach on a sunny day and do nothing but stare out over the vast watery expanse. He would never admit to his fondness, since in his eyes it was silly of a noted warrior to dote on the Great Water. Yet he could not help himself.

This last trip was supposed to have been like all the others. Broken Paw had stopped at the Dalles and traded for oil and otter hides. He had gone on to the Great Water and spent five sleeps at a secluded cove. Then he had started back, and everything had gone wrong, quickly.

When Broken Paw had struck the trail of the golden-haired white man and the short woman, he had counted it as good fortune. Unlike many of his fellows who thought the Chopunnish should stay on peaceful terms with the whites, Broken Paw saw them as invaders who should not be permitted to trap or hunt in Chopunnish territory. When younger, he had met a number of trappers and disliked every one. They struck him as unbearably arrogant. He suspected that many regarded themselves as superior to his people in ways he could not fathom.

So it was not unusual for Broken Paw to go out of his way to make the lives of whites miserable. He especially liked to drive trappers from Chopunnish country. His favorite tactic was to harass them by stealing their horses and provisions right out from under their noses, leaving them stranded. Then he would let them catch sight of his band, which always sent them in panicked flight toward one of the strange wooden lodges where the whites liked to conduct trade. He'd nip at their heels, driving them ahead of him as he might drive stolen horses, never giving them time to eat or sleep. Those who lived to reach the forts were mere skin and bone by the time they did so. It never failed to amuse him.

The warrior wasn't laughing on this particular day as he trailed his quarry into the trackless wilderness south of the mighty Columbia. Inwardly he was fuming, for he had made an unpardonable mistake that would reflect badly on his standing in the tribe.

It had seemed like a good idea at the time. Broken Paw had spied on the mismatched couple for half a day before committing his warriors to their capture. He had planned to keep the female if she proved interesting, and to strip the golden-haired white man and send him on his way, just as Broken Paw had done to so many other mountain men. It would have been a fitting end to his visit to the Great Water.

But his scheme had gone sour. The pair had shown they were tougher and more resourceful than most. They had killed one of the Chopunnish, wounded others. All of which would do Broken Paw's reputation no good since he was the leader of the band. The Chopunnish would talk among themselves, speculating that his medicine was not as powerful as it had once been. Maybe, some would say, it was a sign that he was not worthy of being a leader.

Broken Paw was going to prove them wrong. He intended to follow the pair for as long as breath remained in him. Eventually he would have them both at his mercy. He would exact retribution for the life lost and redeem himself in the eyes of his people.

Now, impatiently waiting for the best tracker in the band to return, Broken Paw munched on a piece of jerked buffalo meat and moodily contemplated storm clouds gathering to the west. He tried to ignore old Long Ghost when the gray-haired warrior came over and stood near him, but as always Long Ghost was like an annoying mosquito who could not be ignored no matter how hard Broken Paw tried.

"This is wrong. We should turn around and go home."

Broken Paw refused to answer, even though the other warriors turned toward him to hear his reply. He took another bite, stalling.

"Already we have lost one man. Little Shield was my friend. His death is an omen. I know, because I have lived longer than all of you and can read signs better than you."

Broken Paw did not like being reminded for the tenth time in as many sleeps of their age difference. He ascribed it to jealousy on the old man's part. Long Ghost had lived over fifty winters, yet had never distinguished himself in any respect. He had never become a leader and never would.

"We are not far from the Kooskooskee. Let us leave this unfamiliar country before tragedy strikes again," Long Ghost declared.

Some of the others whispered among themselves, inducing Broken Paw to say, "The only tragedy will be if we fail to honor our fallen brother by taking the lives of those who killed him. I will personally count coup on the yellow hair who put an arrow into him."

"Count coup," Long Ghost repeated, lacing the two words with blatant scorn.

"We have heard it all before." Broken Paw tried to forestall the usual tirade, but he should have known better.

"It was a bad day for the Chopunnish when we took up the ways of the tribes on the prairie," the old warrior intoned. "I know, because I have lived under the old customs and the new. The old were better." He sucked in air and fixed the younger men with a stern gaze. "You laugh at me behind my back. You think I am foolish for not embracing the new life with my whole heart. But why should I, when the old ways worked so well?"

"Did they?" Clown Horse spoke up. "The Blackfeet, the Cheyennes, the Sioux, they did as they pleased to us, driving us from our country into the mountains. Only when we learned their ways, and fought them as they fight us, did we regain our pride."

"Our pride should be in the fine horses we raise, not in how many scalps we take, or how many enemies we kill," Long Ghost said.

"Everyone knows the Chopunnish own the best horses anywhere," Clown Horse said. "Even the whites say there are no horses like ours."

Long Ghost stared at the handsome animals, with their dark brown spots on a roan background. "I would gladly give up all the horses I own to live as my father lived, and his father before him."

Broken Paw spotted someone jogging through the pines toward them, and smiled. "Enough of this idle talk. Here comes Thunder Hoop."

The tracker's features mirrored his success. He cradled his fusil in his left elbow and announced, "I have found where the yellow hair went in search of the woman, but I cannot find her tracks. She is like a fox, that one. She walks so lightly that her feet seem to float on air."

"This is a mystery," Broken Paw said. "What could have happened to her? Do you think she left the white man to strike off on her own?"

"And leave her horse behind?" Thunder Hoop said. "No, I think something happened to her. I found part of a print, like the one we came across before."

"The naked track?" Woody Hill said.

Long Ghost seized the opening. "No ordinary man could make such a track. You all saw the size of him. It is another sign that we are doing wrong. We must turn back."

Broken Paw stood and gestured with ill-concealed contempt. "You turn back if you want. The rest of us are not afraid to go on."

It was an insult few would tolerate, yet Long Ghost merely smiled an enigmatic smile, then bobbed his chin at the clouds. "Soon it will not matter. The rain will erase all tracks, and you will have no choice."

Regretting that he had brought the old warrior

along, Broken Paw mounted. His gaze lifted to the crest of the mountain to the south and he spied what he took to be a pair of elk crossing a barren tract below a gap. Squinting, he saw they were horses, not elk. "There!" he cried gleefully, pointing with his quirt.

"They are coming this way," Thunder Hoop said.

"If we hurry, we can ambush them," Clown Horse proposed.

Broken Paw had the same idea. He applied his quirt and streaked toward the slope, anxious to bring the pursuit to a close. The riders up above descended to the tree line and were lost to sight. Soon he was among the pines himself.

The slopes were steep and dotted with deadfalls. Only master horsemen could have scaled that mountain as rapidly as the Chopunnish. Broken Paw rode with one hand on his bow, holding an arrow in place.

Yet as fleet as the Chopunnish mounts were, swifter still were the dark clouds sweeping in from the Great Water. Laden with moisture, as black as night, they unleashed a torrent of rain on the warriors when they still had hundreds of yards to climb.

To be frustrated by the elements when he was so close to his prey was almost more than Broken Paw could bear. As cold drops splattered on his head and shoulders, he threw back his head and snarled at the traitorous sky. He slowed, and his companions clustered around him, awaiting his decision.

"Spread out!" Broken Paw shouted. "We cannot let them slip past us!"

The warriors moved to do as bidden. Broken Paw rode forward slowly, his head bent low to keep out some of the rain. The downpour intensified, limiting visibility to less than the length of his horse. Since he could hardly shoot his bow accurately under such adverse conditions, he slid the shaft into his quiver, slung the bow across his soaked chest, and tugged his tomahawk loose.

Broken Paw went around a wide trunk. He glanced to the right and spied Clown Horse; to the left, a wall of rain. The wind had risen. Limbs creaked and crackled under the onslaught, some snapping with loud retorts like those of guns. Somewhere, a tree went down with a resounding crash that spooked his mount. He struck the animal with his quirt to ensure that it behaved, and went on.

Unexpectedly, there was a brief break in the deluge. For the time it would take a man to count to ten, the drops lessened, the wind died, and Broken Paw saw a pair of horses above him. Riding the lead animal was the woman. She was looking over her shoulder but turned as the storm resumed in all its savage fury. He had no idea whether she had spotted him.

Breaking into a gallop, Broken Paw plowed through the brush to the spot where the woman had been. She was gone. He wheeled his horse, seeking her silhouette amid the trees, but the rain was heavier than ever and he could not see his fingers at the end of his arm.

Broken Paw knew she had seen him. She was clever, that one, and for the time being she had eluded them.

He was not about to give up, though. Eventually the storm would end, the hunt would resume. Eventually he would get his hands on her, and then all the cleverness in the world would not spare her from the fate he had in store for her.

Chapter

— 12 —

Singing Wolf, chief of the Burning Heart Band of the Tsistsistas, would never be the same man again. As he sat astride his paint and gazed forlornly at the bloated bodies and ruined lodges, he felt his heart break within him. He went numb all over, as if from a physical blow, and became so light-headed that he thought he would fall.

The warriors with him were equally stunned. Forgotten were the leisurely, happy days just spent in the high mountains. Forgotten were the many pack animals laden with dried elk meat, enough to last the village all winter long, if rationed.

"This cannot be!" Hairy Hand broke the awful silence, voicing the sentiments of them all.

Singing Wolf nudged his horse over to the blackened remains of his lodge. A few strides from it lay his wife, her features horribly bloated, her body ravaged by scavengers. He could not bear to look and jerked his head away, saying under his breath, "Nesting Bird!" Tears came, tears he choked back, refusing to shed them in front of the others. Public displays were not the Tsistsista way.

The chief put both hands on the back of his paint to steady himself. He swallowed to relieve a knot in his throat, then looked up and wished he hadn't.

Not far off lay the old healer, Little Otter, and Feather from the Sky. Apparently he had been helping her to safety when both had been shot from behind. The bullet wounds in the back of their heads had festered and were crawling with maggots.

Singing Wolf closed his eyes and fought off an urge to be violently sick. When he could lift his head, he rode in a slow circuit of the camp, counting the dead. He was chief. It was his duty, no matter how much the task tore him apart inside. Some of the warriors joined him; others simply sat and stared, as motionless as the corpses, the life seemingly drained from their bodies.

"Who could it have been?" Hairy Hand wondered. "The Shinni? The Pawnees? The Dakotas?"

Long Forelock was scanning the encampment intently. "It will be hard to tell. I see no arrows, no lances, other than those of Tsistsistas."

The statement shattered Singing Wolf's mental paralysis. He reined up and confirmed the younger man's assessment. There were many weapons scattered about, some broken by the tread of horse hooves, some intact, but every single one had clearly been fashioned by Burning Heart hands. After a pitched battle like the one fought here, discarded weapons from both sides should have littered the battlefield. Often the victors took their pick of the spoils, but some weapons were always left behind. Broken arrows, in particular, were rarely retrieved because repairing them was impractical.

Since no two tribes made their weapons in exactly the same manner, it was possible for a third party to tell who had been involved in a fight by the markings on the arrows, the style of fletching, the size and shape of the lances. Whoever had attacked the Burning Hearts should have left clues to their identity.

"Everyone look for sign," Singing Wolf directed. "We must learn who did this." He began to take note of how his people had died. Most, he was surprised to discover, had been shot. Others had been tomahawked or stabbed. Many had been mutilated.

"Look here!" Lame Deer shouted, pointing at a patch of bare earth untouched by the flames. "See these tracks!"

Everyone gathered around and took a turn examining the pair of clear footprints. As with weapons, no two tribes crafted their moccasins exactly the same way. Heel and toe shapes were invariably different. The Tsistsistas, for instance, preferred soles cut narrow at both ends, wider through the middle. Pawnees liked their moccasins broad at the front. Arapahos wore footwear wider than any other tribe, while the Crows cut their soles so the moccasins were slightly curved.

Singing Wolf squatted and ran a finger along the uniform outline of one of the prints. The toes pointed outward, not inward, as would be the case if the track had been made by an Indian. "These were made by a white man," he announced.

Murmuring broke out. The warriors scattered to hunt more evidence and were not long in finding dozens of similar footprints. They also found hoofprints made by shod horses.

Gradually the terrible truth dawned on all of them. They looked at one another, disbelief wrestling with reality.

Singing Wolf fluctuated between fury and dazed astonishment. *White men!* Yellow Hair had warned him that many whites were not to be trusted, that some roamed the countryside in large packs like marauding wolves, picking off the weak, the helpless. But never in his wildest imaginings would he have thought any whites capable of the atrocity that had befallen the Burning Hearts.

Suddenly Singing Wolf became aware that Hairy Hand was addressing him. "What did you say, brother?" he asked.

"What should we do about the bodies? Do we dare try to move them? In their condition, they would fall apart in our hands."

Before Singing Wolf could decide, a gleeful yip to the south drew the attention of every warrior there. Rushing toward them across the blackened plain was a small boy of eight or nine, his grimy face glowing with pure joy, his arms waving wildly.

"That is Looks for Home, son of Long Forelock," Hairy Hand said. "Where did he come from?"

The overjoyed father let out a yip louder than the boy's and dashed to meet his son. They embraced, then danced in a circle, hand in hand.

Singing Wolf led the rest of the hunters over to the reunited father and son. He hoped against hope that since the boy had survived, others had as well. When father and son paused to catch their breath, he immediately asked, "Looks for Home, are you alone?"

"No," the excited child answered. "Fourteen of us have been hiding in a gully half a day's walk to the south. The women have been saying you would come back. Over and over they have told us we would be safe again."

"How many are there?" Hairy Hand inquired.

The ears of all those present were pricked to hear the answer. On it depended the future of the Burning Heart Band. "Twelve women, your wife among them. Three girls over fourteen. And seven young ones like me."

Some of the sorrow drained from Singing Wolf. Twelve out of thirty-four was such a small number, but it was enough to rebuild. And the girls were old enough to take husbands. In a year there would be many new mouths to feed, and as often as nature allowed after that until the band was at full strength again. "No men survived?" he interjected.

Looks for Home's happiness diminished. "They all fell trying to defend the village." He paused, his lower lip trembling. "It was terrible. The white men gave us no warning. The men did not have a chance."

Long Forelock clasped his son's arm. "You saw these whites with your own eyes"

"Some of them, Father. And one there was who seemed to be their chief, but he was not white. His skin, his hair, were different."

"How different?" Kicking Bear asked.

"Darker. I saw him shoot Rattle Tail. He laughed when he did it, like he was having great fun. Then he stuck her in the eyes with his knife and laughed some more."

Singing Wolf had one more important question to pose. "Twisted Leg, my daughter-in-law. I did not see her body anywhere. Is she at the gully?"

There was no need for the boy to respond. His expression was adequate.

Singing Wolf shook himself and turned. "We have lost many loved ones, many friends. I know that all our hearts are heavy, but we must be strong now for the sake of those who depend on us." He paused and glanced up at the dozens of circling buzzards that had flapped into the sky earlier at the band's approach. "We will honor the memory of the dead later. Now it is important that we see the survivors to safety. We have enough meat to last for many sleeps, so we can travel to the northwest without delay."

"What of the whites who butchered our families?" Kicking Bear interrupted. "Do we let them go unpunished?"

"My blood cries for vengeance, just like yours," Singing Wolf admitted. "If we only had ourselves to think of, I would not rest until the butchers were destroyed. But we must put the welfare of the women and children who lived through this nightmare before revenge. The living are more important than the dead."

No one argued with his wisdom.

"We will head into the hills and set up a new camp," Singing Wolf went on. "Buffalo are plentiful there at this time of the year. We will collect many hides, build new lodges. In a moon or two, the village will be as it was. In time, the Burning Hearts will thrive as before." He swept them with a sharp gaze. "But our lives will never be the same again. Things have changed forever."

"Because of the whites," Hairy Hand said bitterly.

Lame Deer cleared his throat. "What of Second Son and Yellow Hair? How will they find us if we go so far from our usual haunts?"

The reminder seared through Singing Wolf like a burning brand. He spun toward Looks for Home. "Their son, Wolf Sings on the Mountain! Is he with you?"

"No," the boy said. "My mother saw him ride off early the morning of the raid. He went to the west, the same direction the whites came from. And he never came back. We think the whites must have killed him." Looks for Home nodded to the south. "We have been taking turns at watching the village, and we have seen no one else."

Singing Wolf recalled how sad he had been the day his father, Buffalo Horn, died. It had been the single worst day of his life, until now. His wife was gone. The son he cherished and the daughter-in-law he adored were gone. His beloved nephew was gone. His sister and her husband were probably dead also, or they would have returned long ago. All his family was gone. He was alone in the world.

Then Singing Wolf saw the hopeful eyes fixed on him, and he knew his thoughts had led him astray. He wasn't alone and would never be alone as long as there were Burning Hearts who needed his counsel, who relied on his judgment. They were more than just his people. They were his family now, and he must devote himself to them more deeply than ever before.

"Come," Singing Wolf stated. "The women and children wait. We must give them cause to be happy, to see that life will go on."

Hairy Hand grunted in disgust. "I know you are right, but I would still like to track down the white dogs who did this."

"They are long gone," Long Forelock said. "They must be many days' travel from here by this time."

The warrior was wrong. Camped among the low hills to the east were the objects of their wrath. On the crown of one hill overlooking the incinerated prairie and the site where the village had stood, two men were flat on their stomachs with spyglasses pressed to their right eyes.

"Do we attack them, boss?" Rafe Hancock asked out of dread that they would. Going up against old men, women, and kids was one thing, tangling with seasoned warriors quite another. Besides, the odds were about even and he liked to have them stacked in his favor.

"Are you insane?" Julio Morales responded. "I want the Bennetts, and I don't see them with this bunch." He watched through the telescope as the warriors galloped to the south. "I wish we knew where that boy came from, eh? There must be others who got away. Too bad we couldn't find them before the warriors came back."

Rafe lowered his spyglass. "How much longer do you aim to hang around here? Some of the boys are getting a mite restless."

"Some?" Morales said sarcastically. He had listened to their grumbling for days and knew he had better commit himself to a plan of action soon.

"All right. All of us are damned tired of twiddling our thumbs," Rafe confessed. "And can you blame us? Every day we waste here is a day we could be plundering pilgrims bound for the Oregon country. We didn't throw in with you to stay poor the rest of our lives."

Morales shifted onto his side. "*Bastardos.* This is the thanks I get for all I have done?" He spat in the grass. "Until I came along, these renegades barely stole enough to keep their powder horns filled. Under my leadership they have done better than ever before, yet still they doubt me."

"I didn't say—" Rafe began, but stopped when the other held up a hand.

"*Silencio.* I am not done." Morales folded his telescope and sat up. "You would all do well to trust me more and your fears less. You are like pampered *niños* who are so used to getting what they want that they throw fits when events do not move rapidly enough for them."

Rafe held his tongue. Riling the Mexican was a surefire means of slashing one's life expectancy dramatically, and he aimed to live to a ripe old age.

"Sometimes you whiners disgust me," Morales said, and was disappointed when Hancock refused to take up the gauntlet. He liked a good quarrel. They served to remind the others of who was in charge. "I am always thinking of new and better ways to line our pockets, but does anyone appreciate my effort? No."

"We're not exactly a Christian outfit," Rafe mentioned offhandedly.

"What does that have to do with anything?" Morales demanded. "*El diablo* claimed us the day we were born, amigo. None of us are religious and it is too late for us to change our stripes." He stood and brushed dirt from his leggings. "Enough of this foolish talk. Let's go back. I have an announcement to make."

The cutthroats were taking their ease, hungry faces focused on an antelope haunch slowly roasting on a makeshift spit. Red was doing the honors. "Another few minutes and we can make dog of this meat," he declared for all to hear. Poking it with a finger to test how well it was done, he then licked his finger and smacked his lips. "Hell. Painter can't shine with this."

"I never heard a body brag so on his own cookin'," Webber said. "And all you did was light a damned fire."

Red glowered. "I'd like to see you do any better. Every time you cook, we end up with meat so raw a wolf would spit it out."

A dispute was imminent, but Morales nipped it in the bud by striding to the center of the ring. "Quit your squabbling, children," he said with just the right touch of malice. "I have something important to say."

That shut them up. Morales put his hands on his hips and stated, "Either the band we attacked were not the Burning Hearts, or Cleve Bennett and his red bitch have gone elsewhere to live. Whichever, I think it is time we went on about our own business. Tomorrow at first light we head for South Pass."

General cheers greeted the news.

"*C'est incroyable!* At last!" Landis cried. "I was beginning to think I would spend the rest of my days watching grass grow."

Red wagged his butcher knife. "I just hope all the yarns we've heard about these here pilgrims were told with a straight tongue. It would upset me something awful to get to the Green River country and not find a single greenhorn."

"Some will show, sooner or later," Morales insisted. He winked and grinned. "If they do not, so what? There will be another rendezvous in a few months. Trappers will come from all over, and some will have more plews than they need."

Rafe chuckled. "I'm sure we can persuade them to share with us if we ask real politelike."

The discussion turned to how much money they hoped to make, and how best to attack a single wagon as opposed to attacking several wagons at once. In all cases trickery was called for. The renegades were masters of the art, none more so than Julio Morales. He laid out exactly how they would proceed, everyone marveling at his craftiness.

A watch was posted, and shortly before midnight the last of the killers turned in. Morales slept nearest the fire, as befitted his position as leader, a pistol clasped firmly in his right hand as was his custom.

Breakfast consisted of leftover antelope, gulped cold with cups of coffee to wash it down. Morales ate a light meal. He wasn't fond of riding long distances on a full stomach.

The prairie was swept with spyglasses before the gang moved out into the open. Morales was wary of clashing with the warriors he had seen since they were bound to be out for blood.

From the hills, the renegades rode to the river, then bore westward at a brisk pace, Morales and Rafe Hancock in the lead. Morales gave the village a last, lingering look and sneered at the black circles that marked where the lodges had stood. Wiping the Cheyennes out had been a lot easier than he had anticipated. It was food for thought. What he did once, he could do again. Only next time he would pick a village rich in prime animal hides.

Buzzards covered the bodies even at that early hour. Others waited for their turns to feast. Morales saw one bird rip off a sizable chunk of putrid flesh with its big beak, then, with a deft flip of its ugly head, slide the morsel down its gullet.

The men were in fine spirits at the prospect of killing and robbing again. They talked quietly among themselves and Morales didn't object. He was in rare good humor, too. Despite not having slain the

Bennetts, he had added to his formidable reputation by doing what no other man had ever done. When word got out, he would have more men riding with him than he knew what to do with.

They were abreast of a gravel bar when Morales spotted recently made horse tracks. Holding up a hand, he stopped and slid off his sorrel. Judging by the prints, a pair of horses had watered at that spot many times over a number of days. He guessed that the last time had been less than a week ago.

"Hey, lookee there!" Webber called out, pointing at a dark hole in the bank. "What do you make of that?"

At a gesture from Morales, several of the cutthroats climbed down and converged with their rifles leveled. A man named Cain crawled inside, was gone all of five seconds, then poked his head out to say, "Someone hid out here for a spell, but they're not here now."

Morales investigated for himself. Embers of a small fire in a corner of the cavity testified to repeated nights spent huddled in the sanctuary. A depression against the back wall showed where a man had lain for many days. Most intriguing of all were the footprints.

"A kid made most of these," Red remarked.

"Yes," Morales said, poking at a discarded pile of bloodstained bandages. "A man was hurt and the kid tended him." It sparked an idea. Could it be, he asked himself, that the wounded man was Cleve Bennett and the kid was Bennett's breed brat, Billy-Wolf? It would explain their absence, if not that of the squaw. "Find which way they went," he commanded.

The men fanned out along the bank. The horses had been sheltered among cottonwoods close by.

Tracks were found leading to the spot, but none turned out to lead away, except to the gravel bar.

"There has to be some sign," Morales said. "Keep looking until I say to stop."

Grumbling, the killers complied. Landis, one of the better trackers, walked a score of yards upriver and halted beside a strip of mud. His ear-piercing whistle brought everyone on the double. "See these, *mon ami*," he said. "They are the freshest of the lot, I think."

Morales knelt to study them. He wasn't as good at rating the age of tracks, but he would take Landis's word for it. The former *voyageur* was rarely wrong. In this case it appeared the two horses had entered the river single file at an angle that revealed they were heading westward.

"They're making for the mountains," Red said.

"The same as we are," Morales said, and grinned. Fate had looked favorably on him again. If he pushed the men, they would overtake the pair in four or five days. At long last they would have his revenge on Cleve Bennett. "Mount up. Let's ride."

Morales was a good hater and knew it. He'd learned at an early age. When only six, he had grown to hate his mother for her antics when his father was away. She had invited strange men to their house and always locked him in his room so he would not bother them. Later, his father had learned of her affairs and killed her.

Morales had thought that would be the end of it, but his father had to flee and Morales was given into the care of an uncle who drank himself into a stupor every night. The man had worked Morales from dawn to dusk and cuffed him brutally if he objected. Morales had hated anew.

For six years Morales had tolerated the abuse, then, one stormy night, he had slit his uncle's throat. Drifting steadily northward, he had met other men he hated, but none as much as he hated Cleve Bennett and Second Son. Thinking of them always gave him a warm feeling inside, such as he had that time he twisted a kitten's neck to silence its mewing.

How Morales would love to do the same to the Bennett clan! Over the next several days he followed the river to the northwest and twice came on camps made by the boy and the man. Soon, Morales told himself while rubbing his palms in bloodthirsty anticipation. Soon his enemies would learn what it meant to earn the hatred of Julio Cardenas Morales!

Chapter

— 13 —

It had been four days. Second Son was very worried. She squatted between the small fire and her unconscious mate, folded her arms across her knees, and studied his rugged face. How much longer before he came around? she reflected.

Maybe he never would. Second Son remembered an incident from her childhood, when a noted warrior by the name of Leaps Fast did not quite leap fast enough one day when charged by a bull buffalo. Leaps Fast had been bowled over, then stomped repeatedly.

One of the blows had struck his skull. Although the Burning Hearts did everything in their power, and their best healer, Little Otter, had exhausted herself trying to save him, Leaps Fast never recovered. He lay as one dead, day after day after day. His body wasted away to the point where it could no longer support life, and Leaps Fast's spirit soared to the Great Beyond.

Would the same thing happen to her Cleve? Second Son placed her palm on his forehead to see if his fever had returned. His temperature was as it should be.

A faint rustle told the warrior that her shadow was back. She glanced around to find the giant Modoc standing there with a dead doe over his wide shoulder. He grinned, touched the deer, and addressed her at length.

"What am I going to do with you?" Second Son responded in her own language. Since neither spoke the other's tongue, and since the Modoc had no knowledge of sign, communicating was hard. She had to resort to exaggerated movements to get her ideas across.

Second Son was still not comfortable having the outcast around. She bore him no malice for his treatment of her, but she did not know how far she could trust him, if at all. He had made no attempt to harm her. Rather, he lived to make her happy. The Modoc was the one who did the hunting, who gathered wood, who was ready to do her bidding at any time of the day. It was like having her own personal slave.

But this was different. Second Son could not decide whether the Modoc entertained a romantic interest in her, or whether he had adopted her as a sister. There was a third possibility, but she thought it ridiculous that a man so huge and capable, even if dull-witted, should feel the need for a pretend mother.

"Thank you," Second Son said, smiling and pointing at the doe.

The giant puffed out his chest in pride and set the dead animal down. Placing a callused foot on the body, he gripped a rear leg with both hands, then wrenched. So great was his strength that he tore the leg clean off. Beaming like a five-year-old, he proceeded to skewer the haunch with a sharpened stick so he could roast it.

Second Son had to admit that the Modoc was of great help. In addition to everything else he did, he had taken it on himself to protect her from her enemies. When she had nothing else for him to do, he would go off into the lodgepole pines and keep watch for Broken Paw.

The Nez Percé had not given up. Of that Second Son was sure. She had nearly been caught unawares once, during the thunderstorm, but she would not make the same mistake again.

Second Son looked at Cleve, wishing he would groan or whine or twitch a finger, to show some sign that he would soon rejoin the world of the living. She picked up the cup of broth she had made the evening before and let some trickle into his mouth. His throat automatically bobbed, but that was the only reaction.

Depressed, Second Son put the cup down and rested her brow on her arms. They couldn't stay there forever. Eventually the Nez Percé would find them.

She had to get her man out of there even though moving him might worsen his state.

For one of the few times during their danger-filled marriage, Second Son pondered how her life would be without Yellow Hair. She could not abide the thought. Until he came along, she had believed herself to be complete unto herself. She had needed no one, and secretly regarded her married sisters with amusement. She had never understood why so many women took men into their lives when doing so sometimes brought endless disputes and aggravation.

Then the golden-haired white man had been taken captive by the Tsistsistas, and on seeing him for the first time Second Son had felt alien stirrings in her breast. She had resisted them, for they meant that she was no different than the sisters she laughed at. But there had been no resisting the terrible, lonely ache that formed in her breast when Yellow Hair left the Burning Heart Band to resume his life as a trapper.

Being alone, Second Son had learned, was the worst affliction a person could endure. And there was only one certain cure. It was called love, the deep, abiding love of a man and woman who united their hearts and souls and were determined to withstand all life threw at the two of them, as one. To be without Cleve was unthinkable.

Second Son tried to remember all the times she had witnessed Little Otter conduct healings and to recall whether any of the treatments would benefit her man. There were none she could think of, which made her feel worse. It was disturbing to be so helpless.

The Modoc was staring at her like a devoted puppy,

as he always did. When she looked up, he jabbed a thick thumb at Cleve, then northward, at a high, jagged peak. He said one word several times, dipped two fingers to the ground, and moved them as if they were tiny legs.

Second Son was not quite sure of his meaning. Twice now in the past two days he had done the same thing. She deduced that he wanted to take her to that mountain, but his reason remained a mystery. And she could not see going there unless it would be of benefit.

The hollow in which they were camped was well hidden from prying eyes. Second Son had picked the spot. A spring supplied water. Lush grass afforded ample grazing for the horses.

A light northwesterly breeze shook the trees lining the rim. Second Son stared at the starry heavens, hoping it did not portend another storm. No haze surrounded the moon, and the sky appeared clear.

The night was uneventful. Second Son slept on her back beside Cleve. Several times she awoke to check on him and saw the giant still awake, his eyes glued to her. Shortly before dawn she awoke for the final time. The Modoc was gone.

Second Son knelt at the spring and washed her arms and face. She carried a handful to Cleve and splashed it on his cheeks and neck. The horses were astir, Socks already on his feet.

Early morning was one of Second Son's favorite times of the day. It was when the birds came alive, robins, jays, sparrows, and more warbling in an avian chorus. She loved to listen to the songs; their carefree melodies were contagious.

Then the birds did something they shouldn't do. Every last one fell unaccountably silent. Second Son was on her feet in a flash, the lance she had made in her hands. Only two things would quiet the birds; the presence of a predator—or men were abroad.

The sun peeked above the horizon, flooding the forest with golden shafts. Second Son stepped to the east side of the hollow, where the ground formed an earthen ramp. She crept to the top, careful to keep her head below ground level. Daring a peek, she scanned the rough terrain.

The movement, when it came, was so lightning quick that Second Son almost missed it. A figure had darted from one tree to another, approximately seventy-five yards away. She did not get more than a glimpse, but it was sufficient to warn her the figure was that of a Nez Percé.

Second Son spotted a second warrior, a dozen paces farther back. They were scouring the ground, seeking tracks. One had a rifle, the other a bow. Soon they would reach the bowl, putting Yellow Hair at risk. She opted to take the fight to them.

Slipping over the rim, Second Son melted into the shadows. She had the lance and her knife, and they would have to do. Molding her body to the trunk of a pine, she poked an eyebrow past the trunk. The Nez Percé were huddled next to a set of tracks, whispering. When the man carrying the rifle stood, Second Son drew back and firmed her hold on the lance. She would only get one clear thrust.

The soft thread of moccasins drew near. A shadow took form several paces to the left. Second Son looked for a second shadow but did not see it. She did not like having one of her foes unaccounted for, but she could not stand there and let the closest man go by. She had to act.

The Nez Percé was young, no older than twenty winters. His youth made him blunder, for in not taking his eyes off the tracks he followed, he left himself wide open.

The moment the warrior appeared, Second Son took a bound and drove the fire-hardened tip of her lance at his throat. By a sheer fluke he deflected the blow when he tried to jerk aside and brought his rifle up from his waist. The smack of metal on wood was loud.

Second Son shifted, recovered her balance, and speared her weapon at his chest, giving him no time to set himself or to use his fusil. He frantically retreated. His ankle caught on a low bush, throwing him to one side, making her miss. She reared to plunge the tip into his stomach, but her intuition blared and she spun to confront the second warrior. The spin saved her life.

A speeding shaft whizzed past Second Son's shoulder, missing her by the width of a feather. She heard a yelp behind her as something struck her a glancing blow on the back. Knocked onto one knee, she twisted and saw the first warrior with the arrow jutting from his side. The man had one hand on the shaft and was desperately scrambling backward to put distance between them.

Second Son had to let him go. There was a bowman to deal with. She dived at the very moment he fired another arrow, which nearly clipped her head. Rolling to the right behind a tree, the warrior rose. In order to use the lance, she had to reduce the range.

As Second Son broke from cover toward another tree, she saw a hulking form rear up behind the bowman. He sensed his doom and tried to turn, but the Modoc's enormous hands closed on his back and he was lifted bodily high into the air, above the giant's head. The Nez Percé struggled in vain. He was like an infant in the grasp of a grizzly. He screeched as the Modoc drove him straight down, into the Modoc's bent knee.

The crack of the spine was as loud as a gunshot. The Nez Percé gurgled once, then went limp, like wet reeds.

Second Son sought the fleeing warrior and spied him in full flight to the southeast. "After that one!" she shouted, and pointed so the giant would get her meaning.

The Modoc had hunkered next to the dead warrior and was shaking the dead man's arm and giggling like a kid.

If Second Son wanted it done, she would clearly have to do it herself. Putting on a burst of speed, she chased the wounded brave. He could not be allowed to escape, to report to Broken Paw.

It was a source of pride to the Burning Heart Band that their renowned warrior woman was one of the fleetest in the tribe. When the Tsistsistas held grand gatherings of all the bands, footraces were a common contest. Second Son had won many of them, starting in her twelfth year when she beat a man known as

Long Legs, whose stride had given him many previous victories.

Second Son put her speed to the test now, flying after the wounded warrior. He was running, but stiffly, impaired by the shaft in his torso, using his fusil as a crutch so he wouldn't fall. She swept around the pine and saw him look over a shoulder. His own speed increased.

The man had wonderful stamina. Stricken as he was, he maintained a swift pace. Second Son closed in on him and was perhaps a stone's throw away when he suddenly halted, spun, and raised the fusil. She threw herself behind a log and waited for the blast of the rifle. When none was forthcoming, she hiked her head high enough to realize that the Nez Percé had duped her. He had only pretended to fire, then had run on when she hit the ground.

A clever devil! Second Son mused as she renewed her pursuit. She dared not let him deceive her again, but neither could she ignore the deadly danger the rifle posed. When he pointed it at her a second time, she dodged behind a pine, quickly peeked out, and took off again since he was doing the same.

Gradually, Second Son narrowed the gap. She passed drops of blood scattered on the grass and brush. The man was gravely hurt. It amazed her that he was still on his feet, but then, he was racing for his very life.

A new element was added when Second Son caught sight of a pair of horses in a clearing up ahead. The superbly trained animals had their ears pricked and were ready for flight. She gritted her teeth and put all she had into overtaking her quarry before he reached the mounts.

For the third time the Nez Percé whirled and brought the rifle to bear. The frantic look in his eyes was proof that he was not going to try another bluff. Second Son hugged the earth as the boom of flintlock echoed off across the valley. When she regained her feet, the wily warrior was at the horses, trying to climb on one.

Second Son raised the lance and charged. The man was impeded by the arrow, unable to mount as he ordinarily would. He had to twist his body sideways, then jump. She came within throwing range and was on the verge of doing so when her wily adversary cut to the left and plunged into the woods.

As before, Second Son was left with no choice. She sprinted up to the horse left behind. The animal spooked and would have run off had she not wrapped her fingers on the trailing reins. Her arms were almost torn from their sockets, but she held on and brought the 'Paloose to a stop.

Meanwhile the Nez Percé was gaining. Smiling, too, in the belief he had shaken her.

Second Son intended to prove him wrong. Clamping her hand on the animal's mane, she pulled herself onto its back. A slap of her legs was all that was needed to send it galloping after the other horse.

The Nez Percé realized he wasn't safe yet and knuckled down to the chore of guiding his horse through the verdant maze. He hung on to the useless fusil since it was much too valuable to discard. Twice he tried to reload, but it was impossible.

Ducking under branches, prudently avoiding briars, Second Son closed on her enemy. They flew across a bottom, up a slope, and along a barren ridge. The warrior began to lose ground and urgently beat his horse on the head and shoulders.

At last Second Son thought she had him. The level ridge enabled her to get close enough to hurl her lance. She straightened, threw back her arm, and centered on a spot in the center of the warrior's back.

Beyond the Nez Percé, more riders materialized, seven in all, Broken Paw in the lead. On seeing her, they vented piercing war whoops and rushed to the aid of their fellow.

Frustrated by the development, Second Son hauled on the reins, turned her horse, and fled. Two of the Nez Percé stopped beside the wounded man, but the other five came on rapidly. One held a rifle and was trying to fix a bead.

Bent low over her mount's back, Second Son took the slope much too fast. Her horse stumbled, righted itself, stumbled worse, and tottered toward the bottom, its legs pumping. She thought for sure that she would be unhorsed but they reached the bottom unharmed.

The Nez Percés followed, taking more care than she had, the man with the rifle forced to concentrate on his riding. The tall leader, Broken Paw, scowled and shook a fist at her.

Second Son's first impulse was to head back to the bowl and her mate, but she wisely went in the opposite direction. An arrow flashed over her head. Another seared the flank of her mount and sent the horse into a panic. She had no need to goad it to go faster. All she had to do was hang on as the animal raced along as if a cougar nipped at its tail.

The war party spread out, Broken Paw at the middle of the line. Those with bows notched barb-tipped shafts.

Arrows did not start raining down until Second Son neared a thickly forested hill. The warriors were firing on the fly and doing a commendable job. Most of their shafts came close. A few nicked the horse, yet none entered its flesh. Second Son was spared, but she knew her luck wouldn't hold forever, and she was glad when the canopy of trees formed a protective barrier above her.

Slanting to the north, Second Son stuck to the roughest ground she could find. The thicker the undergrowth, the more it suited her purpose. Most warriors refused to waste arrows, which required a lot of time to make to perfection. They only shot when they believed they could hit their target. By keeping trees and thickets between her horse and those of her pursuers, she kept them from shooting. Not all of them, however. One warrior especially seemed to have a limitless supply of shafts and kept on firing when the others stopped.

Second Son racked her brain for a way out of her predicament. Every stride was taking her farther from Cleve, who was utterly helpless. She yearned to get back to him. But how to do it, without losing her life?

The hill gave way to another, and another. It became apparent that her horse was becoming winded and would soon give out. Second Son slackened her pace so the animal would last a little longer.

The Nez Percés continued to whoop and holler. A number of them had clear shots, but they didn't fire any more arrows. Second Son suspected that they could tell her horse was at the end of its rope, and they were now intent on taking her alive. Oh, they would kill her, in time, but not until after they made her suffer.

Moments later Second Son pounded over the crest of a third hill and was shocked to see an open plain to the east of it. If she kept on going, there would be no cover, nowhere to hide. Eluding the war party would be impossible.

With the insight came action. Second Son veered to the south and pushed her mount even though the consequences could be dire. She had a wild idea, but she could not put it into effect unless she had a substantial lead.

A wide strip of manzanita gave Second Son the chance she needed. By then she was a hundred yards in front of the yipping warriors. She barreled into the heavy growth, ignoring the many cuts she sustained, and when she felt she was completely hidden from their view, she reined up and hopped off. A whack of the lance on the animal's rump sent it fleeing.

Second Son crouched and scooted to the right a dozen steps. She flattened at the base of a manzanita and felt the earth tremble to the drumming of the Nez Percé mounts. They flashed past her, a few so close she could have dropped the riders with her lance, but she let them go by. As soon as the vegetation closed around them, she pushed to her feet and jogged westward.

Second Son counted on her horse leading the Nez Percés on a merry chase. But she had hardly gone far up the slope of the hill when she looked and saw that the animal had halted out of sheer exhaustion and was surrounded by the warriors. Broken Paw angrily issued orders and the men rode back into the manzanita to find her trail.

Outrunning horses was out of the question. Second Son had to stay sharp or her enemies would catch her. One factor in her favor was the hardness of the soil; the tracks she left were few and far between. She came to some pines and squatted to mark the progress of the warriors.

They had spread out even more than before. Some were poking lances into thickets. One man occasionally stood on the back of his horse to see better.

Dropping onto her elbows and knees, Second Son snaked along, always watchful. She covered a lot of ground without incident. The Nez Percés had drifted to the south of her position. When she was satisfied none were anywhere near her, she rose and ran. The forest thinned, allowing her to move as swiftly as a bounding antelope.

Again and again Second Son glanced over a shoulder to see if the Nez Percés had guessed their mistake and were coming toward her. She was so intent on the warriors to her rear that she failed to keep in mind the wounded Nez Percé and the two who had stopped to help him. The oversight nearly cost Second Son her life.

She was threading among pines when the trees ended at a short earthen drop-off. Since to go around would waste precious time, and since the drop was no more than the height of a lodge, she resolved to throw down the lance, slide over the edge, hang by her hands, and fall. But then, as she dangled from the lip, the nicker of a horse made her look down into the trees below.

The wounded warrior and his two friends were on their way to join the others. They were talking softly, the wounded one bent double, his buckskin shirt bearing a large crimson circle. Should any of them lift their heads, they would see Second Son.

Left with no recourse, the Burning Heart warrior simply hung on. She moved nothing except her eyes, marking the course of the trio. When they reined up, she thought she was done for. But they only stopped long enough for the wounded man to spit up some blood. Then they rode on.

Second Son let go when she felt they wouldn't hear her land. Scooping up the lance, she darted into the woods. Her lungs ached, but she refused to slow down until she reached Cleve. Twice she heard yells behind her. Evidently the Nez Percés had lost the scent, which pleased her immensely.

But her good mood did not last long. Second Son presently spied the warrior whose back had been broken, then the grassy bowl. She wondered why the Modoc had not tried to help her and figured it had something to do with his fear of horses.

At the ramp leading down into their sanctuary, Second Son discovered she had been terribly wrong. Horses had nothing to do with the giant's failure to help her. He was gone. The Modoc had deserted her.

And he had taken Cleve.

Chapter

— 14 —

Billy-Wolf Bennett held out a roasted rabbit leg to his cousin and said, "Here. You need to fill your belly."

The somber countenance of Rakes the Sky with Lightning became darker. Without bothering to so much as glance at the offered food, he responded curtly, "No. I am not hungry."

"You have to be." Billy-Wolf refused to be put off. "You have not eaten a bite in a day and a half. I stopped early today just for you, Lightning. You must eat to keep your strength up."

"No," Lightning insisted, and would have rolled onto his side so he did not have to face the boy had it not been so keenly painful for him to move. He closed his eyes and hoped Wolf Sings on the Mountain would leave him alone.

Reluctantly, Billy-Wolf set the morsel down and folded his arms around his legs. He was at his wit's end. No matter how hard he tried, Lightning shut him out time and again. From the moment the warrior had revived, days ago in the hole in the bank, Lightning had been acting as if he no longer cared whether he lived or not. "I do not want you to die," Billy-Wolf said.

Lightning made no reply. His impassive features never changed.

"Did you hear me?" Billy-Wolf said.

"I do not want to talk."

Billy-Wolf leaned forward to peer above the crackling flames that separated them. "You do not want to eat, you do not care to talk. What *do* you want to do? Just waste away to nothing? Because that is what will happen if you do not get on with your life." He paused, too choked with emotion to speak. "Why did you agree to come with me if all you want to do is kill yourself?"

Lightning sighed and turned his head. The simple motion lanced agony through his body. He had to grit his teeth to resist an urge to cry out.

Tears brimming the boy's eyes stopped Lightning from voicing the harsh words he was about to utter. He knew that he could not blame Wolf for being so upset. But he did not know how to explain himself to the boy's satisfaction.

"Well?" Billy-Wolf prompted.

"If you ever lose someone you love more than life itself, then you will understand," Lightning said. It hurt to move his lips but not as severely as it had pained him just several sleeps ago. He was mending rapidly, despite himself. There would be scars from the ordeal, but eventually he would be able to go on with his life, providing he cared to.

"I may be young but I am not stupid," Billy-Wolf said. "I know what you have gone through. I would be just as sad if the same thing had happened to me. But there is no excuse for trying to kill yourself. Not after all the trouble I went through to save you." An idea came to Billy. "Twisted Leg would not have liked to see you this way."

Jarring memories of happier times flooded through Lightning. The knot of misery he had carried in his breast since the attack on the village expanded, threatening to engulf him in torment. "Do not mention her name," he choked out.

Prying himself from between the dogs, Billy-Wolf walked around the fire. He decided it was past time for him to bring matters to a head. He feared that if he did not, he would wind up burying his cousin long before they ever reached California.

Billy hadn't counted on events unfolding the way they had. After lingering for days in the hole in the bank, hoping that survivors of the raid would show or that Singing Wolf would come back from the elk hunt,

Billy had made up his mind to leave, to go find his folks.

He had delayed going as long as he could. Every day Billy had crept close to the village and kept vigilant watch for hours at a time. His stomach had churned, seeing the bodies of those he loved and respected slowly rot away or be devoured by scavengers. From hiding, he had chucked rocks at the buzzards to drive them off, but they had always returned, each time more brazen than the time before.

All this time Billy had also been taking care of Lightning. He had applied mud packs to the burns and made herbal poultices as his mother had taught him, to help the warrior mend. He had made a clay bowl in which he carried water from the river to quench Lightning's thirst.

It had been an uphill battle. At first the warrior had only lain there, refusing to swallow a thing. Billy had been forced to make Lightning eat and drink. Later Lightning had grown strong enough to refuse, but Billy had persuaded him to eat at least a little every day.

Now, though, Lightning would not accept a thing, and Billy wondered if he had made a mistake by leaving. Perhaps he should have waited longer to see if the hunting party came back. Perhaps he should have lit signal fires to attract the attention of other survivors. Perhaps he should have left Lightning behind and gone westward alone.

Perhaps. Perhaps. Perhaps.

There were so many things Billy could have done, but one he had been unable to do was delay hunting for his folks any longer. At night, lying in the dank, cramped hole, he had thought about them constantly. During the day, while watching at the village, he had daydreamed of the glorious times they'd shared together. It had filled him with a longing that could no longer be denied. Billy *had* to find his parents. He would not rest until he learned their fate.

When Billy had presented the idea to Lightning, he'd expected the warrior to decline, to say that it was important for them to wait for Singing Wolf so they could tell him what had happened. To Billy's surprise, Lightning had fixed him with an odd stare, then made an odder comment.

"Yes, we will go. It would be better on the trail. The sun, the wind, the rain. It is not fitting in this hole."

Billy had been too overjoyed to question the strange statements, but now he wished he had. Hindsight told him that Lighting had planned all along to die on the journey. Which he could not let happen.

"We need to talk whether you want to or not," Billy said, and lightly placed a hand on his cousin's shoulder.

"I would like to be alone," Lightning declared, wishing the boy would let him nurture his grief in peace.

"After we speak with straight tongues," Billy boldly stated. Sitting, he picked his next words most carefully. "You talk about losing someone you love. I may have lost my mother and father. The only way I can find out is if I go find them. And I cannot do that without you. I am too young to go all the way to the Great Water alone."

Lightning did not want to, but he glanced at the

boy and felt his heart tear. "You can do it alone," he said more gruffly than he intended.

Billy-Wolf snorted. "You have never lied to me before, Lightning. It saddens me that you would do so now." He sat back. "My father once told me a saying of the whites. The best I can translate it is, 'A man should never bite into more meat than he can chew and swallow.' That holds true for everyone."

"So?"

"So we both know I stand little chance of reaching the far country where my parents went, on my own. I can live off the land as good as the next person, but I am not full-grown yet. There are things you know, things you can do, that I cannot. Without your help, I will probably die."

Billy-Wolf was not trying to deceive the warrior. He was being honest. He had thought it out thoroughly. There were over a thousand miles to cover, with beasts and hostiles a constant menace. Grown men did not attempt the trip alone, for good reason. He would be foolish to try.

Lightning squinted against the harsh glare of the afternoon sun. He had regained the use of his left eyelid, but bright light made the eye ache at times. Disregarding the pang, he looked at the boy, prepared to admit the truth, that he had no desire to live and it would be best if Wolf just went on. But the eloquent appeal of the youngster's face stopped him.

"I suppose I should not ask this of you," Billy-Wolf said. "You have your own life to live. Yet we have been friends for many winters. I think of you more as an older brother. And you are the only one I can turn to."

The warrior thought of his aunt and her husband, who had always treated him kindly and with the utmost respect, even when he had been a boy. Before they left, they had asked him to watch their offspring. He had promised them he would. And despite all that had happened, how could he go back on his word? How could he betray their trust?

"If you want to think it over, I understand," Billy-Wolf said. "I am not asking an easy thing. It will take us many sleeps to reach our destination, and we cannot be sure that we will find Second Son and Yellow Hair even if we get there."

A vivid image of Twisted Leg filled Lightning's mind. She had always been the kindest of persons, always willing to help others in need. What would she have him do, if she were still alive? The answer tore at him. His conscience warred with his sorrow, and he gnashed his teeth in raw misery.

To Billy-Wolf, it seemed his cousin was in moral anguish. "Are you all right?" he asked.

Lightning wanted to pound his fists on the ground and screech his impotent rage at the sky, but his hands were still in bad shape and it did not become a Tsistsista warrior to indulge in childish temper tantrums. "I am as fine as can be expected," he rasped.

"I did not mean to upset you," Billy apologized. He assumed he had made his friend's condition worse than it already had been, and he was upset with himself. "I will let you rest now," he said. "We will finish our talk when you are ready." Propping a hand under him, he went to stand.

It took intense effort, but Rakes the Sky with Lightning moved his arm and touched the boy's elbow. "Wait," he said weakly. Wolf had been right about his strength ebbing. If he did not eat soon, he would become too weak to ride. "I have something to say."

"I am listening," Billy-Wolf said anxiously.

"You are a lot like your father," Lightning said. "Both of you talk with a straight tongue, yet you can tie others up with your words." He sighed. "You are also wise past your years. You knew just how to make me see how wrong I have been."

"Does this mean you are not going to try and kill yourself?"

"I gave your parents a pledge that I would safeguard you until you saw them next. I owe it to their trust to do what I can to help you find them." For the first time since the attack, Lightning cracked a grin, and promptly regretted it. The charred half of his mouth felt as if it were still on fire. "We will find them together."

"Thank you!" Billy-Wolf so forgot himself as to throw his arms around his cousin's shoulders. When Lightning stiffened, he jerked back and blurted, "I am sorry. I forgot about your blisters."

"Why worry about me killing myself when you are doing such a fine job," Lightning joked, and looked at the fire. "Now, what happened to that rabbit meat?"

Across the clearing, Blaze and the stray sorrel that Billy had caught in the vicinity of the village both lifted their heads when the boy cackled crazily.

• • •

"How much longer are we going to play hide-and-seek with the breed and the Injun?" Rafe Hancock asked irritably. He had grown bored with the plodding pace and couldn't wait to finish the pair off. Stopping in the middle of the afternoon had been the straw that broke the camel's back.

Webber nodded in agreement. "You promised us we would head for the Green River country. Instead, all we do is sneak along behind these two."

Julio Morales was about to accept a coffee cup from Red. Glancing up sharply, he was pleased when the two who had questioned his leadership averted their gazes. They might dispute him, but they still feared him, and so long as they did, his position as leader was secure.

"I have explained this once before, *sí*?" Morales said. "There is a chance the brat will lead us to his father and mother. We will wait awhile yet, and see if he does." His next statement cracked like a whip. "I want them *dead*, and I will not let anyone stand in my way!"

"We were just askin'," Webber said. "There's no need to get all touchy."

Morales would have liked to slap both men senseless. The band grew more restless every day, and it would not be long before he had to decide between vengeance and leadership. Not that there was any question which of the two he would pick. He had to hope the boy hooked up with his parents in the next few days or he would have to settle for killing the brat.

Red came walking into camp, a telescope in his left hand. "They've made themselves real comfortable.

Had them a palaver for a while, and now the kid is dishing out supper. It made me hungry."

"So you came back before I sent someone to relieve you?" Morales asked, standing.

"What harm can it do?" Red said. "They're not going anywhere until morning. I'd stake my life on it."

"You just did," Morales said, and before any of them quite realized his meaning, he had whipped out his butcher knife and thrown it. Few were his equal with a knife. The blade hit into Red's chest with a thump, penetrating clear to the heart.

Red gaped at the hilt, then at Morales. "Damn you!" he sputtered, flecking his lips with dots redder than his beard. "You had no call—"

The rest was lost to posterity as Red oozed to the earth and quivered like a reed in the wind. His last breath grated from his lungs. He tried feebly to stand but was unable to lift himself to his knees and pitched onto his face.

Morales placed a hand on one of his three pistols and eyed the rest of the renegades. "Is there anyone else who thinks he doesn't have to do as he is told?"

Rafe Hancock, Webber, and the others were hardened killers to whom violence was a daily part of life. But they liked to be the ones who did the killing. Secretly, each and every one resented the high-handed tactics of their leader. Not one, though, felt brave enough to confront the Mexican.

Rafe blinked a few times and made a point of not looking up until he had his feelings well hidden. "Wouldn't a knock on the head have been better? Now we're a man short."

"There are still fifteen of us, more than enough to handle any trouble that comes along," Morales said. He yanked his blade from the body. "And since you're so concerned about Red's welfare, Hancock, you can drag him out onto the prairie and leave him for the coyotes and buzzards to find."

"Me?" Rafe argued, but bent to obey when he saw the Mexican's eyes narrow and Morales's hand tighten on the butt of the pistol. Grumbling under his breath, he clasped Red's wrists and slowly backed through the strip of woodland toward the high, gently waving grass. The renegades went on about their affairs as if nothing out of the ordinary had taken place.

Rafe's dislike of Morales was growing by leaps and bounds. Were it not for the outstanding job Morales did of finding plunder, Rafe would have put a lead ball through the man's brain long ago.

It was too bad, Rafe mused, that none of the others would make as competent a boss. Maybe the next time he went to St. Louis, he would keep his eyes peeled and his ears open, either for someone bold enough to cross the greaser and skilled enough to stay alive afterward, or for another gang looking to hire new recruits.

Rafe stared at Red's lifeless features. "You should have known better, partner," he said regretfully. "That nasty cuss is rattler mean when his dander is up. Maybe in your next life you'll have the sense not to flap your gums when you shouldn't."

At the edge of the trees, Rafe stopped to survey the countryside. Despite Morales's assurances that they were in the clear, Rafe would not rest easy until they had covered a lot of miles. The Cheyennes weren't about to take the massacre lying down. Just to think about a war party creeping into camp while he slept was enough to make his skin crawl. He knew all about the various tortures Indians liked to inflict.

If it weren't for the rotten savages, Rafe reflected, white men would be able to sleep a lot easier at night. President Andrew Jackson had the right notion a while back when he told the American people that they would be better off if every last red devil were exterminated.

Rafe chuckled at the remembrance. He shouldn't feel bad at all about wiping out those Cheyennes; he had just been doing his patriotic duty. Why, Old Hickory would probably pin a medal on him if he knew!

Rafe had planned to drag his friend a fair piece out onto the plain, but as he stood there gazing at the waving grass, he imagined dusky savages lurking out there just waiting for a member of the gang to show himself. He glanced down at Red and shrugged. "I reckon it doesn't matter to a dead man where his bones bleach in the sun."

Turning, Rafe took a few steps, then drew up short. "I must be getting forgetful in my middle age," he commented. Squatting beside the corpse, he stripped off Red's powder horn, ammo pouch, and possibles bag. A search of Red's pockets turned up a poke crammed with coins and a few bills.

"Why, look at this," Rafe exclaimed, gloating. "And here you told me that you were plumb broke. You canny liar, you."

Rafe hid the poke at the bottom of his own possibles bag, then headed back, whistling happily. He shut up when Morales shot him a suspicious look. To cover himself, he dropped the powder horn, ammo pouch, and bag at their treacherous leader's feet. "I suppose you'll want to divide these up as you see fit."

Morales picked up the possibles bag and rummaged through it. "Nothing much here," he said. "You would think he would have had a few pesos cached away, eh?"

"Not old Red," Rafe said glibly. "That hoss couldn't hold on to a cent if his life depended on it." Acting as innocent as a newborn babe, he strolled over to the fire and poured himself a cup of coffee.

Julio Morales closed the possibles bag and tossed it to a man named Byers. "Never say I never gave you anything, amigo." He passed out the other items, then strolled to where Hancock squatted. Out of the corner of an eye he saw the other man fidget nervously, and he smiled to himself. *"Pajaros de la misma pluma."*

"What was that?" Rafe asked.

"Birds of a feather, I think you would say," Morales explained. "You and me, we are much alike. All of us are, or we would not be doing what we do."

"True enough," Rafe said, unable to see where the conversation was leading. He suspected that Morales guessed the truth about his theft, but he wasn't about to turn over the poke unless pressed. He'd known Red longer than the Mex, so he figured that he had just as much right to the money as any of them. More, even.

"Yes, we are birds of a feather," Morales stressed. "That is why we share and share alike when it comes time to divide the spoils we work so hard to acquire."

Rafe started to rise and go sip his coffee elsewhere, but their leader gripped his sleeve.

"What is your rush, friend? I am not done yet," Morales said. Letting go, he made a show of slowly drawing his knife, then traced small circles in the dirt with the tip. "We all have our faults. I know I do. But one fault I do not have is being stingy. I have always divided the plunder evenly, have I not?"

"Yes," Rafe conceded, feeling more uncomfortable by the second. The others sensed that something was up and were watching intently.

"The same is expected of all of us," Morales said loudly so everyone heard. "We share fairly. Anyone not willing to do so would be better off on his own, *sí*?"

Rafe offered no reply. He wanted to lower a hand to one of his pistols, but that glittering knife rooted him in place. He could see dry splotches of Red's blood on the metal.

"I only mention this, señor, because I think you are holding out on us, your amigos," Morales said pleasantly. Raising the knife, he held the razor edge inches from Hancock's throat, as if he were examining it. "I would like to think that you have not held out on us on purpose. I would like to think that you simply forgot."

Rafe was furious but helpless. The slightest move and he would be slit from ear to ear.

"Did you forget, *compadre*?" Morales asked.

"Now that you mention it," Rafe said, using all of his willpower to keep his voice level, "I did. Let me show you." Ever so slowly, he stuck his hand into his possibles bag and drew out the poke.

"*Gracias,*" Morales said, grinning wickedly. He sheathed the knife in a blur, then rose. "You see, my friends? We are all brothers here. Remember what this man has done if you are ever in the same situation." Patting Hancock on the shoulder as he might a pet that had performed well, he added, "Just one thing, amigo. I will overlook your memory lapse this time. But never forget to share with us again, or we might think you do it on purpose. And you would not want that to happen."

"No, I wouldn't," Rafe agreed, and walked off so no one would observe the rage that came over him. Morales had humiliated him in front of everyone, and he wouldn't stand for being put to shame by anyone, ever. "You made a big mistake, Mex," he said under his breath. "You're going to regret the day you did this. Mark my words."

Chapter

— 15 —

Second Son was pushing herself as she had never pushed herself before. Legs churning, her lungs aching with every breath, her body caked with sweat, she scaled the steep slope of the jagged mountain at a pace few could have matched. Yet it wasn't fast enough.

The Modoc was somewhere above her, with Cleve. She had readily found the giant's tracks down in the bowl, found where he had lifted her mate onto a shoulder, and made for the mountain at a brisk gait. For most of the morning and afternoon she had been pursuing them on horseback. Then the slopes had become too steep for the horses, so she had left them and gone on afoot. As yet, she had not so much as glimpsed the Modoc.

Second Son did not know why the giant had taken Yellow Hair. She tried to tell herself that he must have had a good reason, and that her mate would come to no harm. But the truth was that she didn't know the Modoc all that well, and trusted him less. He had treated her kindly after Cleve was hurt, but he might have been acting. Maybe he wanted her all to himself; maybe he had just been awaiting his chance to dispose of Cleve, his rival.

An added worry was her man's condition. Second Son feared that moving him would only make him worse, and might, in fact, kill him. She was tempted to shout in the hope the Modoc would hear and stop, but if he had sinister intent, the shout would only warn him and he would try harder to elude her. So she ran on, ever higher, her strength beginning to wane.

This mountain was different from most. It was higher, darker, and covered with thicker growth except near the summit, which unlike the majority of peaks was not a smooth crown but a sheer rocky height.

Second Son noted the position of the sun, which hung two hands' width above the western horizon. Once it set, she would not be able to track unless she used a torch, which the Modoc would see. Even though she had drained herself to near the point of exhaustion, she redoubled her effort.

Then came the moment Second Son longed for. High up on the mountain, near the rocky crest, a vague figure moved, lumbering along like a great grizzly. Only this wasn't a bear. It was the Modoc, and he still had Cleve. She saw a patch of yellow hair.

A surge of newfound energy flowed through Second Son's limbs. Relying on the lance to steady her balance, she climbed steadily. The pines gave way to scrub growth, the gnarled scrub to barren stone. She went up over a lip onto a wide shelf and stopped in surprise.

The shelf was dotted with peculiar pits, some as deep as she was tall, others shallow. Piled high near them were the huge stones that had been scooped out when the pits were made. Several of the stone pillars were six feet or more. Only someone with enormous muscles could have accomplished such a feat.

Second Son had never seen the like. It was worthy of closer study, but she had a higher priority. Going on, she was dwarfed by towering boulders as she jogged along a narrow game trail that wound among them. The boulders blotted out the sun. She moved in murky shadow. Here the air hung as still as death. It was much cooler, too.

A scraping sound brought Second Son to a halt. It came from somewhere ahead. On cat's feet she advanced, keeping her back to boulders so no one could jump her from behind. She heard another noise that was repeated a few times, a strange sound she could not identify at first. On drawing closer, she was reminded of water being splashed about. But that was ridiculous.

A few moments later Second Son learned otherwise. She came to the end of the trail and discovered a spacious clearing, in the center of which was a pristine spring. Kneeling at the edge was the Modoc. Beside him were piled clothes, *Cleve's* clothes. And, to her horror, the Modoc was lowering her naked mate into the water.

A strident Tsistsista war whoop issued from Second Son's throat as she raced forward. The giant twisted in alarm, saw her face, and tried to bring his hands up to defend himself.

Second Son was not to be denied. She still held the lance as if it were a walking stick. Instead of raising it to her shoulder to spear the tip into the Modoc, she swung her weapon as if it were a club and caught the giant on the temple. All of her power and weight went into the swing.

With a resounding crack, the lance snapped in two. The Modoc toppled, blood trickling from a gash.

Second Son had eyes only for Cleve. The giant had dropped him and his body was almost entirely submerged. His head and one shoulder were all that remained on solid ground. She saw him slide farther into the water and squatted to grab his shoulders before his face went under.

Cleve was a big man, packed with muscles. Second Son had forgotten how heavy he was. She dug in her heels and pulled, but her palms slipped on his wet, slippery skin, and he sank in up to his neck. No!

her mind screamed in defiance. Firming her hold, she heaved upward and backward. She had him half out of the spring when her left foot slid out from under her and she fell onto her back, with Cleve on top.

Pinned, Second Son went to push her man to one side so she could rise. She heard movement, and craned her neck to see over her shoulder.

The Modoc had recovered and risen into a crouch. Blood smeared his temple and cheek. He touched his wound, stared at his red fingers, then looked at her.

Second Son was helpless. She slipped a hand under Cleve to try to get to her knife, but the giant reached her before she could draw the blade and stood directly over her, his knobby fists clenched. His hands unfolded and his thick fingers swooped down. She tensed, certain he was going to strangle the life from her. To her amazement, the Modoc grabbed hold of Cleve and effortlessly lifted him up.

Scrambling off the ground, Second Son was set to hurl herself at the giant. But he was staring down at her mate. She glanced at Cleve to see if he was all right and could hardly believe her eyes when she saw that his eyes were open and he was gazing fondly at her.

"Second Son."

The words were croaked. Cleve slowly raised an arm to reach for her, but he was still too weak to do more than lift his forearm off his chest.

Second Son started toward him, then caught herself and swung toward the Modoc. The giant gave a bashful sort of smile and stepped back, motioning at her and Cleve. She held her ground until he was a safe distance away; then, and only then, did she sink down next to the one who meant more to her than anything.

"What is going on?" Cleve asked. "The last I remember, you were fighting that guy and I tried to help. I think I recall flying head over heels, and then everything went black."

"You hit your head," Second Son disclosed. She confirmed that he had no fever or fresh bruises or cuts, and asked, "How do you feel? Do you hurt anywhere?"

"No. I feel awful weak, is all. And thirsty."

Second Son turned and dipped a hand into the spring. She had not noticed before, but the water was ice-cold, as frigid as a Rocky Mountain lake in the middle of winter, so cold her skin tingled. She cupped a palmful to Cleve's lips and let the liquid seep slowly into his mouth.

"Mmmmm, that's good," Cleve said. "I could down a gallon. Give me a hand."

Although she had reservations, Second Son helped him shift around so he could drink on his own. She made a point of not losing track of the outcast, who had taken a seat at the base of a boulder and seemed content to observe the goings-on.

The warrior recollected how the Modoc had twice before tried to get her to bring Cleve to this very peak. It occurred to her that the giant had never intended to harm anyone. The Modoc must have intended to dip Cleve into the spring all along. Perhaps the Modoc knew that a dash of cold water oftentimes brought unconscious people around, and in his dull, plodding way he had figured that the spring would do the same for Yellow Hair. It was the only explanation that made any sense.

Cleve drank for over a minute. He would have liked to drink more, but his belly ached. His mind had sharpened a little, and as he sat up he felt a draft chill his privates. "What the hell!" he declared. "Where are my britches?"

"You just had a bath," Second Son said. She retrieved his buckskins, then had to practically dress him as he was unable to do so himself. She did not let on, but his persistent weakness bothered her. She remembered a Tsistsista once struck by a Blackfoot war club who had ever afterward been as feeble as a sickly child. Would her mate be the same?

"I must have really rattled the old noggin," Cleve said, pressing a hand to his forehead. "Give me a few days, though, and I'll be as fit as a fiddle." He looked around. "Where are the horses? I think I can ride on my own."

Second Son propped her shoulder under his. "Lean on me. I will guide you." As she straightened she received a shock. The Modoc was gone. While she had dressed Cleve the giant had slipped soundlessly off.

Cleve also noticed. "Where did the walking mountain get to? Is he a friend or an enemy?"

"A friend, I think," Second Son said.

Going down the mountain proved even more grueling than going up it. Cleve was a shadow of his former self, so weak he could not manage a single step on his own. Second Son had to support the both of them the entire distance, and by the time they were halfway down, her legs were leaden, her thighs shrieking in agony. She willed herself to forge on.

Socks and Shadow were right where they should be. Second Son steered Cleve to his horse and gave him a boost up. He swayed, grabbed the mane, and held on by the skin of his teeth.

"Tarnation," he complained. "What the hell is the matter with me?"

"You have been through a lot," Second Son said. "Give yourself time to mend."

Mounting, Second Son bore westward to swing around the peak. Try as she might, she saw no sign of the Modoc. She wondered if she had truly seen the last of him or whether he was up to his old trick of shadowing her.

"So fill me in," Cleve said. He knew his woman well enough to know she was deeply troubled, which in itself was cause to fret. She hardly ever let anything get to her. "What happened while I was out?"

Second Son provided brief details, concluding with, "The Nez Percés will not give up easily. Broken Paw will keep hunting until he finds us."

"If we can hold them off until I'm feeling better, we'll make that bastard mighty sorry he didn't leave well enough alone," Cleve vowed.

Twilight had bathed the world in shades of gray when Second Son called a halt for the night in a clearing among spruce trees. A check of their back trail turned up no trace of the Modoc. "It might be best to make a cold camp," she proposed. "The war party is somewhere in this area."

"Too bad," Cleve said, grimacing as he sank down. "I could go for a hot meal. I'm starved enough to eat a bear raw."

A man in his shape needed food. Against her better judgment, Second Son took a downed limb and whittled the end into a sharp point. "You watch the horses. I will find your supper."

It was almost too dark to hunt. Second Son stalked through the pines, on the lookout for a rabbit or grouse. She would have to get close to employ her crude spear, which was difficult enough to do in broad daylight.

Game was scarce. Second Son snaked into every thicket she came across, searched patches of grass from end to end, and the only creature she flushed was a doe, which sped off so quickly she had no time to throw. In due course she had to admit to herself that she was wasting her time. Upset for Cleve, she hastened toward their camp and still had a few yards to go when the acrid scent of smoke and roasting meat wafted to her on the breeze.

Cleve had scooped a hole next to a log and made a small fire in it so the flames could not be seen from any great distance. He had a spit set up and chunks of meat turning on a slender length of broken limb. "You did right fine." He grinned at her. "Where did you get to after you tossed me the rabbit?"

Second Son gazed at the skinned animal. "I would like to take credit, but I cannot."

"Then who . . . ?" Cleve said, raising the stick to look at the meat.

"I would guess the Modoc," Second Son said, joining him. "He is watching over us, helping us as he helped me when you could not be revived."

"Why? Has he taken a shine to you?" Cleve asked. The prospect didn't worry him. Second Son had handled forward men before, in her own inimitable fashion. If the giant overstepped himself, he'd be minus his testicles before he could blink.

"I honestly do not know," Second Son admitted. "I think he likes me, but he has never tried to take advantage the way Terrebonne once did."

Cleve grunted. Jules Terrebonne had been an avowed enemy of theirs who once tried to force himself on Second Son.

"He is like a child, this one," Second Son went on. "A very lonely child. I think he wants to be around others."

"Then why doesn't he show himself?" Cleve wondered, scanning the forest. It gave him a spooky feeling to think that the giant was out there at that moment, watching their every move.

"Earlier I thought he was trying to drown you, so I hit him," Second Son said. "And you rode your horse into him, remember?" She absently reverted to her own tongue. "He must think that we do not like him."

"Well, whatever his reason for sharing the rabbit, I'm grateful for the eats." Cleve lowered their supper to the flames, his mouth watering at the delicious aroma.

Second Son walked to the edge of the clearing and scoured the woods. She swore that she could feel the Modoc's presence, close by, but she doubted that he would show himself if she called out to him.

To the southeast, a tiny ball of reddish-orange light flickered. Second Son studied it awhile, until Cleve said her name. He had divided the meat and offered her a short stick.

"Dig in. I know I haven't eaten in a spell, but I'd swear this is the tastiest rabbit on God's green earth."

Second Son took a bite, chewed lustily, and swallowed. Her stomach rumbled, betraying her hunger. Before she ate more, she commented, "The war party is camped on the north side of the mountain with the spring at the top. They will be after us at first light."

"Then we have to be on our way before then," Cleve said, unruffled. He snapped his fingers. "Say! Where the blazes is my rifle?"

"Broken," Second Son replied, and detailed the loss. "I will make new lances for both of us. They will have to do until we slay a large animal and I have enough sinew to string a bow."

"Make that two bows," Cleve corrected her. "When the time comes, I aim to do my part." He wolfed down another bite and smiled at her. The truth was, though, that he felt far less confident than he let on. The meat, while delicious, was doing little to relieve the woozy feeling that had plagued him since he came around. He hoped that he'd be able to hold up his end when the war party struck.

. . .

Several miles away someone else entertained similar thoughts, if for different reasons. Long Ghost, seasoned Chopunnish warrior, stared into the inky wall of night and recalled the disturbing dream he had the night before.

Dreams were important, Long Ghost reminded himself. Often they were the means by which the spirit world made contact with this world. Sometimes they were omens, warnings for those wise enough to heed them.

Long Ghost shivered as he thought of the images that had made him toss and turn and finally leap up off his blanket, his body slick with perspiration. The dream had started straightforwardly enough, with the war party still on the trail of the she-cat and her man. They had entered a valley and followed the tracks to a stream.

Suddenly Broken Paw had spotted the woman and the golden-haired white, watering their horses. At his command the band had attacked. They had swooped down on the pair, hacking them to bits with tomahawks and knives. And then they had stood around, gloating over their prowess.

That was when the dream turned into a nightmare, when a monstrous shape rushed out of the woods and tore into the Chopunnish warriors like a living whirlwind. Long Ghost could hear their terrified, tormented screams, see the fresh blood squirting from their crushed bodies.

It had been a sign, Long Ghost believed, a sign that they should give up, should leave the woman and the man in peace. He stared at their leader and stated as much.

"How many times must you bring up the same thing?" Broken Paw snapped. "How many times must I tell you that we will keep on until we have avenged our brother?"

Long Ghost nodded at Plays with Badgers, whose side was heavily bandaged. "Today we lost Crooked Ears and almost lost Plays with Badgers. How many must die before you admit this is a mistake?"

Broken Paw began to rise, but stopped. "I tire of your prattle, old one," he said, sinking down. "The woman was lucky, that is all. If she had not turned when she did, Plays with Badgers would not have been hit by Crooked Ears' arrow."

"And what of the creature Plays with Badgers saw?" Long Ghost asked. "What of the giant who was part man and part bear?"

"There is no such creature," Broken Paw spat. "Plays with Badgers is in pain. He only thinks he saw it."

The wounded warrior took offense. "I know what I saw. I am not a child who imagines things because I happen to be hurt. The creature rose up out of the earth and broke Crooked Ears' back as easily as you or I would break a twig."

Broken Paw noted the effect Plays with Badgers was having on the others and restrained himself from doing something he would regret. Even though he led the band, he did not have the right to impose his will on them. The Chopunnish prided themselves on their independence. Each man was free to do as his heart dictated. In order to keep them in line, he must persuade them that he was right, the old warrior and the wounded fool wrong.

"I did not accuse you of acting like a child," Broken Paw began. "If you say you saw someone kill Crooked Ears, then you did. But you had an arrow in you at the time. It might be that you saw a man, maybe the white man, and mistook him for a creature." He held up his hand when Plays with Badgers went to protest. "No matter who or what you saw, we owe it to our two slain brothers not to give up."

Clown Horse, as always, agreed. "You speak my mind, too. I will ride with you however long you need me."

"And I," Thunder Hoop said. "I also think Plays with Badgers was mistaken, but not because of the arrow in his side." He swept them with a glance. "I think all of you have forgotten the huge footprint I found, the one made by a barefoot giant."

"He must have been the one who killed Crooked Ears!" Broken Paw exclaimed. "Which means he is in league with the woman and the yellow hair."

Woody Hill tapped his tomahawk. "Crooked Ears was my best friend. Hear my vow. I will slay this giant and hang his hair in my lodge."

Delighted, Broken Paw said, "It makes me proud to have warriors like you at my side. Together, we will run the three of them into the ground."

Long Ghost realized that he had lost, but he had one last objection to offer. "What about Plays with Badgers? He is in no shape for hard riding or fighting.

And it would not be wise to leave him alone with a giant in the woods."

Broken Paw would have liked to crow with glee. The old warrior had played right into his hands and didn't even know it. "You have a point, Long Ghost. Perhaps it would be best if Plays with Badgers returned to the Chinook village, where our other wounded brothers wait for us. Chillarlawil will greet him with open arms."

"He should go alone?"

"That would not be wise," Broken Paw said, resisting a smug grin. "You should go with him, you and"—he paused to pick the old warrior's closest friend among the members of the band—"Raven Tail. There should be two so that one can rest at night while the other keeps watch."

"I will go," Raven Tail said.

Long Ghost had lived too many winters not to guess Broken Paw's strategy. "I commend your wisdom," he said sarcastically, but no one seemed to notice. "We will reach the village safely. I hope the rest of you will do the same."

"There are still four of us and only three of our enemies," Broken Paw said. "we are less than a day behind them. So I will make a vow to my own. Before the sun has crossed the sky two more times, their blood will be mixed with the dirt of the ground."

"May it be so," Long Ghost said sincerely. As much as he disliked Broken Paw, their leader was still Chopunnish. They all were, and as such he could not help fearing for their lives. He gazed at each of them in turn, at Clown Horse, Woody Hill,

Thunder Hoop and Broken Paw, saw them joking and laughing, saw them brimming with confidence and vitality, and a horrible feeling knifed through him that despite their combined prowess, despite their grim determination, he was not gazing on four vital, powerful warriors in the prime of their lives, but on four men who were dead and who simply did not know it yet.

Chapter
— 16 —

Wolf Sings on the Mountain and Rakes the Sky with Lightning reached South Pass and crossed over without incident. They traveled on a beeline across the prairie to the head of the remote Wind River country, and then up to the sandy saddle first discovered by a hardy trapper named Fitzpatrick. Once on the far side of the high wall of the majestic Rocky Mountains, they entered the verdant Green River country, where many trappers had plied their trade for over a decade.

Lightning made a remarkable recovery. Thanks to

the herbal poultices and the rarefied mountain air, the burns healed much faster than Billy-Wolf expected. The boy had figured that the warrior would be a virtual invalid for several months and require his constant care, yet by the time they came to South Pass, Lightning had regained much of his former vitality and strength.

The Kit Fox warrior would never be the same man again, though. He would carry scars with him for the rest of his life. Those on his back and legs he covered with new buckskins made after Billy dropped a large buck. But those on the left side of his formerly handsome face could not be concealed. Lightning saw them every time he lowered his head to a stream or spring to drink. Now and then Billy-Wolf caught his cousin running a hand over the wrinkled skin, a haunted look in Lightning's eyes.

By mutual agreement they avoided everyone. When they spotted campfire smoke, they swung well around it. When they glimpsed roving bands of Indians, they lay low until the bands were gone. At all times they exercised extreme caution.

It was not long after they crested South Pass and were winding down to a lower elevation that Lightning twisted and studied the skyline.

"What is the matter?" Billy asked.

"I do not know," the warrior answered. "For many sleeps I have been bothered by the feeling that someone is following us. But there has been no sign of anyone."

"We cannot take your feeling lightly," Billy said. "This is Blackfoot country. They will kill us on sight."

The country was more open than they would have liked. A series of sloping grades brought them to a narrow valley floor where a belt of trees lined a narrow river. They drew rein in the shade and spent over an hour watching the slopes above them without spotting a soul.

At last Lightning shrugged and climbed onto the sorrel. "I was wrong. I am sorry," he said in disgust. "The fire has made my brain feeble. I worry over things which are not there."

"My father likes to say that a man can never be too careful," Billy-Wolf mentioned, and a deep longing tugged at his heartstrings. It would be many weeks before they reached California, but he could not help champing at the bit to get there.

Lightning saw the boy's sadness and had to close his mind to his own. As long as he blotted out any and all memories of that dreadful day, he was all right. It simply hurt too much for him to think of Twisted Leg or any of the other Tsistsistas he had known and loved. On those few occasions when his guard dropped and he thought of his wonderful wife and their unborn child—mostly in the middle of the night, when he woke up in frequent cold sweats—the searing torment made him curl up into a ball and whine like a baby. It was just too much to bear.

Thankfully, Lightning had the boy to look after. By dwelling on their journey and not the past, he could make it through the day without undue suffering. On most days, at any rate.

That evening, as they were busy making camp, Lightning had another lapse. He was leading the horses to a stream when a pair of doves took wing and flew off to the north. Doves had been Twisted Leg's favorite birds. She often remarked on how mating pairs stayed together for life, and how she wanted her married life to be the same.

Lightning bowed his head and closed his eyes as waves of excruciating emotion washed over him. It would not do for him to go on like this, but he did not know how else to cope. When a person lost the one who gave their whole life meaning, they could not go on as if nothing had happened. He wished for a distraction, something to take his mind off his loss. And he got his wish.

Blaze and the bay whinnied at the same time, and Blaze stopped.

Lightning was still in motion. The hard tug on his arm threw him off stride. He glanced at the agitated animals, both of which were staring intently at a cluster of cottonwoods and brush off to the left, their nostrils flaring. He sniffed, but the only smell he detected was the stale odor of skunk that had passed by sometime during the previous night.

The warrior hauled on the reins. Only the sorrel took another step. Blaze continued to watch those trees, his ears pricked.

Billy-Wolf was gathering wood for their fire. As always, Jase and Snip were at his side. Suddenly both dogs stopped, faced the cottonwoods, and growled as they had that time they challenged the bull buffalo.

"What is it?" Billy asked softly. "What's in there?"

As if in answer, a dusky brown shape materialized

in the middle of the stand, a huge shape half as high as some of the saplings.

Lightning saw and understood. Whirling, he shouted, "Get on your horse! We must leave at once!"

It was too late. A deafening roar rent the crisp evening air and the slender cottonwoods shook as if in a powerful wind. The next instant a female grizzly hurtled from cover, her lips drawn back to reveal her large, tapered teeth. She paused once to repeat her roar, saliva dripping from her chin.

The horses were thrown into a panic. Both reared, their front legs flailing, and it was all Lightning could do to hold on to their reins.

The tableau rooted Billy-Wolf in place. He knew that he should go to the warrior's aid, but he couldn't seem to get his legs to move.

Then the grizzly shot toward Blaze and the sorrel and both mounts tore loose and bolted to the north along the riverbank. The bear darted past a startled Lightning, frozen in the act of reaching for the ash bow he had made back in the Wind River country. It would have pursued the horses had the two dogs not entered the fray.

Barking savagely, Snip and Jase closed on the behemoth. Billy shouted for them to stop, but either they couldn't hear him above their own barking and the roars of the riled bear, or they had no intention of obeying. Bestial instinct had them in its grip.

Jase reached the bear first, dashed in close, and nipped at a hind leg. Displaying astounding agility for a creature so immense, the grizzly slid to a stop and spun. It was the perfect picture of ferocity. Slavering and bellowing, it swung at Snip when the yellow dog rushed at its neck, and only the dog's astounding reflexes saved it from having its head ripped off. Both dogs crouched and growled just out of reach.

Meanwhile the horses had fled far enough to be safe and were still in full flight. Lightning glanced at them as he unslung the bow. He was raising it to shoot when the boy cried his name and pointed behind him. Fearing the female had a mate, he pivoted.

A pair of fat cubs were waddling from the cottonwoods. They were not at all alarmed by the commotion and acted as if they were taking a leisurely stroll. On seeing Lightning they stopped abruptly. One tripped over its own paws and collided with its sibling.

For some reason, the little ones made Lightning think of the child he would never know. Shaking his head, he swiveled toward Wolf. The cubs were no threat. He had no desire to kill them.

Billy-Wolf had dropped his armload of deadwood and was sprinting toward the dogs. He wanted to get them out of there before they were torn to shreds. In his anxiety over their welfare, he neglected to think of his own. He waved his arms and called out, "Snip! Jase! Heel!"

The grizzly was rapidly being driven berserk. Again and again it lunged at the dogs, again and again they darted aside. Their nonstop barking made it even madder. Snarling hideously, it went after first one, then the other, its mammoth paws missing by a hair. When a new sound fell on its ears, it whirled toward the source and charged.

Lightning's breath caught in his throat. The thought

of losing someone else close to him was more than he could bear. But he was too far off to reach his cousin in time. "Wolf!" he shouted. "Run!"

Petrified by the sight of the monster bearing down on him, young Billy-Wolf stood as rigid as a block of ice. He saw the bear's huge, glistening teeth, saw its wicked claws each as long as one of his fingers, and paralysis seized him again, if only briefly. On hearing his name yelled by the warrior, he whipped around and fled toward several small pines.

The mother bear roared once more and Billy swore he could feel her hot breath fan the nape of his neck. He was a yard from the pines with the grizzly right behind when he leaped for all he was worth. He'd hoped to sail over the first tree, but he hit it instead. The slender trunk bent as if in a storm, then catapulted him to one side. It saved his life.

Billy-Wolf heard the bear slam into the pines. A sharp snap told him one of them had been broken in half by the creature's massive bulk. Landing on his right shoulder, he pushed to his feet and fled down the river, certain the beast would be on him before he went five yards.

No claws bit into his flesh. No teeth tore and rent. Billy looked over a shoulder and was astounded to behold the grizzly ripping apart the tree it had plowed over. Pine needles and wood fragments flew every which way. So long as it focused its wrath on the vegetation, Billy stood a prayer of reaching the water and hiding in the reeds lining its bank.

Lightning ran to meet the boy. He hadn't fired a shaft yet and hoped not to. Never in all his years of hunting had he heard of a single arrow bringing a bear down. Shooting this one, he mused, would only make the grizzly madder than it already was.

The bear had reduced one pine to splinters and was beginning on a second. Billy-Wolf observed it closely. He had less than thirty feet to cover when Snip and Jase launched a united attack on the grizzly's hindquarters. The bear promptly forgot all about the trees and turned on them.

"No!" Billy yipped, stopping. "Leave it alone! Come with me!"

The dogs, embroiled in a fight for their lives, failed to heed. Constantly in motion, biting and barking and clawing in a frenzy, they swirled around the grizzly, running first in one direction, then another.

The enraged bear lashed out over and over but could not draw blood. It would lunge at one dog and miss. Then, before it could press its attack, the other dog would take a bite out of its flank or side. The grizzly would whirl to confront the new threat, and the pattern would repeat itself all over again.

Billy-Wolf started to go help his pets. He took no more than two strides when a strong arm looped around his waist and he was hauled toward the river. "Let me go!" he shouted. "They need me!"

"You were spared once," Lightning said. "Do not think you will be so lucky a second time." Wolf resisted, pushing and kicking, but Lightning held on. He would save the boy, despite himself.

A cloud of dust had partially swallowed the fierce combatants, and a chorus of growls rose from the cloud's core. Billy saw the bear spinning every which way. Glimpses were all he had of the dogs. He was mad at the warrior for denying him the right to help them, but he stopped resisting since he did not want to hurt Lightning.

A wavering howl punctuated a booming roar, the howl of a dog in severe pain. Billy-Wolf renewed his frantic attempt to break free. He had no idea which dog had been hurt. It didn't matter. They were his friends and they needed him.

The cloud broke in half and out of the opening reared the grizzly, eight feet of rippling muscle and sinew, her front paws dripping blood, more blood rimming her gaping maw. She threw back her head and uttered a rumbling snarl. Head cocked to bite, she went to lower herself to the ground when one of the cubs let out a mewling cry.

Lightning was almost to the water. He stopped when the grizzly burst from the dust and pushed the boy from him. If the bear came after them, he would take the brunt of the charge. He notched his shaft and firmly planted his feet.

The mother bear was apparently satisfied with the damage she had done. She sped to the cubs, licked each once, then made for the depths of the cotton-woods with her little ones in tow.

Billy-Wolf could not wait until they were out of sight before he moved. He raced madly toward the settling dust, afraid that both of his loyal companions had been slain. He forgot to hold his breath and wound up hacking when the dust got into his lungs. Swinging frantically in an effort to disperse the cloud so he could see clearly, he turned one way and then another, seeking some sign of Snip and Jase.

The moment came, and Billy thought his heart would stop. The dogs were side by side, Snip's tongue lolling, his nose pressed to Jase's cheek. Snip whined and looked up at Billy, his eyes pleading for something to be done. But there was nothing Billy could do, nothing anyone could have done.

Jase had been torn open from the front shoulder to his hindquarters. The grizzly's claws had dug three or four inches into his flesh, leaving wide furrows that exposed the dog's ribs and internal organs. Jase was alive and raised his head to stare at his master.

"Oh, no!" Billy cried, falling to his knees. He gently cradled the dog's head on his thigh. "Please, no." Jase licked his hand, then tried to rise, but Billy-Wolf held him down. "Lie still, boy," he said, choking on the words. Tears gushed, and he blinked so he could see. "Just lie still. Soon the pain will go away."

Rakes the Sky with Lightning stood to one side, his shoulders slumped. He did not understand the white tongue, but the boy's anguish was plain. It brought back memories of the first pony he had owned, a gift from his grandfather. How he had pampered that little calico mare! Three times a day he had taken it to drink. He had always made a point to seek out the sweetest of grasses for it to eat. He had ridden it everywhere, and would have taken it into the lodge at night if his father had let him.

Then, two winters after Lightning was given the gift, dozens of horses were driven off by raiding Shinni. Among them was his cherished calico.

The Burning Heart warriors had given chase. Because Lightning's animal had been one of those stolen, his father let him go along. So he had been with them when they found his horse, transfixed by three arrows. The little mare had been unable to keep up with the bigger animals, so the Shinni had shot her dead as a sign of their contempt for the Tsistsistas.

It had broken Lightning's heart. Over the next several days he had wandered out onto the prairie a number of times to be alone, to cry until he was dry. Now, as he watched his young cousin wrestle with tears caused by a similar loss, those old feelings came back as strong as ever and he nearly shed some himself.

Billy-Wolf tenderly stroked Jase's brow and lightly rubbed a drooping ear. The red pool spread from under the dog toward his leggings, but he did not try to move. He watched Jase's heaving sides, watched and suffered as they heaved less and less. Jase attempted to lick him again but was too weak.

"That's all right, boy," Billy said. "You just rest. You did more than enough tackling that bear. I'm right proud of you."

The dog's coat was slick with blood. Billy caressed Jase's chin and thought of the day long ago when his pa and he had journeyed to far-off Missouri to visit his pa's kin and he had received Jase as a present. That had been one of the happiest days of his life.

Snip lay next to him, whining pitiably. Billy laid a hand on the dog's head, but there was no consoling the animal. Snip knew.

When Billy glanced back at Jase, it was all over.

Jase's sides had stopped heaving and his tongue lolled from his mouth. Billy shut his eyes to keep more tears from coming, but it was like trying to hold back a flood. He'd held them in when the village had been attacked, held them in day after day afterward when he'd kept watch and seen the bodies of those he cared for begin to rot away. He'd held them in on long nights when he couldn't sleep for worrying about his parents. Now he could hold them in no longer.

Billy-Wolf bent his head to Jase's and wept as he had never wept before.

"What the hell are they doing now?" Rafe Hancock asked.

Webber adjusted the spyglass and clucked like a hen. "If I didn't see it with my own peepers, I wouldn't believe it."

"What?" Rafe persisted, glancing down at the valley. From their lofty perch on a slope to the northeast they enjoyed a sweeping view of the whole countryside.

"Appears to me they're buryin' one of their mongrels," Webber said. "The boy done dug himself a hole and now the buck is helping the brat lower the dog down in."

Rafe squinted, but the clearing by the river was too far off for him to see more than stick figures. "What do you reckon happened to it?"

"How the hell should I know?" the testy renegade answered. "Maybe the cur acted up and the buck fetched it a good one with his tomahawk. Injuns won't stand for dogs that don't listen."

They had arrived at their perch a short while ago,

after being sent ahead by Morales to scout the land and find a suitable spot to camp. "Damn their hides for not going on. It would have been nice to camp down yonder where the trees block off the wind and there's plenty of fresh water for us and our horses."

Webber snickered. "We could sneak on down there right this minute and slit their throats. No one would ever know. We'd blame it on the Blackfeet. And then we could give up this damn-fool goose chase and get to plunderin' pilgrims like we figured on doing."

Rafe looked at him. Of late, more and more members of the band had been talking behind Morales's back of getting on with the business at hand. They were sick and tired of shadowing the brat and the buck. Only the fact that the pair had headed for the Green River region, which had been the bands' original goal, had kept the men in line.

"Well, what do you say?" Webber prodded. "It's no secret you feel the same way I do. The rest of the boys will be in our debt."

"And what about Morales?" Rafe asked. Not that he cared. His dislike of their leader had grown into overpowering hatred. He would as soon kill the Mex as he would spit on him.

From above them a rasping voice declared, "Yes, what about Morales? I would like to hear your answer, Webber."

The two renegades turned. Julio Morales held a rifle and seemed on the verge of using it. He stalked toward them, bent low so his silhouette would not be visible from below. "I do not like it when my men talk about turning against me," he said.

"Who did that?" Webber exclaimed, acting innocent. "I sure didn't. All I said was that I'd like to get this over with and plant the two bastards we've been followin'. Is there something wrong with speakin' my piece?"

"So long as that is all you were doing, no," Morales said. "But I have heard the muttering that goes on. I know that some of you are too impatient for your own good."

Rafe barely held his temper in check. No man had the right to dictate to him as if he were a slave. He had tolerated all he was going to. Somehow, soon, he would slip his knife into Morales and be done with all the foolishness.

"I will keep watch for a while," Morales said, plucking the telescope from Webber's grasp. "Coffee is on. Go have some." He stepped aside so they could pass at arm's length, then stretched out on his side where Webber had been and watched them closely until they disappeared over the ridge.

Morales shook his head in disgust. It was all falling apart. All his scheming, all his treachery, all the killing he had done to reign as leader, and those he once thought completely under his heel were close to turning against him.

Indirectly, the accursed Bennetts were to blame. Morales had never lost hope that eventually their son would lead him to them. Back on the prairie, when it became obvious that the brat and the buck were heading for South Pass, Morales had taken it as a good sign. "See?" he had told his men. "You want to go to the Green River area, and we will."

Morales had figured they would stop complaining, but he had figured wrong. As soon as the voices of dissent increased, he had nipped them in the bud. But the harder he cracked down on his men, the more they resented it. Now there wasn't one man in the bunch he trusted not to slay him if the opportunity presented itself.

And all because of Cleve and Second Son.

Morales scratched his chin. Maybe, he reflected, Webber had the right idea. Maybe they should go down there and slay the pair. He shifted and went to raise the spyglass, then blinked on seeing a sorrel ground-hitched a few hundred feet below him. Recognition brought him to his knees and he saw something else, much closer.

It was the Cheyenne warrior, who promptly whipped a bow up and loosed a shaft.

Chapter

— 17 —

"Maybe he got tired of dogging our steps," Cleve Bennett speculated. "I didn't figure he'd stick around forever."

"I did," Second Son said while studying the woodland they had just passed through. It had been days since the Modoc slew the rabbit for them and there had been no trace of him since. "We are the only friends he has."

"That's downright pitiful, if true," Cleve said. "You have me feeling half-sorry for him." He pressed a hand to his lower back and stretched to relieve a cramp. "It's a shame we had to push on so hard in order to lose the damned Nez Percés. He probably couldn't keep up."

Second Son kneed Shadow alongside Socks. "How are you holding up? Feeling any different?"

"How I wish," Cleve grumbled. "I'm all right for half an hour or so after I wake up. But I tire too damn fast and spend the rest of each day as weak as a kitten. It's humiliating. The Bennetts have always prided themselves on being as strong as oxen."

"You need rest," Second Son said. "A lot of it. We should have put you to bed and kept you there right after you hit your head. Once we shake Broken Paw, we'll stop until you are fit enough to go on."

"I won't be babied."

"And I will not return to the Broken Hearts alone. When I won you as my wife, I planned for us to live a long life together."

"Yes, husband," Cleve said in mock meekness.

They shared a laugh and forged eastward. Since the Walters-Beeville expedition had taken a different route to California, this was virgin territory to them. Cleve drank in the sights. The rolling mountains, while high, were nowhere near the height of the regal Rockies. There was a greater variety of plant life, and game was exceptionally abundant, due in part to the heavier rainfall the region received.

Cleve recalled that midway between the Pacific Coast and the Rocky Mountains, near the junction of the Portenuf and Snake rivers, stood an isolated outpost known as Fort Hall. Originally built by a trader named Wyeth, the post had been taken over by the Hudson's Bay Company.

It was Cleve's hope that they would be able to arrange credit at the fort. He counted on obtaining a new rifle, a brace of pistols, and a packhorse laden with supplies. Properly outfitted, they would have no trouble safely reaching Burning Heart country.

Provided, of course, Cleve's health improved. He was much worse off than he had let on to Second Son and fretted that the condition might be permanent. Being an invalid was frightening. He knew of others who had been hit hard on the head and ended their days as pale shadows of their former selves. That must not happen to him.

Second Son was not fooled. She had lived with Yellow Hair too long and knew him too well not to see through him. But she did not make an issue of his state, for to do so would only sting his pride.

She was constantly on the lookout for herbs with medicinal properties. Two obstacles hampered her search. One, few of the plants that grew in the land of the Tsistsistas also grew in this new land, and two, they were on the move from dawn to sunset, allowing her no time to hunt for a cure.

Before them stretched a lush valley. A small herd of mountain buffalo grazed to the north. To the southeast several deer foraged. Soaring high overhead on the air currents was a large red hawk, which every so often uttered a piercing shriek.

The tranquil setting caused Second Son to relax a little. For days her nerves had been stretched taut since she always had to be on her guard for the war party. At night she had been losing sleep because Cleve could not sit guard for more than two hours without dozing off. The main burden fell on her shoulders.

It had been so long since Second Son saw the distant fire of the war party that she was beginning to think the warriors had given up the chase. A few more days and she could go back to getting a good night's sleep. Thinking of it made her yawn.

The grass grew waist-high, swishing against the legs of their horses as they rode toward a knoll at the far end of the valley. Cleve was in the lead. He tried to stay alert, but his eyelids were leaden even though it was only the middle of the morning. He took to dozing for short spells.

Second Son thought of calling out to waken him but did not. He needed rest. Tossing her hair back over her shoulders, she surveyed the surrounding mountains. All appeared peaceful. A few of the buffalo were staring at them but did not seem disposed to stampede. The deer were slinking into the pines while the red hawk had soared to the west, seeking prey.

Blackberry bushes covered the knoll. Second Son was sorry it wasn't the time of year for the berries to be ripe. Socks walked to the north to go around and she did the same. Cleve raised his head, blinked a few times, snorted, and dozed off again. He sagged to the side and was in danger of falling off.

"Yellow Hair?" Second Son said softly. Her words brought no response, so she moved up beside him, on the right, between Socks and the thorny bushes. She put a hand on his shoulder and shook. "As you like to say, rise and shine. Or would you rather eat thorns?"

Cleve sluggishly lifted his head and looked at her. His dull eyes flared to anxious clarity when he saw a figure rising up out of the briars. "Look out!" he bellowed.

At the selfsame moment Second Son felt someone or something to her rear. She shifted, or tried to. Corded arms closed around her waist and she was jerked from the mare. Automatically, she kicked and slashed an elbow backward. It threw her assailant off balance and they tumbled into the bushes. There was a yip of pain and the arms fell away.

Second Son tried to push to her feet, but the briars clung to her clothes and tore at her skin, impeding her. Her hand swooped to the hilt of her knife. As she drew she felt her hair grabbed by iron hands. The next she knew, she was being flung. Thorns ripped open her wrists and hands. Her feet felt the ground and the world turned upside down. Then she smashed onto her right shoulder.

Pain exploded in her head. The knife went flying. Nearby, a commotion had erupted. Valiantly Second Son struggled up to help Yellow Hair, but she had barely gotten her bearings when two heavy forms rammed into her, one high, one low. It was as if she had been buried under a rock avalanche. Her arms were pinned. Her captors roughly hauled her upright.

A leering, painted face materialized before her. Second Son had never seen this man close up before, but she knew it was Broken Paw. Two of his warriors held her. A fourth stood over Cleve, who lay unconscious, with blood trickling from his mouth.

"Now you ours!" the tall warrior signed, gloating, and put his hands on his hips.

Second Son held herself still and made no attempt, yet, to free herself. If they expected her to cower and quake and beg for mercy as some women would have done, they were about to be disappointed. Holding her head high, her chin jutting in defiance, she waited calmly for them to make the next move.

Broken Paw glanced at Clown Horse and Woody Hill and said in their tongue, "Look at this one. She pretends that she is not afraid. She must think that she is a warrior."

"She fights like one," said Woody Hill. "And she is fast. If not for the thorns, she would have knifed one of us."

Clown Horse admired the fit of her buckskins. "Now she is ours to do with as we please. I, for one, want some time with her alone."

"I will decide what to do with both of them," Broken Paw declared testily. As leader of the war party, he believed it only fair he have that right. He stared into the woman's dark eyes and nearly flinched. Smoldering fury lurked at the core of her being. They had caught themselves a wildcat.

Second Son had listened closely to the exchange, but she had not picked up any clues to their intentions. The one on her right was giving that hungry look women knew so well. Their leader seemed upset, but she did not know why.

"I called Broken Paw," Broken Paw signed. He

wanted the warrior woman to know the name of the man who had outsmarted her. "Question. You ready die?" He thought his taunt would inspire fear, but she showed none whatsoever. Truly, he mused, this was a most remarkable woman, unlike any other he had ever met. His original plan had been to have fun with her, then strangle her with her own intestines. But now he had second thoughts. Clown Horse was right. The woman was very attractive.

"Do we stand here all day?" Thunder Hoop spoke up. "And what about this one? Should I kill him or do we test his manhood first?"

Second Son noticed all the warriors focus on her mate. The stocky warrior standing next to him held a bow and trained the barbed-arrow tip on Cleve's chest, then made as if to pull the string back.

There was no way for Second Son to tell whether the Nez Percé intended to go through with the execution. Since she could not afford to wait and see if it was a bluff, she lashed out. She kicked Broken Paw squarely in the groin, which sent him staggering back into the stocky warrior who had drawn the bowstring almost to his chin. They both went down, their legs entangled. The bow twanged, the shaft thudding into the earth near Cleve's head. Second Son made no further moves. The pair holding her firmed their grips and gave her a violent shake as if to teach her a lesson.

Broken Paw rose slowly, a hand cupped over his manhood. He knew that he was red in the face, but he could not help himself. It felt as if the woman had crushed a testicle. Limping, he walked in a small circle to try to relieve some of the pain. He glanced at the woman to see if she was smiling at his expense, but she betrayed no emotion. She was smart, this one.

"Want me to kill her?" Thunder Hoop asked. He had notched another arrow, extended his bow.

"And end her life in the blink of an eye after all we have gone through to capture her?" Broken Paw replied in disgust. Wincing as he accidentally jostled his organ, he snapped, "No one touches either of them yet. We will take our time and do this right."

Clown Horse snorted like his namesake. "Just so I get to show this pretty one why Nez Percé women are so content with their husbands."

"You and me," Woody Hill said eagerly.

"But you do not have a wife," Clown Horse reminded him.

"I need the practice for when I take one."

They all chuckled, even Broken Paw. He sent Thunder Loop after their horses, then shuffled to a flat spot and took a seat. It relieved more of the agony but not all. "We must find a spring so I can soak in it," he mentioned.

"You were fortunate she did not ruin you for life," Woody Hill said. "We will have to stake out her arms and legs when we are ready."

Clown Horse let go with one hand to trace the outline of her lips with a finger. "Forget her arms and legs. It is her teeth you must watch out for. Forget yourself, and you will be minus your tongue."

"I hope she does fight back," Woody Hill said. "I like it when women scratch and claw."

Broken Paw watched Thunder Hoop enter the trees and congratulated himself on his brilliant tactic. Since the pair had been heading steadily eastward for days, he had reasoned they would continue to do so for some time yet, enough time for the band to swing swiftly to the south and loop past the pair in order to set up an ambush. It had worked flawlessly.

"Maybe we should take them back to our village," he proposed. "Our women could use the man as their slave, and this woman would make some warrior a fine wife."

"Would she?" Clown Horse said. "We both know she would turn on whoever took her. Her kind does not tame easily. One morning we would wake up to learn she had fled after sticking a knife into the man."

"She would not stab me," Woody Hill boasted. "I would beat her like I do horses which do not listen. In less than one moon she would drop everything to grant my every wish."

Broken Paw let the younger man rave on. Woody Hill would learn soon enough that taking a woman into his lodge meant more than having his meals prepared on time and his belongings kept in order. Women acted as sweet as honey when first wed, but in time they were the ones who ruled the nest. It was a sad fact of life that even the mightiest of warriors was no match for a clever female.

"Before we go home, we must go back to the Chinook village for our brothers," Clown Horse commented. "By then, Plays with Badgers and the others should be fit enough to ride."

Second Son could tell by their manner that they did not intend to kill Cleve and her right off. So long as they didn't lift a finger against Yellow Hair, she wouldn't resist. She'd seen one of their number leave, undoubtedly to fetch their horses, and it gladdened her. On the trail it would be easier to take them by surprise.

Just then Cleve groaned and moved an arm.

"Is he waking up?" Woody Hill asked.

Frowning because he had to move, Broken Paw hobbled to the white-eye. "No, he is still unconscious. Which is strange. I did not think I struck him very hard."

"He is white," Woody Hill said as if that explained everything.

"So?"

"Whites are weaker than us. They are all cowards at heart."

"The Blackfeet say that is not so, and the Blackfeet should know better than anyone," Broken Paw said. "Have you not heard of the time, many winters past, when they captured a trapper, stripped him naked, and gave him a head start? All their best men raced after him. Not only did he slay the fastest man in the tribe, he eluded the rest. Only a brave, strong man could have done that."

"Since when do you speak in defense of whites?" Woody Hill wanted to know.

"I have a better question," Clown Horse said. "Where is Thunder Hoop? He should have returned by now."

Broken Paw faced the forest. The tracker was nowhere in sight, yet the horses had been tied less than an arrow's flight away. "That is so," he remarked.

Second Son sensed they were troubled and guessed why. Could it be? she wondered hopefully.

Neither Socks nor Shadow had run off. The horses did not resist when the tall leader gathered their reins and stood still while he hoisted Cleve onto the mare. In a group they headed toward the trees.

Second Son was half pushed, half carried. Once she tripped and received a knee in the back to goad her on.

"Thunder Hoop!" Broken Paw bellowed, but received no response.

"I do not like this," Clown Horse said.

Broken Paw agreed. The tracker was always dependable; he had gone for their mounts, he should have come back. Drawing his tomahawk, he slipped quietly toward the glade where the horses had been tied.

"There!" Woody Hill suddenly whispered, and so forgot himself as to release their captive and point.

Thunder Hoop's bow lay in the grass, an arrow next to it. A few steps farther were several broken shafts. A few more, a small puddle of blood.

"An animal got him," Woody Hill declared, unlimbering the fusil he carried slung across his back. "A bear or a big cat."

"No animal could have taken Thunder Hoop unaware, let alone killed him without making noise," Broken Paw said.

Clown Horse put a hand on the hilt of his long knife. "Thunder Hoop thought there might be a third one. Remember the track made by the big man who went barefoot?"

No sooner were the words out of the Chopunnish's mouth than a gigantic figure crashed through the brush and into their midst. Broken Paw was rooted in place in amazement, a mistake that cost him when the Modoc rammed a backhand into his face and sent him flying into a tree. Spinning, the giant rushed the remaining two.

First to come alive was Clown Horse, who arced his blade overhead. Second Son leaped, caught hold of his wrist, and twisted, attempting to make him drop the knife. The warrior held on grimly to his weapon. He drove a punch at her mouth, but she snapped aside and his knuckles only grazed her cheek. Locked together, they fell.

Second Son landed on her side, facing the third Nez Percé. She saw the Modoc rear above him and heard the fusil go off. The giant must not have been hit because his knobby hands closed on the warrior's head, then wrenched to the right. There was a sharp pop.

Second Son had to forget about the Modoc and preserve her own life. The warrior she was grappling with had slipped astride her chest, wrapped both hands on the hilt, and thrown all his weight into lancing the blade into her chest. The tip was a palm's width from piercing her. She locked her elbows and exerted herself to her utmost. Bit by bit, though, the man edged the knife lower.

At the very instant Second Son saw triumph light the warrior's features, the Modoc materialized above them.

The giant seized Clown Horse by the scruff of the neck and brutally yanked him into the air. Clown

Horse jerked around, lunged, and buried the blade. He drew back the knife to stab again, but the Modoc's hand closed on his throat.

Second Son heard a loud squishing sound as she leaped to her feet. Before she could turn to the Modoc, Broken Paw hurtled at her with his tomahawk poised to cleave her skull. She skipped backward and the blow missed. Another nearly took her leg off at the calf.

Broken Paw was beside himself. After all he had gone through, he was not going to let the woman live. She would pay for the lives of his fellow Chopunnish with her own.

Unable to tear her eyes from the enraged avenger, Second Son retreated under an onslaught of wild swings. She dodged. She ducked. She danced backward. The tomahawk clipped her buckskins but not her body. She held her own until she inadvertently backed into a tree.

Broken Paw tasted victory. Snarling like a savage beast, he swung the long-handled steel tomahawk at Second Son's forehead, certain the honed metal edge would cleave her head in half.

But the Tsistsista warrior had not lived as long as she had by giving up easily. Shifting to the side, she managed to move just enough to cause the Nez Percé to miss. The tomahawk sheared several strands of her hair and embedded itself in the trunk.

Second Son tried to dart to safety. Her enemy snaked out a leg, hooking her ankle. Arms rigid to absorb the shock, Second Son sprawled onto her hands and knees. Her gaze alighted on an object lying in front of her. Grabbing it, she glanced back just as the Nez Percé tore the tomahawk lose and leaped at her.

Timing was critical. Holding the arrow she had found close to the feathers, Second Son whirled while at the same time taking a step to the right. The tomahawk slashed empty air, but the arrow sliced into Broken Paw below his arm and speared up into his chest. It scraped one of his ribs, sank deeper, and hit something soft. His heart.

Black astonishment etched Broken Paw's features. He froze, then opened his mouth to speak. Blood, not words, gushed forth. He looked at her as the light of life faded, looked at her with a pathetic, questioning gaze. Letting go of the slick shaft, she stepped back and Broken Paw crumpled.

Second Son inhaled deeply. That one had been too close. She turned to see how the Modoc had fared and found him on his knees, his hands pressed to his side. The fusil had blown a hole in him the size of a melon.

Going over, Second Son touched his sloped brow. The Modoc looked up and mustered a thin smile. He sadly said a few words in his language, then held his hand out for her to see the wound. "There is nothing I can do," she said softly.

Slowly, timidly, the giant reached out to her. Second Son let him. He lightly rubbed his finger along her jaw and spoke two short words. Even though she could not speak his tongue, she knew what they meant: *thank you.*

The Modoc suddenly quivered and clutched his abdomen. A groan wavered on the breeze. He gazed at her and kept on gazing as his enormous bulk folded in half. His misshapen forehead hit with a low thud, his rippling arms dropped to the grass, and he stopped moving.

Shadow whinnied. Second Son listened to footsteps and a hand fell on her shoulder.

"Is he . . . ?"

"Yes."

"He tried to save us, didn't he? Why?"

"We were his friends."

Cleve stepped forward, trying to read her expression. It was one he had never seen before. "Do we bury him or leave him for the coyotes?"

"Need you ask?"

It took over an hour. The hole had to be twice the size of an average man's. Cleve insisted on helping to lower the Modoc, then stood back while Second Son filled in the grave. When she was done, he clasped his hands and remarked, "We didn't even know his name, but I reckon a few words ought to be said." He paused, and for lack of anything better to say, concluded, "May he rest in peace."

Second Son straightened. "At long last I think he is."

Chapter
— 18 —

Rakes the Sky with Lightning had detected movement on the slope above the valley and instantly gone to the sorrel. "I suspect we are being watched," he had told Wolf. "Wait here."

Using what cover there was and approaching the spot in a roundabout fashion, Lightning reined up below the high bench and crept up the slope. Two thirds of the way to the rim, he heard low voices and crouched.

Only then did it occur to Lightning that he was being rash. He was in no shape to confront enemies. And thanks to his burned fingers, which were almost but not yet completely healed, his speed with a bow was less than it should be. Still, he was too close to turn back now. Padding forward, he paused a dozen paces from the lip.

Lightning heard three different men speak. Judging by their tones, they were not the best of friends. The voices fell silent and he thought the men moved off. Cautiously, he advanced, setting each foot down silently. He was only five steps from the bench when a head poked into sight.

Recognition came instantly. Wolf Sings on the Mountain had told Lightning about the pack of vicious white men who wiped out the Burning Heart band, about how this pack was led by a *Mex-i-khan*, as Wolf called him, a swarthy, small man whose features were carved into the boy's memory and which Wolf had detailed exactly. The man's name had proven too hard for Lightning to pronounce, so the pair had taken to calling him Evil Heart.

This man was that *Mex-i-khan*. This man was Evil Heart. Lightning was sure of it. The rest of the butchers had been white and the man staring in astonishment at him was definitely not.

With the insight came swift action, perhaps too swift. Lightning whipped up his bow and fired, but his unsteady fingers trembled just enough to throw his aim off and the shaft bit into the earth just below the rim, causing the butcher to duck down.

The warrior charged. He grabbed another arrow from his quiver and was trying to notch it to the string when Evil Heart jumped up with the stock of his rifle already tucked to his shoulder.

Lightning acted without thinking, swinging the bow at the gun. By sheer luck he deflected the barrel just as it discharged. The ball flew off into the sky and Lightning flew into the killer. Both of them crashed down.

All Lightning could think of was Twisted Leg, of the kindest, sweetest woman who had ever lived, of the devoted wife and loyal partner whose life had been so savagely ended by the vile man under him. He literally saw red. A blind rage filled him with intoxicating fury. Obsessed with squashing the life from the slayer of his people, the warrior pounded wildly away with his fists, neglecting the knife that hung at his side.

Julio Cardenas Morales believed he was up against a madman. The Cheyenne's flushed face was contorted in feral hatred and there was a maniacal gleam in his eyes. Morales warded off a deluge of blows while striving to land a few of his own. Suddenly it dawned on him that the Indian's blows were having little effect, that the Cheyenne must still be quite weak.

Morales knew that the warrior had been burned, and burned badly, during the attack. Many times when he'd spied on the pair, he'd observed the boy applying ointments to the wounds. Now, realizing he had an edge, Morales slammed a fist into the Cheyenne's jaw that rocked the warrior backward.

Lightning's head spun, but he refused to give up. Locking his fingers on Evil Heart's throat, he sought to choke the life from his foe. Morales tried prying at the fingers but could not loosen them. In desperation he threw himself to the right, then the left. They rolled back and forth, Lightning continuing to squeeze, Morales delivering punch after punch.

Neither paid any attention to where they were rolling. Lightning felt them go over the rim and was able to brace himself. Morales had the breath knocked from him by the warrior's knee, then they were tumbling like a pair of tumbleweeds locked together, over and over down the slope until their momentum was spent and they were on their sides facing one another in the high grass.

Morales rammed a foot into the Cheyenne's stomach. Speared through by searing pain, Lightning lost his grip. The Mexican kicked again, and for a few moments Lightning's vision was chaotic. When it cleared, he saw the butcher on his knees, a knife gleaming in the sunlight, poised to stab into his chest.

"Morales!"

The high-pitched cry cut through the renegade like the icy finger of death itself. Morales jerked his head up and saw the Bennett brat ten feet away. The boy held a bow. "Breed!" Morales hissed.

Billy-Wolf Bennett had disobeyed Lightning and followed at a discreet distance. Having just lost Jase, he was not going to risk losing his cousin. He'd decided that they should face their enemy united.

Never in a million years would Billy have figured on it being Morales. Now, sighting down his arrow at the man who had brought so much misery to his family and more to the Burning Hearts, at the man who had callously slaughtered helpless women and children and infants and laughing while doing it, Billy-Wolf felt an emotion new to him: a fiery, calculated desire to kill another human being. The arrow was in flight before he realized he had let go.

Morales shrieked when the shaft ripped through his torso. He gaped in disbelief at the feathers, unable to accept the reality of the experience. Other men were supposed to die, but not him. He was supposed to live to a ripe old age. This couldn't be happening, he told himself.

As if in slow motion, Morales saw the brat nocking another arrow. Dropping his knife, he clawed at one of his pistols. Oddly enough, his fingers would not respond the way they should. His grip slipped. Then his body was jarred by the second shaft, which pierced him right above the first.

Billy-Wolf took a step and sighted down another arrow. Dimly, he was aware of Lightning watching him, of harsh shouts in the distance. He saw the renegade fumble and drop the pistol, then grab for another.

"*Bastardo!*" Morales screamed as he cleared his belt and elevated his arm. He was convinced that he would live if only he disposed of the brat. So far there was no pain, which made him think his vital organs had been spared. He'd known many a man who had survived being shot and he would do the same.

Tsistsista boys were taught how to use a bow as soon as they were strong enough to lift one. Day after day, year after year, they practiced shooting from every conceivable position—standing, kneeling, squatting, lying down, and from horseback at a full gallop. They could hit a man-sized target at one hundred yards nine times out of ten. From twenty feet or less, they rarely missed any target.

Accuracy was just part of their training. They were also taught how to shoot rapidly, how to put a second arrow in flight before the first hit.

Billy-Wolf Bennett had learned his lessons well. Now he loosed three arrows in swift succession, one right after the other. At the *thud-thud-thud* of impact, his family's despised enemy keeled over.

Julio Cardenas Morales stared at the vault of blue above him and wondered why his body refused to obey his mental commands. His arms would not move. His legs would not move. And a bizarre black veil seemed to be expanding outward from the center of his chest. Then a pair of faces appeared above him, those of the breed and the buck. He worked his mouth, trying to spit at them, but he could no longer feel his tongue or his lips. Hollow words fell on his ears.

"This is for my mother and my father," Billy-Wolf said formally, "and for all the Burning Hearts you slew." He paused. "And this is for me."

Morales saw a knife appear above his eyes. Vaguely, he felt his scalp itch and tingle and something moist slide down across his brow. The knife reappeared, coated with blood. Next to it was a small, greasy mat of slick black hair, dripping red drops. His brain was growing sluggish. It took him a few seconds to realize the greasy mat was his scalp.

Then the Cheyenne warrior bent down and Morales felt a ticklish prick along his throat. He told himself that the buck had simply jabbed him, not slit his throat. He assured himself that any second now, sensation would return to his body and he would jump up and shoot them both. He was still assuring himself when the black veil engulfed all that he was and ever had been.

"He's gone," Billy-Wolf said. "Good riddance."

Lightning had pivoted to listen to the yells, which were growing in volume. "We must go. Quickly," he said, grabbing his cousin's arm.

Darting to their horses, they mounted and fled down the slope with Snip loping alongside Blaze. Hardly were they astride their animals when gunfire shattered the evening and lead balls swarmed after them like riled hornets.

Rakes the Sky with Lightning took the lead. He rode in a serpentine pattern to make it harder for the whites to hit them, and once he was among the trees made straight for the pile of wood his cousin had discarded earlier. Sliding off, he barked at Wolf, "We must build a fire, the biggest fire ever made."

"Why?" Billy-Wolf said, confused. He failed to see what good a fire would do them against the bloodthirsty band that would soon be on their heels.

"They will gather around Evil Heart's body and waste many words before they think to run for their horses," Lightning explained. "We have time if we hurry."

No less puzzled, Billy jumped down and scurried to gather as much wood as he could. A check of the slope showed a knot of renegades clustered around Morales just as Lightning had predicted. The knot was still there when he brought his third armload to where the warrior was bent low over kindling, blowing gently on a tiny flame.

"More wood," Lightning broke rhythm long enough to say.

Billy obeyed, adding armful after arumful to the growing pile. After Lightning had a small fire going, he leaped up and helped bring additional dead branches over. The pile was as high as the warrior's waist when more shouting broke out above them.

"Now throw all the wood on the fire at once," Lightning directed. Hands flying, he did just that.

In minutes the cutthroats would be closing on the spot. It seemed the height of folly to Billy for them to be making a bonfire when their lives would be forfeit if they did not get out of there. The flames flared steadily higher, leaping and crackling as if alive. Still Lightning added limbs, one arm raised to shield his face from the blistering heat.

Billy heard a horse nicker to the northwest. "I think they are on their way," he warned.

"Come," Lightning said. He scooted to the sorrel, swung on, and rode into the trees to the north. Instead of angling to the river, he surprised Billy and angled to the east, until they were near enough to the slope to see the renegades, who were south of them, galloping toward the fire.

"What are we doing?" Billy whispered when the warrior drew rein.

"Watch and learn."

Hunched low over Blaze, Billy saw the pack of human wolves spread out, then slow down as they neared the strip of woodland. One of the men gestured and several broke off to either side. Billy guessed they would circle around and flank the fire. Apparently the renegades believed the two of them were near it, an illusion created by the dancing shadows.

Rather abruptly, Billy realized that this had been Lightning's plan all along. The fire was a lure, drawing the killers as surely as a flame drew moths.

"Tie your horse," Lightning whispered. "Bring your bow and make no noise."

More mystified than ever, Billy-Wolf did as he was told. He notched an arrow when the warrior did and glided through the trees to a point where the bonfire was clearly visible. By now the flames were shooting seven feet into the darkening sky, illuminating the woods for yards around and casting a bright glow that probably could be seen from miles off. Lightning dipped to one knee, so Billy did the same. Snip squatted beside him.

Shadows flitted toward the fire. As if at a prearranged signal, they all went to ground, and for a while the night was still save for the roar of the fire. Finally a solitary figure stepped warily into the light, rifle leveled. Glancing this way and that, he moved a few more feet, then straightened and slowly lowered his gun. He shrugged his shoulders, turned, and called out, "Looks to me like the coast is clear."

Other renegades appeared. Presently all of them ringed the bonfire. They looked at one another in confusion.

"What is this, Rafe? Where the hell did they get to?" one man snapped.

"How the hell should I know?" Rafe answered. "I could have sworn I saw them right here a minute ago."

"Why'd they make this fire so big?" asked another.

"Maybe so they could see anyone sneaking up on them," suggested a fourth.

"Or maybe just to draw us off their trail," a husky specimen declared.

The man called Rafe nodded. "Well, we'll show them that they can't pull the wool over our eyes. Bring the horses, Webber!"

A pair of grizzled butchers came out of the gloom leading two groups of horses.

Billy-Wolf's elbow was nudged and Lightning spoke in his ear. "Shoot the men holding the horses. I will shoot the animals."

The horses? Billy thought. Surely he can't mean the horses. Then Lightning's bow twanged. A horse vented a shrill whinny while rearing into the night. It threw the other horses into immediate panic and many tried to bolt.

"Shoot the men!" the warrior said.

Moving more out of habit than design, Billy sighted on one of the renegades trying to keep the mounts under control and relaxed his fingers. The man turned just as he fired. His shaft thumped into the cutthroat's back, propelling him into the frightened animals.

Swiveling, Billy sent an arrow zinging at the other horse holder. This one had seen his companion fall and was trying to bring a rifle to bear with one hand and hold on to eight reins with the other. He screamed when his throat was pierced, released both the flintlock and the reins, and toppled to his knees.

The rest shook off their initial surprise and blasted away, firing at anything and everything they mistook for an attacker. Lead flew in all directions. Two of them were accidentally shot by their fellows.

By this time Lightning had downed five of their mounts. As much as it pained him to have to shoot horses, he had no choice. It was either that or allow the white men to give chase, and that was not part of his plan. He wanted the whites to remain at that spot until well past daylight. If their horses were scattered to the four winds, they would take half the morning rounding them up.

Moments later the horses scattered, fleeing into the dark despite the efforts of several renegades to stop them. Other men ran to help the wounded while the rest reloaded and fired as rapidly as they could.

"Fall back into the trees!" Rafe shouted. "We're sitting ducks next to this damned fire!"

Billy-Wolf got off one last shot before the butchers disappeared. He aimed at the center of a burly man's chest, but as he let the arrow fly the man dropped a ramrod and bent to pick it up. The shaft pierced the renegade's forehead and burst out the back of his cranium in a gory spray of blood and brains.

As suddenly as the fight commenced, it ended. Silence reigned, broken by the nicker of wounded horses and the sighing of the wind.

"You did well," Lightning said softly, remembering how much compliments had meant to him after his first battle. He smiled at his cousin. No longer should he think of Wolf as a boy, he mused. Wolf Sings on the Mountain had shed blood, had counted coup. From that day forth, Wolf deserved to be treated as a man.

"Do we leave now?" Billy-Wolf asked.

"We must keep these whites pinned down until first light," Lightning disclosed. "Then we will go."

Once again Billy could not see the logic in staying there when they could be fifteen or twenty miles behind them by dawn. The renegades would never catch up. He had learned, though, to trust his cousin's judgment, so he offered no objections.

Snip fidgeted and growled softly until Billy placed a soothing hand on his neck.

"Shush, boy. We can't let them hear us."

"How would you like a rifle?" Lightning expectedly asked. He knew his cousin was a fine shot, having witnessed shooting matches set up by Yellow Hair.

"My father took ours, remember?" Billy-Wolf responded. It had been Cleve's contention that he would need a spare on the long trek, but he had promised to buy Billy one of his own as soon as he returned from California.

"I see three you can take your pick from," Lightning said, pointing.

It was true. Three rifles lay in plain sight not far from the fire. So did three bodies.

"No one could reach them without being seen," Billy commented. "It would be certain death to try."

Lightning set down his bow and noiselessly unslung his quiver. "I can get you one if you want."

"No," Billy declared. "It is too dangerous. I have gone without a gun this long, I can go without one awhile longer."

The warrior smiled. "The Tsistsista half of you thinks of my safety, but the white half of you desires the weapon of your father. Do not move from this spot. I will be back before the stars have traveled the length of your arm."

"No—" Billy protested, but it was too late. The warrior blended into the foliage as if part of it. Billy began to rise, to cry out, but stopped himself before he blundered. Settling behind a bush, he counted the arrows he had left, then let Snip place his head on his knee.

The renegades had learned from their mistake. They made no noise and did not show themselves.

Billy wondered if maybe some of them were working their way around toward him and dismissed the idea because they had no idea where the arrows had come from. Their frantic shooting had proven that. Keeping his eyes peeled for Lightning, he idly stroked Snip and tried to hold back the fatigue gnawing at his mind.

Time dragged as if weighted by boulders. Billy-Wolf had to shake himself to stay fully alert. They had spent a long day in the saddle, then tangled with the she-bear and the renegades. All that, combined with the loss of Jase, had him feeling terribly tired.

Mostly Billy stared at the three rifles. Eventually Lightning would try to grab one and he wanted to be ready in case the whites spotted the warrior and opened fire. He would do what he could to protect his cousin.

In the mountains to the south a wolf howled a lonely refrain and was answered by others. A wayward coyote joined in for a while. As if not to be outdone, a mountain lion high on a mountain screamed long and loud, sounding just like a woman in the worst pain of her life.

All these were sounds Billy knew and ignored. The crack of a twig was another matter. Stiffening, he scanned the vegetation to his right. Something was there, sure enough, as a slinking shadow showed.

Billy-Wolf dropped low and eased an arrow out. It could not be Lightning, since none of the rifles were missing and the warrior would not return empty-handed. He held his breath, waiting for the figure to slink nearer. The man did move, but toward the fire, not toward him, and was bathed, briefly, in the shifting glow when the flames unaccountably soared higher.

It was an Indian. Billy's eyes became the size of walnuts. The warrior's hair, his buckskins, his painted face, and especially the red shield he carried, adorned with eagle feathers, pointed to him being a Blackfoot. He stared at the bonfire awhile, then turned and was one with the night.

Billy let out his breath and slowly sat up. Where there was one Blackfoot, there were bound to be plenty more. A roving war party must have spotted the fire from afar and sent a man to investigate. He could hardly wait to tell Lightning.

A glance revealed that one of the rifles was gone. Billy did not see how his cousin could have stolen it, yet he had. The wait now became almost unbearable. He dreaded more Blackfeet would come before his cousin did.

As if sprung from the earth, Rakes the Sky with Lightning materialized. Not only had he brought a rifle, he had a powder horn and ammo pouch stripped from a corpse. "As I promised," he whispered with a smile, which faded on being told about the Blackfoot. "I did not expect them so soon. We must leave, now."

"You *expected* them?" Billy said, flabbergasted.

"Why else do you think we made such a big fire?"

Billy smiled in appreciation of the full extent of Lightning's cleverness. Staying close to him, Billy crept to the horses. The warrior insisted that they lead the animals rather than ride. At the river they climbed on their mounts and forded a shallow pool. Beyond, a hill reared. They rode to the other side, where Lightning guided them into a dry wash.

"We will stay here tonight."

"Is that wise?" Billy asked. "The Blackfeet might find us."

"They will have eyes and ears only for the whites. And we must be sure."

"Sure of what?"

Lightning did not reply. They made themselves as comfortable as they could, Billy huddled next to Snip for extra warmth. Unable to keep his eyes open, Billy-Wolf soon slumbered. He thought he had only been dozing for a few minutes when the caterwauling of the mountain lion woke him up. On sitting up, he discovered that he was wrong, twice over. Dawn streaked the eastern sky with bright bands of pink. And the terrible caterwauling was not issuing from the throat of a cougar, but from the throats of men being savagely slain.

"Is that . . . ?" Billy asked, shooting up.

"It is," Lightning confirmed.

The warrior and the boy listened to the war whoops, shrieks, and wails until the sounds faded. Then, mounting, they flew to the northeast as fast as they could go.

Chapter

— 19 —

From then on, Rakes the Sky with Lightning and Billy-Wolf Bennett were more cautious than ever. They took to traveling at night and lay low during the day in order to reduce the odds of running into another Blackfoot war party. Nighttime, though, was when grizzlies and the big cats liked to prowl. Now and then they would hear one of the fierce predators near at hand, but they reached the Green River without being attacked.

Here the warrior called a halt so they could hunt for

elk. Lightning tracked a small herd and brought down a young bull with a single arrow at seventy yards. They made racks to smoke the meat.

Shortly after this, while they were at the river watering the horses, Billy-Wolf spotted a large party of trappers crossing a ford south of them. They promptly took cover and stayed hidden until the trappers were gone.

It bothered Billy, though. His conscience pricked him for shunning men his pa would likely call friends. For all he knew, some of those men might have made his father's acquaintance at one time or another.

Lightning, on the other hand, was glad they had not made contact. His cousin had explained to him that the whites who destroyed the Burning Heart village were not trappers, like Yellow Hair, but vicious men who preyed on others, white and red. Even so, Lightning did not know if he would ever trust a strange white man again.

As soon as they had all the jerked meat their horses could comfortably carry, the pair moved on, bearing westward. Neither had any firm idea which route was best. Since the Great Water was known to be far to the west, that was the direction they took.

At length the warrior and the youngster came to a high ridge overlooking a large lake some sixty miles in circumference. Billy recollected hearing tales from his pa about a certain body of salt water reputed to be in that general region. "I wonder if this is the Big Salt Lake the trappers talk so much about?" he mused aloud in English, and then mentioned the same in the Tsistsista tongue.

It turned out not to be. They found evidence of a recent large encampment of over two hundred lodges. Lightning discovered a discarded parfleche and studied its design. "I think these were Shoshone," he speculated. "They went south."

They pushed on. The beautiful country beyond rose gradually into a high range of mountains. By sticking to the bank of a winding river, they passed through the range without having to seek out a high pass and came to a spot where a perpendicular high rock towered above them. Billy noticed odd white patches up near the crest. As he watched, one of those patches scampered across the sheer face with incredible agility. "Look!" he cried.

"Mountain sheep," Lightning said. "I hunted them once."

The next day they stumbled on five peculiar springs, no more than small holes in the ground, the likes of which neither had ever seen. First they smelled a rank odor, then they heard a bubbling sound. Lightning spotted the springs and they climbed down to inspect them. Billy could not resist dipping a finger in each. Several had a bubbly, pleasant taste, but the others were sour and sulfurous.

From another ridge they finally caught sight of the Big Salt Lake. It's immensity staggered them. They had little time to appreciate it because they came on more and more signs of Indian activity and had to be extra wary.

At the mouth of the river, on the east shore of the Salt Lake, they elected to rest their horses for two days. Billy was delighted to learn that the area swarmed with huge flocks of geese, brants, ducks, and swans. Most fascinating of all were the hundreds of ungainly cranes, which he had rarely seen before. He spent many an hour lying on his belly, observing their antics.

Lightning was treated to his first ever meal of scrambled eggs, courtesy of Billy. The warrior was skeptical until he swallowed a bite. The very next morning he wanted eggs again.

Here they made a crucial decision. Since the Salt Lake barred their path, they had to bear either to the north or the south to go around it. Lightning was of the opinion that they ran a worse risk of encountering hostile tribes if they went south, so they picked north.

They remembered a stream that had branched north from the river and retraced their steps to it, traveling by day again since they were out of Blackfoot country. The next evening they spotted fresh hoofprints in a gravel bar. Some of the horses had been shod.

"White men," Lightning commented. "Maybe more like Evil Heart."

"Or just trappers," Billy said.

Several days later the pair came to a wide, verdant valley watered by the biggest river they had yet seen. They were about to swing to the west again when Lightning spied smoke spiraling from two campfires not half a mile to the east.

"We should take a look," the warrior advised. "If there is a large village in this valley, we must hide until dark and then go on."

Presently they learned the source of the smoke, but

it was not rising from a village. From the top of a hill they gazed down on a structure unlike any they had ever beheld. It was an enormous stockade, eighty feet square, built from cottonwood trees set on end deep in the ground. The walls were fifteen feet high, and there were eight-foot-high guard bastions at two corners. From a pole at the center of the stockade fluttered the Stars and Stripes.

"I'll be!" Billy exclaimed. "It's a fort. An American trading post!"

The excitement in Wolf's voice drew Lightning's head around. "Do you want to go down there?"

Billy had not entertained the notion, but the idea appealed to him. It seemed like ages since last they had talked to other people. And he was sure they would get a friendly reception, him being half-white and all. Plus, there were dozens of lodges pitched near the fort, which proved the trappers were on good terms with friendly Indians. "Will you come also?"

Lightning hesitated. He could see white men lounging near the gate, and there were bound to be many more inside.

"I will not go if you do not," Billy declared.

The warrior had known for some time that his young cousin hungered for companionship. He did not want to deny Wolf the opportunity, but he could not help thinking it was a mistake, that they would be throwing their lives away.

"Please," Billy persisted.

Lightning made up his mind. If they were to die, so be it. They would die together and go down fighting as befitted Tsistsista warriors. "We will go."

In order to reach the gate they had to pass through the village. Many of the Indians were abroad, and most gave them a close scrutiny. Billy-Wolf, in the lead, cradled his rifle in the crook of his elbow and held his head high. None of the Indians spoke to them until they drew abreast of a large lodge bearing the likeness of a white bird. A handsome warrior raised his hand in salute.

"I called White Raven," he signed fluidly. "I Flathead chief."

Billy had heard of the Flatheads but never met any. He remembered his pa saying they were one of the friendliest tribes around. "I called Wolf Sings on the Mountain. My friend called Rakes the Sky with Lightning."

"Question. You Arapahos?"

"We Cheyennes."

"Question. You hungry? I have plenty food. Come eat with us when sun low."

Billy-Wolf glanced at Lightning, who answered.

"We come when sun low. Now talk white men."

White Raven moved aside and they went on. Billy could not resist grinning at his cousin and saying, "See? Not everyone wants to take our hair."

"What about them?" Lightning responded, nodding.

Five grungy, buckskin-clad mountain men were watching the pair approach the fort. A surly sort who sported a brown leather patch over his left eye hefted a rifle and moved to intercept them. "Hold up there, young hoss. Do you savvy English, by any chance?"

"I speak it well. I am William Wolf Bennett, son of Cleve Bennett and Second Son," Billy announced. "I would like to learn if there is any word of my parents in this country. Let us pass."

The mountain man's good eye narrowed and the corners of his mouth crinkled. "Well, now. Ain't you the proper gentleman. A breed, ain't ya?" Snickering, he motioned at his companions. "What do you think, boys? Do they look dangerous? Think it's safe to let 'em in?"

Before anyone could reply, another man appeared. This one was sturdily built and had on homespun clothes rather than buckskins. Buckled at his waist was a sword. On seeing him, the loungers sobered and straightened.

"Pardon me," the newcomer said, addressing Billy. "Did I overhear correctly? Your name is Bennett?"

"It is," Billy-Wolf answered, and was troubled when the man gave him the sort of look a hungry mountain lion might give a lost fawn.

"I'm Courtney Walker. I'm in charge at Fort Hall. You will be so kind as to accompany me, immediately," the man said. At a nod from him, the one-eyed trapper and the rest quickly spread out to form a ring around Billy and Lightning.

The warrior tensed. The moment he had dreaded had arrived. He had his bow in hand but had not thought it best to ride through the Flathead camp with an arrow notched. He resolved to wait for the whites to lower their guard before he grabbed a shaft and made them pay for their treachery.

Billy-Wolf was likewise upset. Walker had an air of command about him that could not be denied, but the boy did not like putting himself in his hands when he did not know Walker's intention. "Why should we go?" he boldly demanded.

"You will understand shortly. Come along."

Left with no recourse, Billy entered Fort Hall. Whites were everywhere, toiling at a variety of jobs. Courtney Walker angled toward a long, low building and walked up to an open door. Halting, he pivoted, stared somberly at Billy a moment, then shouted, "Get your mangy carcass out here. You have a visitor." Stepping aside, he grinned.

Billy was at a loss to understand until a large frame filled the doorway and a golden-haired man bellowed in a voice he knew as well as his own, "Walker! You have some gall. What the hell was that all about? What do you mean, a visitor?"

Father and son set eyes on one another at the same instant. Cleve let out with a roar that would have done justice to a grizzly bear and reached Blaze in two bounds. Sweeping Billy-Wolf into his arms, he practically shrieked, "Second Son! He's here! Our boy is here!"

Then all three of them were hugging one another, and try as they might, not one of them could resist the tears that trickled down their faces, not even Second Son, who could count on one finger the number of times she had cried in her life. Snip yipped and licked and went into a frenzy of ecstasy while Walker and the trappers stood around chuckling at the grand trick they had played.

Only Rakes the Sky with Lightning did not cry or smile. He refused to show emotion in front of the whites, whose chuckles he mistook for laughter at the expense of his aunt's family. Dismounting slowly, he waited for Second Son and Yellow Hair to notice him. The latter gave him a cheerful bear hug, while Second Son, having recovered her composure, simply put a hand on his shoulder and smiled.

Second Son's smile faded when she got a good look at her nephew's face. The scars were testimony that something awful had occurred, which the haunted look in his eyes confirmed. "What has happened?" she bluntly asked.

Lightning glanced at the whites. He did not relish breaking the news in their presence and stated as much.

"We will go over to the west wall," Cleve suggested. "The man who is chief here has kindly let us stay in a lean-to while I have been on the mend." Turning to Courtney Walker, he translated, adding, "I suspect he's a bearer of bad news."

"If there's anything I can do, you have only to say the word," Walker responded.

Billy-Wolf could scarcely contain himself. He wanted to know all about what had happened to his folks since last he saw them, but he damned up the deluge of questions while his cousin related the massacre.

Cleve and Second Son listened, aghast. Their soaring joy had evaporated, replaced by overpowering heartache. When Lightning told about the Mexican who had led the butchers, Cleve looked at their son. "Was it Julio Morales?" he asked in English.

"It was him, all right," Billy-Wolf said. "But he got

his in the end, Pa. Someone turned him into a pincushion."

"Who?" Second Son inquired.

"Me."

Wife and husband exchanged startled looks. They had thought to be there when their son killed his first man.

Second Son swelled with pride. She could not get over how much Wolf had grown. When they departed for California, they had left a small boy behind. Now, he stood on the verge of manhood and had proven he would make an outstanding warrior.

Until well into the night the four of them talked, sharing their many adventures and their bittersweet memories. At last Cleve squared his broad shoulders and said, "In a few days we were going to head for Tsistsista country. Now I wonder if we should. All those who meant anything to us are gone. The Burning Heart Band is no more."

"But what of Singing Wolf?" Billy-Wolf said. "We never did learn what happened to him."

"My brother should have returned long before you left," Second Son said sadly, and looked at each of them. "I am afraid that we are the last of the Burning Hearts."

For a while melancholy claimed them. Snip fidgeted, disturbed by their sorrowful silence.

Presently Cleve cleared his throat. "That being so, I see no reason for us to go back. We have to get on with our lives." He gestured westward. "A whole new land waits for us outside that wall, a land rich with game and opportunity. I say we do some exploring and find a new place to call home."

"I agree," Second Son said, although it upset her to do so. She had always been close to her brother. "Like two peas in a pod," as Cleve would say. It would be a long while before she adjusted to life without him. But she still had her husband and her son, and Lightning. People who cared for her, and for whom she cared deeply. With them by her side, she would face whatever the future had to offer.

The Chinooks actually existed and did have a village at the Dalles. While there is no historical record of their being fluent in sign, it is a known fact that they traded extensively with the Nez Percé and Shoshone, who were. It only stands to reason that some of the Chinooks, especially their leaders, would have mastered so vital a means of communication with the plains and many Rocky Mountain tribes.

Chillarlawil is a historical figure whose kindness to Lewis and Clark is well documented.

The Chopunnish, or Nez Percé, were indeed perhaps the most outstanding horse breeders in all of North America. It is safe to say that the arrival of the horse changed their way of life forever. Where formerly they had lived much like other peaceful plateau peoples, they soon adopted the customs of their warlike neighbors to the east, the Blackfeet, and became little different from a typical plains tribe.

The attack on the Burning Heart village has as its basis similar attacks too numerous to list, most but not all conducted by militia or military forces who believed they were wiping the Indians out for the greater good and glory of their country.

Fort Hall existed. Actually, there were three. First came the trading post mentioned in this story, which was run by the Hudson's Bay Company for a number of years after being built by Wyeth. Later, a second Fort Hall was set up three miles north of the original post by two companies of Mounted Riflemen under orders to protect settlers on the Oregon Trail. It was soon abandoned because of the scarcity of forage. Two decades later, in 1870, the Interior Department ordered a third Fort Hall built east of the original post. This one was used to keep the Shoshone and Bannock Indians in line until so many whites moved into the region that it was no longer needed.

If it is true that biological evolution conforms to the adage "Survival of the fittest," then perhaps it is equally true that cultural evolution might best be summed up as "Conquest by the fittest."

Such has it always been. Maybe, one day, if we're

lucky, we will learn to sow friendship by accenting the similarities between people and not breed hatred by accenting the differences.

Maybe.

One day.

MOUNTAIN MAJESTY BOOK 8
THE SAVAGE LAND
by John Killdeer

After many long, difficult years of separation, Cleve, Second Son, and Billy-Wolf have finally been reunited and are determined to make a new start. Believing their friends on the Plains to be dead, the family heads north, where rumors of plentiful beaver lead them to the Coeur d'Alene Mountains in present-day Idaho. For once the Bennetts are enjoying some peaceful time together, and Second Son has never been happier. Yearning to spend time with her son, Second Son takes Billy-Wolf on a hunting trip north into Canada, where she hopes to reestablish their bond. But before long a new and unexpected enemy crosses their path and shatters the peace they enjoyed.

Driven from their lands by the powerful Crees, a roving band of fierce Chipewyans are looking for a new region in which to settle. They are also in search of women, since they lost most of their own to the Crees. Without Cleve and desperately outnumbered, Second Son is forced to retreat even deeper into the densely forested northland, where she'll wage an all-out battle to preserve her precious freedom and protect her son. With the bitter taste of slavery forever etched in her mind, Second Son's unbreakable spirit is put to the ultimate test.

Look for THE SAVAGE LAND, Book 8 in the Mountain Majesty series, on sale in October 1995 wherever Bantam Books are sold.

THE MAGNIFICENT NEW SAGA OF THE MEN
AND WOMEN WHO TAMED THE MOUNTAINS!

It was a land of harsh beauty and fierce dangers—
and the men and women who made their
livelihood in the Rocky Mountains had to use
every resource of strength and shrewdness to
survive there. Trapper Cleve Bennett and the
Indian woman he loves live a saga of survival
on the high frontier.

MOUNTAIN MAJESTY

WILDERNESS RENDEZVOUS
❏ 28887-3 $4.50/$5.50 in Canada

PASSAGE WEST
❏ 56376-9 $4.99/$5.99 in Canada

FAR HORIZON
❏ 56459-5 $4.99/$5.99 in Canada

by
John Killdeer

From Dana Fuller Ross, the creator of WAGONS WEST

THE HOLTS

OREGON LEGACY _____ 28248-4 $5.50/$6.50 in Canada
An epic adventure emblazoned with the courage and passion of a legendary
family—inheritors of a fighting spirit and an unconquerable dream.

OKLAHOMA PRIDE _____ 28446-0 $5.50/$6.99 in Canada
America's passionate pioneer family heads for new adventure
on the last western frontier.

CAROLINA COURAGE _____ 28756-7 $5.99/$6.99 in Canada
The saga continues in a violence-torn land as hearts and minds catch fire
with an indomitable spirit.

CALIFORNIA GLORY _____ 28970-5 $4.99/$5.99 in Canada
Passion and pride sweep a great American family into anger from
an enemy outside . . . and desires within.

HAWAII HERITAGE _____ 29414-8 $5.50/$6.50 in Canada
The pioneer spirit lives on as an island is swept into bloody revolution.

SIERRA TRIUMPH _____ 29750-3 $5.50/$6.50 in Canada
A battle that goes beyond that of the sexes challenges the ideals of a nation
and one remarkable family.

YUKON JUSTICE _____ 29763-5 $5.99/$6.99 in Canada
As gold fever sweeps across the nation, a great migration north begins
to the Yukon Territory of Canada.

PACIFIC DESTINY _____ 56149-9 $5.99/$6.99 in Canada
Across the Pacific, in the Philippines, Henry Blake—a U.S. government spy—
undertakes a dangerous secret mission.

HOMECOMING _____ 56150-2 $5.99/$6.99 in Canada
The promise of a new adventure draws Frank Blake toward New Mexico
to discover an unexpected destiny.

Ask for these books at your local bookstore or use this page to order.

Please send me the books I have checked above. I am enclosing $_____ (add $2.50 to
cover postage and handling). Send check or money order, no cash or C.O.D.'s, please.

Name _____

Address _____

City/State/Zip _____

Send order to: Bantam Books, Dept. LE 12, 2451 S. Wolf Rd., Des Plaines, IL 60018
Allow four to six weeks for delivery.
Prices and availability subject to change without notice.   LE 12 4/95